THE BONES
OF AMORET

Arthur Herbert

First Edition: April 2022
Printed in the United States

COPYRIGHT © 2022 Arthur Herbert
ISBN: (paperback) 978-1-945263-95-8

Cover Art by: Stuart Bache, Books Covered Ltd.
(Shrewsbury, UK)
https://www.bookscovered.co.uk/

Also by Arthur Herbert:

The Cuts that Cure
Lockdown: A Collection of Dark Tales

For Amy, my real-life Angelica

I'd always figured lightnin' strike
Or rattlesnake or barroom fight
Would do me in, and not some Mexican rose.

The fact is I was hot and dumb
Struck stupid by the sun and love
So on the one hand I guess she played her part

- Max Stalling

Arthur Herbert

Chapter 1

The day Blaine Beckett went missing, the day that started off the whole sordid, miserable chain reaction of events to follow, started off so peacefully you'd have been forgiven for thinking it was an omen for good things, that God wouldn't allow anything to go wrong on a day that had such a beautiful start to it. It was a Monday and I'd had to clear my clinic schedule to see to the day's work. I rose well before the sun and went about getting dressed and making coffee as quietly as I could to let Angelica and Miguel sleep.

Before Jimmy Wayne came to pick me up, I checked on the national news, not long enough even to sit down. I turned the volume so low I had to lean in to hear just two feet from the set. It was all over the television that somebody in Chicago had poisoned bunches of batches of Tylenol, killing a handful of people up there and now folks around the country were wetting the bed about it. That was one of the nice things about our little west Texas town back then in '82, things like that seemed far away, otherworldly from our home in the high desert hills.

My dogs trailed me onto the front porch, keeping me company while I waited. The two mutts would have been, let's see, about three years old at the time. Sonny Fitzgerald owned a scrap metal yard in town— later on, that'll come into the story I'm fixing to tell you— and he'd found a couple of pups beneath a clunker's chassis one morning, as bony as the metal skeleton they were huddled under. Their mama was nowhere to be found and the poor things were starving. His first instinct when he heard their pitiful mewling was to put them down right there on the spot, but something made him stop short and call me instead. One I called Rope Tail, and he grew up lovable but dumb. If brains were hog lard you couldn't have used his to grease a big skillet. But his sister, a brindle I named Maybelline, well, she was special. Thirty-eight pounds of grade-A badass and smart as a whip. Rope Tail would go on to disappear one day in '87. Coyotes got him, I suspect. Maybelline, though, lived to a ripe old age. I miss 'em both, but her more.

Out on the porch, I took in a lungful of the crisp night air. That deep, cleansing breath would have sent me into a coughing fit a few months prior, but it invigorated me that morning since I'd walked away from the cancer-stick habit two months before on my forty-fourth birthday.

In my rocking chair, I sipped coffee while Rope Tail dozed with his chin on my boot, his cheeks sucking in and billowing out in a sleepy cadence. Off to my right, high in the night sky a ring of stage lights lit up a water tower with the name "AMORET" painted on the tank's gunmetal-gray plates in a looping cursive, like the title sequence in a black and white movie.

It was still dark when Jimmy Wayne Hickerson pulled up to my curb in our custom panel truck. In our teens his features had been more pretty than handsome, with long lashes that made girls swoon. But a lifetime in the desert winds had carved lines in his once-delicate face. Jimmy Wayne was an interesting man. He lived his years convinced the moon landing had been faked but alien abductions were real.

"Mornin' Doc."

"Mornin'."

"You ready?"

"I been ready."

I poured him a coffee to go while he twirled the key chain around his finger, then we loaded up and headed through the empty streets toward Shy Mike's place. We'd put a rebuilt engine in the truck two months before— the old motor couldn't outrun a fat man— and Jimmy Wayne was still getting to know it, babying it along through the darkness. We'd made that run many times, so I didn't have to remind him to take the long way, skirting the edges where town met the wide expanse of the caldera and the sweep of our headlights picked up scrub brush and boulders.

Say, ma'am, do you have enough tapes for that little recorder of yours? Telling this'll take a while. Really? "Digital"? Can I see it for a second?

Well, signs and wonders, isn't that something. Man lives to be eighty-four years old, you get to thinking you've seen it all, then something else comes along to prove you wrong.

I have to admit I was surprised when you called from that El Paso newspaper wanting to write something about the fortieth anniversary of all that sadness we had with the Becketts. Lord, forty years. Seems like it was yesterday.

I guess I can understand why you'd want to talk to me, hip-deep in all that business as I was. Plus, I think it's fair to say I've lived a life more interesting than most. I practiced medicine here in Amoret for forty-two years, even making house calls until around the time they got bin Laden. And I watched the border change from a peaceful hunk of desert where people got along, saying live and let live, into the goddamn war zone it is now.

I know you didn't come here to talk about this, but I got shot down once in Viet Nam when the Huey I was riding in took a round to the rotor. Another time when I was taking a trail to Bien Thoc through what was supposed to be safe territory, I stopped to answer nature's call when three VC passed by within twenty feet of where I was squatting against a tree. There was the time it fell to me to bag up the remains of a Buddhist monk after he immolated himself to protest the war, and I delivered three hundred and sixteen babies into this world. Most of 'em brown or yellow, but still. Should you have a mind to hear any of those stories after we're through talking about Amoret and the Becketts, just say so.

Shit, where was I? My mind wanders so. If you really want to write down this story for your paper like you say, you're gonna have to get used to my digressions, which you'll soon enough come to see is another word for my bullshit.

Pulling up to Shy Mike Culverson's trailer, we parked next to an umbrella clothesline and tapped the horn, letting the truck idle to keep the cab warm against the mild October chill. He appeared in the doorway, yawning as he tilted his mesh ball cap back and scratched his shaggy widow's peak. A simple man, Shy Mike was uneducated but smart, unread but capable, and so honest you could play poker with him over the phone.

Audra, his pear-shaped wife, stood just inside, a fuzzy-at-the-edges grayed-out shape behind the mesh screen door. Squinting against the glare of the headlights, she clutched her terry cloth robe closed at the neck and poked her head out, turtle-like, to hand him a plaid thermos and give him a kiss before waving at Jimmy Wayne and me with a smile.

Clutching the handrail, Shy Mike threw a long shadow as he eased his way down the three plank steps, lowering his gimp leg with its immobile knee onto the step below before hitching his weight down on his good leg. Despite only being in his late thirties, he hobbled like an old man. It'd been a decade since he had a promising career as a professional bull rider cut short at a rodeo in Broken Bow, Oklahoma, when his spur got tangled in a flank strap as he was bucked off, leaving him tethered to the enraged animal by one heel and turning his knee into a swivel.

"It was like bein' in the middle of a goddamn blender," he told me afterward as he lay in his hospital bed recuperating from his first surgery. It took only seven seconds for the rodeo clowns to cut him loose— I timed it once, years later when I discovered a video of the ride— but it seemed an eternity watching it in real time. Despite three surgeries the leg never healed right. He was stoic about it, though, I'll give him that. Accepting, even.

We waited patiently while he hoisted himself onto the running board and dropped onto the bench seat next to me. Then he swiveled his bum leg in, fussing with it until he got it situated, like a mother smoothing down her boy's cowlick for a picture.

"Mornin', Jimmy Wayne. Doc." We nodded back as he placed a pinch of tobacco in his lip and poured coffee into the thermos' screw-top cup.

"Trade you a spit cup for a pinch," Jimmy Wayne said, pointing to a styrofoam cup in the holder.

Wordlessly, Shy Mike passed the tin across and both men took turns sipping coffee with one hand and spitting tobacco juice in the community cup with the other. The thought of what that must have tasted like always made me grimace.

"Eleven souls. I got that right?" Shy Mike asked.

"Yup."

"Motel got set up okay?" he asked as he looked out his window at the vastness of the barial stretching off to the dark horizon. This was more to make conversation. We all knew we wouldn't have gotten this far if the motel hadn't been set up okay.

The first of the day's light crept up as Jimmy Wayne pointed the rig due south down a fifty-mile stretch of two-lane asphalt between Marfa and the Rio Grande that was as desolate then as it is now. That piece of the Chihuahua Desert was a bad place to get in trouble— back then, the staties didn't mandate a trooper drive it twice a day looking for folks in distress like they do these days— but that didn't detract from its wild beauty.

If you had a mind to pull over and get out to walk the chapparal, wandering among the yucca with their delicate white blossoms and the nopal cactus with their fat, fleshy leaves; the spiny sotol bushes, the caprock mesas and limestone shelves and stands of cotton wood trees, you didn't have to go far to realize you were looking at the same view the Comanches had back when. I can't speak for others, but it never failed to give me a reverent feeling. I'd already seen my share of man's inhumanity to man by then in my life— and trust me, I'm going to tell you about more— but that pristine desert landscape always seemed to cancel all that out. At least it did for me. Still does.

An hour later, the highway ended in a dusty "T"

at an isolated spot facing the Rio Grande. Along the shoreline, thick bulrushes framed the pretty green-grey water as it runs whenever the country out here's been a week or more without rain. While showers are always welcome 'round these parts, they turn the river water a swollen, ugly brown for a while. But on that morning, there were ripples visible over the gravel sand bars. Long beards of slimy rock moss waved gently in the current, and the sunlight glinted off the water like someone'd spilled a new bag of nickels across the surface.

I'd have liked to take a minute, but my companions weren't contemplative men. Jimmy Wayne barely slowed the panel truck as he took a left to follow 170 as it paralleled the river, so close we never lost sight of it.

Shortly, we topped a rise and got our first glimpse of the Chisos Mountains squatting low on the horizon, a sight we used as our landmark. Jimmy Wayne checked his mirrors as he decelerated, then pulled onto the shoulder at the highway's crest. He killed the engine and got out to stretch before popping the hood. Softly whistling, he propped it with the folding support rod from the engine compartment's liner. The hot motor ticked as it cooled.

Shy Mike fetched the binoculars from the glove box and tossed the strap around his neck where they swung like a pendulum as he swiveled and did his little hop-step to reclaim the ground. He exhaled a fog onto the lenses and wiped them with the tail of his shirt as he hobbled around the front of the truck and straddled the solid yellow stripes.

That spot had a view of the road for a mile and a half in both directions, the reason it'd been chosen. Shy Mike glassed the empty highway, then lowered the binoculars and spat. Wiping his chin with his Carhartt jacket's sleeve, he looked at Jimmy Wayne and me across the open engine compartment and nodded.

I walked to the shoulder's edge where it dropped off to a short escarpment thick with bristly, crimson-flowered ocotillo. Nature's sounds crept out like they'd been in hiding: the burbling of the river at the end of the declivity, the trilling and chirring of insects in the thick vegetation, the breeze rustling through the cane, the sound of grit when Jimmy Wayne's boots turned on concrete.

Wetting my lips, I made an "OK" sign with my left hand and tucked my lips over my teeth. Pushing my tongue back, I emitted a commanding whistle toward the river, strong and clear, rising in inflection at the end. It pierced the desert air, cutting across the pale river plain before echoing off a shale bluff a few hundred yards away.

Nothing moved. The scene below us lay still as a portrait for a moment, and I felt a brief rumble of concern before I caught movement to my left. A young Mexican, short and muscular, stood up from behind a dense huddle of creosote bush fifty yards away and shifted his light backpack before waving. His toothy grin shone through a thick beard, causing me to smile.

He said something over his shoulder, and suddenly the underbrush was alive with activity. Young men and women, all brown-skinned with dirty work clothes and exhausted, pensive faces stood up from hiding places among the desert scrub. I did a quick head count: eleven, not counting my bearded friend Chebo.

"*Venga, venga,*" Chebo urged the group onward, up through the thicket toward the asphalt, twelve miles of hard yards coming to an end. After walking through the night, they looked numb from fear and fatigue.

They fell in single file behind their guide. Chebo picked his way forward along a serpentine path through the thicket, generating a steady stream of inaudible chatter.

While most of the group trudged behind Chebo with their heads down and mindful of their footing, the last person in line shuffled along staring in our direction, not looking where she was going. A slight woman, she appeared dazed, and as the rest of the group advanced, she lagged behind with her head up and eyes locked on the truck. Zombie-like, she scuffed her feet forward, arms dangling limply by her sides until she stumbled on the uneven ground and fell to her knees. She managed to get to her feet, but once upright her eyes stayed fixed on the vehicle like a lost sailor who'd suddenly located the North Star. Then, unnoticed by the group, she inexplicably peeled off at a tangent from their path, blazing her own trail through the underbrush on a beeline for the truck.

Her track took her ten feet from the group's conga line, then fifteen, then twenty. The brambles on her path became thicker. She tried to push through, eyes still up and unwavering as she willed herself forward, throwing one foot in front of the other with a shambling, Frankenstein gait.

The thorny vines clawed and scratched at her, yet she still churned forward robotically until eventually the underbrush won out. When the scrub became an impassable wall, she seemed to realize her predicament, but by that point her exhausted body and mind failed her. Unable to go forward, too fatigued to turn back, she went limp, without even the reserves to call for help, the sharp vines suspending her like a marionette.

I shouted at her, *"¡No se muevea, no se muevea! ¡Le voy a ayudar!"* Chebo had almost reached the highway's asphalt when he heard me, and for the first time turned to see the straggler. I waved him off and made my way down the slope, then when the thorny scrub got too thick, faced backwards and folded my arms to push through to reach her.

Up close she seemed brittle, with buck teeth and wiry hair, pipe cleaner arms and sandals held together by duct tape. As I stripped away the brambles, her scratched face and glassy eyes drifted toward me, then turned back to rest on the matted spikey runners, unable to help me help her. I felt like I was releasing a rabbit from a snare.

Once I had her free, I hoisted her and pulled her in close to shield her bony frame as best I could, then waded backward up the slope as thorns clawed at me. Eventually the spiked vines thinned, and I could face forward again before taking the last few steps onto the pavement at a trot and gently depositing her on her feet. She stood stock still for a few moments, then shambled in the direction of the truck once again without acknowledging me. I followed, picking thorns from my hands and sucking at the worst of the scratches.

The rest of the immigrants surrounded Jimmy Wayne at the back of the truck. He rolled up the cargo bay's sliding door and gestured with a smile toward two large coolers bungeed to the floor. *"Tenemos comida y agua aqui amigos. No se preocupen, todo va a estar bien."* Shy Mike continued watching the highway for any last-minute approaching vehicles.

Chebo approached me with a look of concern,

thrusting his chin in the young girl's direction. "She okay?"

I shrugged. "Dunno yet, she's pretty loopy right now. Probably just dehydrated. I'll give her a good once-over at the motel."

"That's going to have to wait," Chebo said. "I need you to come with me back onto the trail a few miles." He reached into the cargo bay where we kept supplies and rummaged.

"I thought there were eleven today?"

Without looking back at me, he said, "There were. Are."

"So what's going on?"

"I'll tell you on the way." He pulled two bottles of water, some candy bars, then a collapsible stretcher from the stack of supplies. "Trust me, we need to get moving."

I shrugged. "Fair enough." I called out to Shy Mike and Jimmy Wayne as they loaded up the group, "Chebo says me and him gotta head back up the trail for something. Y'all get these folks to the motel. Do me a favor and really push the fluids on that *señorita* I had to fish outta the thicket, would you? Once y'all dropped everybody off and got 'em settled, head back in this direction and wait for us right here."

They nodded and turned away as Chebo and I set off back into that lawless landscape.

Forty-five minutes later, we stood over the object of Chebo's concern. At the bottom of a limestone bluff on a broad wash of gravel lay an unconscious Mexican. With a thin beard and shaved head, he sported a tattoo of a spider web on the left side of his scalp that, under normal circumstances, would have made him appear menacing. At that moment, though, with his lips cracked and tongue swollen, his blistered face appeared vulnerable, almost pathetic. The severity of his sunburn made his age difficult to guess, but I put him in his mid-twenties.

The man's slight frame gave the illusion the massive pack on his back wore him rather than the other way around. I put him at about one hundred forty pounds, while the enormous pack must have weighed sixty. I didn't see any water on him.

It looked clear what had happened. Too much weight. Not enough water. Too much desert.

Shaking my head, I squatted and unzipped the pack's top compartment, knowing what I'd find. Under the nylon flap, crammed to the gills, lay packet after packet of white powder, bound in cellophane and duct-taped into kilos.

Chapter 2

Though I knew it was coming, the sight of all that dope still made me pause. "Son of a bitch."

Chebo leaned against a boulder with his arms folded across his chest, a pinched expression darkening his face. "I found him like this about four hours ago."

My gaze flicked up at him. "I don't want no part of this pack."

Chebo cocked his head and sighed. "If you are thinking about taking him back without it, you could save time and just put a bullet in his head right here. If he shows up without the *drogas*, whoever he works for will kill him. It is why he did not leave the pack behind once he started to get in trouble."

"You think I don't know that? I'm just thinkin' out loud."

Chebo bent at the waist, hands on his knees, and leaned closer to study the man, watching the slow rise and fall of his chest. "By now, he's been missed. Which means they are out here looking for him. If we left him in this spot, how long do you think he would last?"

"Not long."

"How long is not long?"

I pressed two fingers to the side of the man's

neck. His pulse felt like a hummingbird's, a weak flutter. "Maybe make it to sundown. Maybe." Chebo opened his mouth to say something, then stopped short.

I gave the man a hard shake. "*¡Amigo! ¡Abre los ojos!*" His head lolled like a chicken with a broken neck, but his eyes didn't open. I slapped his cheek several times in rapid succession, a sound like polite applause. "*¡Abre los ojos!*" He only moaned, a dry guttural sound.

I said to Chebo, "I call this the poor man's smelling salts." I grabbed the man's nipple through his chambray shirt and gave it a vicious twist that made Chebo wince. I'd hoped this would snap the man awake but he only grimaced in his semi-consciousness, and I cursed under my breath when he barely swatted at my hand in slow motion.

With a heavy sigh I said, "So let me talk this through 'cause I want to make sure I got this straight in my head. If his employers stumble across us on the Mexican side of the river carrying him out with that backpack, we'll likely be shot on sight, no questions asked. If we're caught with that pack on the Texas side of the river, we'll never see another sunrise that doesn't come through prison bars. And if we leave the pack behind, we hand the man a death sentence. That sound about right? I missin' anything?"

Chebo rubbed at his lips in thought. "No. *De acuerdo*. We all three of us got a problem."

I stroked my stubbled chin while I scanned the empty, rolling plains of the surrounding caldera.

We had it all to ourselves.

For the moment.

"What a goddamn fustercluck," I hissed, shaking my head at our bad luck. I spat a wad of phlegm across the trail in disgust, then reluctantly made the decision.

"Okay, gimme a hand puttin' this stretcher together."

What? I see you looking at me strange.

I would have thought you knew about this already, me helping smuggle folks in across the river back in the day. I'll grant it isn't something you expect to hear, a doctor helping coyotes. Hell's bells, I can only imagine what you must be thinking right now. Let me explain.

The porous border's always been a fact of life out here, and most folks back then would agree that both sides benefitted from the arrangement. The problem I saw on a daily basis, though, was that for Mexicans who'd made it across using their legs instead of legalities, they had a hell of a time getting medical care. Unfortunately, what that usually meant was often as not they just did without.

I tried to get funding to set up a no-frills clinic outside Presidio, Texas, right across the river from Ojinaga, Mexico, that would cater to that population. I had a hell of a time, though, as neither Amoret nor Presidio was interested in paying for it. I spent a couple years going around with my hat in my hand, trying to raise the funds privately, emphasizing that I was willing to donate my time without drawing a paycheck, but no luck.

Around the time that goddam peanut farmer was heading out of office, though, a man approached me the name of Pablo. Even after all this time, if it's the same to you, ma'am, I'll keep his last name to myself. He'd heard of my struggles and was sympathetic, saying he had a proposition he wanted to discuss.

Now, smuggling wasn't the business in the late seventies that it is today, but there've always been people trying to make a dollar getting others over. The competition between smugglers has been heated at times, and all of them always looked for an edge. Pablo said he worked for one such group, and his associates were willing to underwrite my new clinic if in return, I'd agree to perform medical assessments on the immigrants they brought over. They figured— rightly, as it turned out— an offer like that would set 'em apart.

I'd be lying if I didn't say I was nervous at the prospect of getting in bed with those boys. It was breaking the law, sure, but I was less worried about that. I was raised to believe there were the laws of God and the laws of man, and when the two conflicted, the former should win out, period. Corny as it may sound, I did see it as a moral obligation to those poor folks. And if I'm being perfectly honest, back then things were a lot more—casual, I guess is the word I'm looking for. I don't want to say getting caught working with a bunch of immigrants would be a speeding ticket, but nor were you likely to wind up on the front page of the newspaper, either.

No, most of what I was nervous about was the simple fact of what it meant to be entering that world. I'd be going from the audience to the arena floor, a passage I suspected was one-way only. There might be life-long consequences to that decision, consequences that at that moment in time were unknowable.

I told Pablo I wanted to meet the folks I'd be working with before I considered the offer any further. Same as now, you heard hellish stories about smugglers, many of whom treated rape as the price of doing business. They'd get some poor young women— or worse yet, children— out in the desert in the dark, scared, no idea where they were, and start, well, let's just call it renegotiating the terms of their deal. I wanted my new clinic badly, and if it came with the chance to help out other folks who needed it, all the better. But I told Pablo I'd have no part of it if I had to deal with any pieces of shit like that.

Two days later I found myself in a Lajitas cantina meeting Chebo.

We drank and talked while we sized each other up. He was so short I could eat peanuts off the top of his head, but Lord could he put tequila away, and we got way deep into our cups that night. With his kind eyes and gregarious as hell, I often think as I look back he might have been the happiest soul I ever knew. Happy and content, through-and-through.

That was good enough for me, and I signed on the next day. Pablo asked if I could recommend two friends to join the enterprise, men who were sympathetic to the cause, trustworthy, able to handle themselves. Jimmy Wayne and Shy Mike more than fit that bill, and the work paid well. We started making those runs to that high point on the highway about twice a month in the summer of '80, so on the day Blaine disappeared we'd been going at it almost two years. I cut the ribbon on the Presidio clinic about a month before they released the hostages in Iran, and though most of the immigrants we brought in kept moving to the interior, some stuck around, and I took care of them in their new home. People are just people, after all. Folks lose sight of that sometimes.

The boys had returned with the cargo truck by the time Chebo and I made it back to the river crossing. Shy Mike kept his binoculars trained on the empty highway while Chebo and I set the stretcher down by the rear of the truck with a thud. The man groaned at the impact but didn't move.

"That what I think it is?" Jimmy Wayne pointed at the pack, his brow furrowed.

"Don't make me lie to you," I said as I rolled my shoulders to loosen them.

"So, what? You decided be a good idea to get us in the dope runnin' business?"

"I decided not to leave a man to die, if that's what you mean."

"Well good for you."

"You'd 'a done the same if you'd'a been there."

"Oh, I would have, huh?"

"Not a doubt in my mind."

"Hell, since we're branchin' out, maybe we oughtta start bringin' in Chinamen?"

"Goddammit, I'm not--"

"Hey, Shy Mike? What do you think? You might could learn you some of that ching-chong talk, make a pretty penny as a translator, maybe."

I paused, staring at him in silence for a moment. "You through bein' a smart-ass?" I asked patiently.

Jimmy Wayne was quiet for a long moment. Then he said, "You know, Pablo's gonna shit himself, we got ourselves mixed up in this."

"You let me worry 'bout Pablo. He'll understand. I know him."

"You used to know him, back when it was just us makin' him money and not lookin' like we was hijackin' loads of dope."

"I know him yet."

"Hear me out. I ain't sayin' we just leave this feller and count on his people findin' him. But what if we stash that pack somewheres out here, and bring him to the motel? You fix him up, and once he's better then we tell him where he can find it and cut him loose."

I thought about that, but only for a moment. "Nope, I can't do that."

"You mean won't."

"Won't then. You know as well as I do that pack'll grow legs out here. It disappears, and then all this is for nothin'."

Frustrated, Jimmy Wayne said, "Shy Mike, speak up. Whatta you think?"

He lowered the binoculars. "You were lucky not to of got yourself shot bringin' him this far." He shrugged, then brought the field glasses back up. "But you want to push your luck a little further, I'll go along."

"*Bah*," Jimmy Wayne swung a hand at the air in Shy Mike's direction. "You ain't got sense enough to lift the lid 'fore you piss."

"You don't wanna hear what I got to say, don't ask."

I said to Jimmy Wayne, "Look, none of us asked for this, but here we are. Now me, Shy Mike, and Chebo're eye to eye on this one. I understand if you don't want any part of this. We can leave you here to hitch your way back and you keep your hands clean. I'll even pay you back your wages out of my own pocket just for your trouble. But I'll tell you like the Good Lord told Peter, it's decision time. What's it gonna be?

Jimmy Wayne's lips pressed into a thin white slash, and he shook his head. "I hope you know what you're doin'."

"Trust me."

"Hmph. I said those words enough m'self to know what bullshit they are when I hear 'em outta somebody else's mouth." He was quiet for several seconds as he looked out into the desert. Finally, he mumbled in resignation, "'Too dumb to live.' That's what they're gonna put on my goddam tombstone after signin' on to this."

Shy Mike nodded, then limped around to the passenger side. "Come on then, we're burnin' daylight."

While Jimmy Wayne dropped the cowling, Chebo and I slid the stretcher with the unconscious man onto the truck bay's floor, then climbed up after it. The cargo door rumbled down, casting the three of us into complete darkness, like a condemned man getting the hood just before the noose. In shadow as black as a dream, I heard the pistol-crack of the trundle door's bolt shoot home, then the engine coughed to life. In the darkness, I shuffled forward and groped at the air for the bulb's dangling, beaded chain. It brushed my cheek and I gave it a yank, snapping on a single sixty-watt bulb that gave the dim cargo hold an eerie quality. It wasn't hard to imagine we were inside a big coffin.

Jimmy Wayne fired up the engine, revving it hard, taking out his frustrations on it. For twenty minutes, our three bodies bounced and swayed in unison to the motions of the road, casting long dancing shadows. Chebo and I kept our balance by clinging to handles we'd MIG-welded to the cargo bay's inner walls. He tried to ease the tension, cracking loud jokes over the creaking of the truck's suspension, but I wasn't in the mood. The dead air tasted of danger.

Soon, I heard the familiar sound of tires skipping in the seams of a bridge's asphalt. Moments later, the truck slowed, then lurched to a stop. The bolt was pulled back on the sliding door's latch and sunlight flooded the bay once again. I winced and threw up a hand to block the glare.

Framed like a painting in the bay's doorway, a neon cowboy with a manic grin gazed down at us against a blue square of sky. He sat astride a bucking bronco, its nostrils billowing glowing smoke. With legs akimbo and chaps fluttering in the cartoon wind, he gripped the pommel with one hand and pointed upward at a sign for the Mustang Motor Court with the other. Below the horse, a fluorescent "NO" glowed next to the word "VACANCY."

The motel was a squat, L-shaped affair nestled just off the highway's apron. No frills, with plywood doors and stamped tin numerals, the rooms opened onto a packed-dirt parking lot. A century-old quarry yawned behind the motel while low cliffs surrounded it on three sides, their faces honey-combed by the black mouths of abandoned cinnabar mines. Those pock-marked *mesas* seemed to keep out the passage of time, preserving the motel in an invisible dome as delicate as a soap bubble.

When the motel's owner, a subdued redneck named Elijah Hardy, fell on hard times years before, he first decided to supplement his income by running a cock fighting ring in the quarry out back. That venture ended with him getting a talking-to from the sheriff. His second entrepreneurial misadventure, though— cooking bathtub speed in room seven and selling it to long-haul truckers— ended with him doin' a nickel at Three Rivers. After making parole, he was all too happy to rent us rooms to stage the immigrants for twenty-four hours because it provided him with two of his favorite things in the world: passive cash and deniability.

Chebo jumped down and left to spread the word that the doctor they'd been told to expect had arrived, and I'd be coming around to examine each of them shortly.

Shy Mike tossed me a room key on a fob, and he and Jimmy Wayne humped the stretcher along behind me. While they situated the man on the mattress, I splashed my face at the sink, scrubbing it hard, then ran my wet fingers through my hair.

My arms still roared with fatigue from toting the stretcher, and it took me two sticks to get an IV in the man's forearm. I took the painting over the bed off the wall and hung a bottle of saline from the nail, letting the fluid run wide open into my moribund patient.

When that bottle was empty, I spiked a second, and again ran it in as fast as it could go. For the third bottle, I thumbed the tubing's clamp back to slow the drip and told Shy Mike to come get me when the bottle got close to running dry.

For the next sixty minutes, I went room to room listening to lungs and looking at tonsils. They were a young bunch, and other than some malnutrition, generally healthy. Some had never seen an actual doctor before, getting their medical care back home instead from *curanderas*, and they appeared curious how a physician compared to those folk healers. I did a little medicine and made a lot of small talk, offering reassurances and giving practical advice. Above all else, I smiled. I wanted them to see a friendly white face ushering in their new lives. Those people were why I did what I did, after all. We made those runs often enough that they tended to blur together, but for those people it'd be the biggest day in most of their lives. They'd carry those memories, good or bad, for years, telling friends and loved ones the stories over and over. I often told the boys, the impressions those poor folks took away from their interactions with us would color their perceptions of Texas as a whole. We couldn't take that responsibility lightly.

Back in the drug mule's room I sat vigil, watching him dream as the hours crawled by until shadows closed in on us. He tossed and thrashed in his sleep, occasionally crying out in Spanish or grabbing fistfuls of sheets, tortured by nightmares. A storm rolled through in late afternoon, and the hypnotic sound of rain thrumming on the covered walkway outside led me to doze in my straight-back chair. It was dark as the Devil's pockets when I was startled awake by a semi-lucid voice croaking, "*Agua.*"

I lifted my chin from my chest and stared unmoving at the mule's sun burned face, his dry lips struggling to form words. Within a minute, the dullness fell away as his consciousness finally broke through. His wide eyes immediately darted to the backpack leaning against the wall behind me. In a whimper thick with fear he managed to beg, "*No me mate.*" Don't kill me.

Propped on the nightstand, my legs had fallen asleep and I stamped my boots hard to get the feeling back. Once I thought I could trust my limbs to support me, I crossed the room to fetch him a bottle of water and he accepted it with an expression of lust. "*Lentamente,*" I said. Slowly.

Backlit by a lightning flash, the mule propped himself on an elbow and took a few tentative sips, then a few more. I took my seat once again and sat watching him with my arms crossed, unsmiling.

When he finished the bottle, he belched loudly and collapsed back against his pillow. Gently touching his face, he winced at the pain, then turned to face me once again. Groaning, he asked, "*¿Dónde estoy?*"

I leaned forward, elbows on my knees and fingers interlaced, a deadly serious expression on my face. "How's your English? English would be better."

He paused. "Me English is hokay."

"Good, because my Spanish is shaky, and I don't want you seeing my translator's face. For that matter, I thought about coverin' my face, but when you think back later about what happened here, you aren't gonna have to be the Mexican version of Sherlock fuckin' Holmes to figure out who I am." I extended a sandwich and a candy bar. "You hungry? You're probably hungry." He tore into both ravenously. I waited until he finished.

"Was that good?"

He nodded warily.

"Not making you feel like you're gonna throw up?"

He shook his head.

"All right. Now then, I found you unconscious in the desert about, oh, sixteen hours ago, almost dead, still about two miles from the river yet. You and that goddamn backpack." I jerked my thumb at it angrily. "You with me so far?"

The mule's eyes suggested he was.

"Me and my people took a big fuckin' chance, bringin' you here. Most folks in our position would have just left you there for the buzzards. You and that pack are like a virus, infecting every man, woman, and child you come in contact with, putting them at risk. You know why?"

He shook his head.

"Because once people meet you, they become what we call in English a 'loose end.' And if there's one thing the men with machetes who're lookin' for you and that goddam pack right now hate, it's loose ends.

"So, the way I see it, you owe me. Yessir, I mean to tell you, you owe me 'bout as big as one man can owe another. You know what that word means, 'owe'? Like, a debt?"

The mule nodded.

"Good, 'cause here's how you're gonna pay me back that debt. It's the easiest thing anybody's gonna ask from you for the rest of however much time the Lord sees fit to give you. You're not gonna tell me your name, you're not gonna say where you're from. I don't want to know anything more about you than I already do. You understand?"

Once again, he nodded. "I understand."

"When I leave this room, you're just gonna lay there in that bed, keepin' an eye on that clock next to the air conditioner. You can eat, drink, sleep, shower, watch television, contemplate the goddam paradox of free will and divine omniscience for all I care. I don't give a shit what you do, but you won't look out them curtains, and you won't leave this room until that clock says eight in the morning. By then, we'll have skedaddled outta here, and you'll have this whole place to yourself. You got it?"

"*Sí.*"

"Okay. Now, earlier I unplugged the room's phone and took it up to the front office, left it with the owner. His name's Elijah, and he'll be expecting you. Come eight o'clock, you can go up there and he'll let you have it back. Bring it here, plug it in, and call your people to bring you home. Now, when you make that call, I don't want you to say nothin' 'bout me or any of this. Far as you're concerned, you and me, we ain't never met. I don't care what bullshit you got to make up, but the word '*gringo*' best not come out your mouth. We clear on that?"

"*Sí.*"

"I said, are we clear?"

"Yes."

We exchanged silences for a moment, then I stood and shook his hand. "I gotta get some sleep, it's been a hell of a couple days. Good luck. And no offense, *amigo*, but I hope we never meet again."

I didn't know it then as I crunched across the gravel toward my room in the dark, but that was a wish that fate would not see fit to grant.

Chapter 3

Before leaving the motel, I made three calls. The first to Angelica to let her know I was all right and on my way back to town.

The second call was to the feed store to leave a message for my ranch foreman, Gilberto Moreno. I owned almost thirteen hundred acres outside Amoret, and Gilberto lived out there year-round after I finished off the back of the barn for him. Humble and competent, the old man had well water and propane gas, but no power or phone— "Just as God intended it," he would say— so the feed store was willing to pass along notes when he came in to buy supplies. I wanted an update on a pink eye infection that was making its way through my cattle, and I didn't have time to go out there myself. The clerk said she'd pass the message along.

The third call was to Pablo.

When I finished telling him the story, there was only the hum of the line. A silence stretched so long I was about to ask if he was still there when he said, "You are too smart a man to have done something so stupid, Doctor. Please tell me you are joking."

"I couldn't leave a man to die when I could help him. Not then, not now. Not ever."

He sighed. "I have heard it said, 'The heart of a

good man is the sanctuary of God in this world.' And I believe that to be true. But the world to which that saying refers is not the one you and I occupy on the days when you go to the river, *mi amigo*. For reasons known only to Him, God tends to punish goodness more than reward it along *la frontera*. I pray that is a lesson you do not learn the hard way. What have you said to this man about you and your people?"

"Not a thing."

"Nothing?"

"Not word one."

"*Bueno*. Although you and the role you play for us is well known."

"Actually, I did make a comment to that effect. But nothin' to be done 'bout that now."

"No, nothing to be done."

While we talked, the first of the vehicles arrived to ferry the immigrants to their next stop, with the goal to have them all moved by dawn. If everything went according to plan, we'd all be long gone by eight o'clock.

Once I hung up, we left Shy Mike to oversee things. I drove the empty rig back toward Amoret while Jimmy Wayne stared out the bug-spattered windshield, lost in his thoughts. Chebo dozed between us, his head lolling on the bench seat.

You see, ma'am, there was always an element of danger anytime we made one of those runs to the river, but usually it was abstract, theoretical. The episode with the mule and his pack had made that danger something I could reach out and touch, though, and that could now touch me back. I'd incurred a risk, and it would be a while before I knew if we were in the clear.

The best way I can explain it, I think, was it felt

like this time about twenty years ago when I was sewing up the face of a drunk in the E.R., some dumbass who got slashed with a broken bottle in a bar fight if memory serves. I was tired as all hell, finishing up a twenty-four-hour shift, and I paused to yawn right at the moment the man sneezed. When his head jerked, it drove the needle right into my opposite thumb. Then come to find the man had hepatitis C, so I got to sweat out blood tests for six months. Relax, it turned out fine. But the worst part was for that whole six months, the first thing I did every morning when I woke up, even before I shuffled over to take a piss, was to check my eyes in the mirror to see if they were yellow. That fresh fear never went away completely during that time, it's just that as days and weeks and months passed, I learned to live with it. And just like then, the sense of foreboding I felt staring at the mule gradually melted as the miles between us piled up. At some point on that drive home to Amoret, I decided that I was just going to have to learn to live with it for a while.

We hit the city limits with two hours to kill before my clinic started. I nudged Chebo. "You boys up for a late breakfast? My treat."

Jimmy Wayne said, "You're speakin' my language now, cousin." Chebo rubbed the sleep out of his eyes and nodded.

We exchanged the truck for Jimmy Wayne's pickup and headed to Penny's Diner on the town square. A long row of backs occupied the counter, so we headed toward a green leatherette booth at the rear. I knew most of the patrons, a byproduct of being the only doctor for fifty miles in all directions.

I worked my way through the crowd, slapping backs, shaking hands, pointing my greetings. Blaine

Beckett's disappearance wasn't common knowledge yet, and I saw Blaine's father Maxwell in the crowd reading the paper with his glasses perched halfway down his nose. His curl-topped cane hung on the chair across from him, and an empty plate bore a thin whorl of runny egg yolk where he'd wiped his toast.

The crusty old man was a transplant from Boston, a widower who'd followed his son and new daughter-in-law to west Texas years before. He largely kept to himself, an unusual fact given how visible Blaine and his wife Darla were in Amoret society. Maxwell had a reputation as a curmudgeon in the way we've all seen in men that age. Over the last several months, Darla mentioned to me that she worried Max may be showing early signs of dementia. I'd offered to check him out at my regular clinic, but they never took me up on it. He still drove, and breakfast at Penny's was his daily routine. As I'd reflect on it over the time to come, he didn't have a look on that morning like a man who knew his boy had vanished into thin air. Least if he did it hadn't affected his appetite. Filing past his table, Maxwell's eyes flicked up from the sports page toward mine and just as quickly down again, his scowl uninviting enough that I kept walking.

Our waitress, a young woman with a lazy eye, wet a pencil with her tongue and took our order, reappearing with three plates of *huevos rancheros*. As we dug in, Chebo asked through a mouthful of food, "When we finish here, would you do me a favor and take me by the second-hand store?"

"What you after?" I asked.

"Need to buy a pair of pants."

"You forget to pack? That's not like you," Jimmy Wayne said as he stabbed his straw into the ice of his empty drink, then gestured to the waitress for a refill.

"No, I did something dumb."

Leaning sideways, I glanced under the table and said, "Those 'uns got a couple holes in 'em but don't look too bad."

"No, these are fine, but I had to give away my only other pair on the trail."

"Well, don't keep us in suspense," I said, sipping coffee.

Lowering his voice so he wouldn't be overheard, Chebo said, "You remember the *hombre* with the big scar on his chin? The one who said he was from Sinaloa?"

"Red-checkered shirt? Jumpier than usual?" Jimmy Wayne asked.

"That's him. So, when we were at the safe house, he must have asked me two or three times about snakes on the trail. How often did I see them? Were the ones here in the Chihuahua as poisonous as the ones he knew from back home? Had any of the people I'd taken through ever been bitten on the walk? That kind of thing."

"How come do you reckon? Anybody makin' that walk's got lot bigger things to worry 'bout than snakes," Jimmy Wayne said, and burped into the back of his hand.

"Who knows?" Chebo said. "But when we started the walk, I decided to have some fun with him.

"We got to that limestone cliff face, you know, the one about four miles in? I always take a break there, let everyone rest. While everyone set down their bags and talked, I took one of the bungee cords off my bedroll. It's dark green and about this long," holding his hands three feet apart.

"Uh-oh," I said, smiling in spite of myself.

Chebo giggled harder, his voice husky as he struggled to keep quiet. "I coiled it up behind the rock

I was sitting on, then called the *hombre* over and motioned him to sit next to me. He sits and we talk for a minute about nothing. Then I said, 'Well, we should start thinking about ... wait one moment, what is that?' I was looking behind the rock, and he was immediately alert, like 'What is what?' I reached down into the dark space behind the rock and said, 'Wait, is that a—?' Then I grabbed the bungee and tossed it in the man's direction. It uncoiled in the air, lit up by the moonlight, and I screamed like a little girl, *'Snake! Snake! Snake!'* It landed around his neck and shoulders."

Jimmy Wayne chuckled, "How'd that go over?"

Chebo didn't answer at first, eyes squeezed shut and coughing as he put his palm on his chest, trying to control the volume of his voice amid his laughter. After a moment, he snorted, "He shit his pants."

I did a spit-take as Jimmy Wayne twice smacked the Formica table with an open palm and kicked one leg straight out. "Like actually shit his pants? Defecated?" I asked, laughing out loud.

Tears streamed down Chebo's cheeks as he nodded. "Yes. And not a little bit. It was like a reverse toilet flush."

The patrons looked back at our booth, wondering about the commotion. I shushed the two men, but it only made things worse, like getting the giggles in church.

"Boy, that's nightmare fuel right there," I chuckled, dabbing my eyes with a paper napkin.

"If we had not been where we were, and no one else knew where we were going, he might have killed me," Chebo said, wiping his eyes as his laughter dissipated. "I felt so bad, and he was so embarrassed, that I gave him my only other pair of pants."

"I guess you better had," Jimmy Wayne

snickered. The waitress topped off everyone's coffee
and laid the check face down next to me as the bell
over the etched-glass door jingled and one of
Amoret's finest, Beau Alexander, strolled up to the
register. Scanning the crowd while waiting for his
takeout, his eyes caught mine. I gave a nod and a
smile, and moments later he walked over holding a
styrofoam box.

"Mornin' Doc. Jimmy Wayne. Chebo."

"Morning, Beau. I'm guessin' that box's full of
donuts?" Jimmy Wayne teased.

"Keep it up, Jimmy Wayne. As it is, I'm already
on the fence 'bout you. That goddamn truck you
drive's so ugly, next time I see it I'm citin' you for
disturbin' the peace."

I scooched against the wall to make room. "Come
on and eat your meal sittin' down like a civilized
man."

Beau shook his head. "Wish I could. I'm comin'
over on actual business." He looked around and
seeing Maxwell nearby, lowered his voice to a stage
whisper. "Doc, you seen Darla Beckett today?"

"No, but I didn't have reason to neither. Why you
ask?"

"We got a phone call from her early this mornin'.
Says she come home from bein' gone since Friday
noon and Blaine wasn't there, his car gone too. She
said that's unusual 'nuff as it is for a Tuesday
mornin', but then she got messages on the answering
machine from the college sayin' he no-showed his
classes yesterday. They's wantin' to know if he's all
right."

Jimmy Wayne shook his head. "A little of that
asshole goes a long way. Ask me, if he done lit a
shuck out of town she should count herself lucky."

"First thing I thought too, believe you me," Beau

confided. " But just 'cause he's 'bout as welcome as a breeze from the outhouse don't mean we don't gotta look for him. Darla says she was off visiting family in San Antone so she don't know how long Blaine's actually been missin', or if he even is. I got her callin' their friends, seein' who saw him when."

"I don't know what to make of that, Beau. I surely don't," I said, brushing crumbs off my shirt.

"Okay. Well, Doc, you hear anything, give me a call pronto if you would."

"Count on it."

Jimmy Wayne tipped his head over his shoulder in Maxwell's direction. "Think his daddy over there knows his boy's missin'?"

"One way to find out," the deputy replied and ambled over to Maxwell's table. Jimmy Wayne turned to watch discretely as the lawman cleared his throat and introduced himself to Maxwell. The old man looked over the top of the paper, then put it down, his face morphing into concern as Beau started talking.

Jimmy Wayne turned back to face us and said in a low voice, "Well don't that beat all."

I changed the subject. "How long you in town, Chebo?"

"Couple of days. Yolanda has her first boyfriend. My family wants me to meet him." I'd gotten to know Chebo's younger sister the year before when he'd invited me to her *quinceañera*. That night under the looped strings of bare sixty-watt bulbs, she'd flitted about in a brocade gown, effervescent and all-smiles, already a beauty with big doe eyes that would break a lot of hearts before it was through.

"They like him?" Jimmy Wayne asked.

"Well enough," he shrugged. "They say he treats her well. He's a few years older, has a good job, works hard. Respectful, believes in the old ways."

"Can't ask for much more'n that in a cuñado," I said.

"His people anybody I'd know?" Jimmy Wayne asked.

"No, they're back in Piedras Negras."

Chebo finished his plate, wiping the dripping residue up on a sodden tortilla. I pushed the plate with my half-eaten meal across to him, and he tore into those remains too, still ravenous. I turned my back to the wall and swung my legs onto the booth seat, propping one boot heel on the other's toe while I sipped my coffee. Jimmy Wayne shook a cigarette out of a soft pack and tapped it against the back side of his wrist as silence settled over the table. Chebo scooped home fries onto his fork, then without looking up from his plate suddenly said, "Beckett is dead."

Jimmy Wayne stopped with the lit match inches in front of his cigarette, startled. He leaned toward Chebo, the cigarette bobbing with his words, and muttered, "You know somethin' 'bout this?"

Chebo still didn't look up from the plate. "That's what my caul is telling me."

"Your what?" Jimmy Wayne asked.

"I was born with a caul on my face, *gabacho*. The *curandera* who delivered me told my parents that meant I will be able to see things other people cannot see." He solemnly tapped a finger against his temple and squinched that eye shut.

Jimmy Wayne lit his cigarette and waved out the match. "Well shit, I thank you for tellin' me 'bout this hocus-pocus of yours in time for the Super Bowl. See, me and the missus got our eyes on this above-ground pool--"

"Laugh all you want."

Jimmy Wayne pressed, "Come on, let's do one right here. I'm thinkin' of a number—"

Chebo flashed irritation. He saw this as a gift, and his faith in it was touching.

"Don't be such a shit-heel," I scolded.

Jimmy Wayne obeyed, letting it drop and smiling as he exhaled smoke in two long plumes, like a cartoon bull. But the mood at the table had changed. The invocation of death made the possibility suddenly real, as though Chebo had brought it to pass.

Chapter 4

The clinic day after a run to the river was always a long one. I had to work through lunch, so as I turned onto our street that Tuesday evening, it was full on dark and I was equal parts exhausted and famished.

Back in those days, we lived in a quiet little neighborhood, modest single-family homes in the middle of town that resembled the folks who lived there: unpretentious and ordinary. With an elementary school nearby and neighbors that still talked over fences, the sound of lawnmowers would fill the mornings and the evening air carried the smell of charcoal grills. There were contests for the best Christmas lights, and at Halloween the neatly-trimmed sidewalks teemed with kids trick-or-treating at strangers' houses. The place reminded me a lot of Mayberry.

Rope Tail and Maybelline kicked up a fuss, bouncing and barking to announce my arrival. Inside, the house smelled of cooking and Carpet Fresh. I kicked off my boots at the front door and padded in my white cotton socks toward the kitchen, flipping through the mail.

At the stove, a woman with a stained dishrag thrown carelessly over one shoulder peered into a saucepan, her back to me. Her hips swayed to accordion-laced Tejano music drifting out of a pocket transistor on the counter. She sang along low under her breath as her long ponytail swung in time with her backside, like a slow metronome. She was my love, my life, my world.

"You can't greet a decent man at the door?" I asked, coming up behind her.

"Oh, did one follow you in?" she asked eagerly in her lightly accented lilt, and peered past me in the direction of the foyer. Then she bent her head backwards over her shoulder to look at me with her beautiful smile and blew me an air kiss. I slid one arm around her waist and kissed the nape of her neck before running my lips gently over the hard beads of the crystal rosary she habitually wore. She smelled crisp and clean, like warm laundry as it comes out of the drier.

Short and thin, pretty and plain, Angelica Villalobos had piercing emerald-green eyes that had seen too much of the universe's brutishness. Not that that was her real name. I guess I could tell it to you now since it doesn't matter anymore, but if it's all the same to you, ma'am, I'll hold off.

What's that? Why won't I tell you her birth name? Well, maybe because it adds to her mystique in this story. If I'm being honest, though, I think I won't just because Angelica Vilalobos is the name she always went by once she crawled up that same slope of ground at the river crossing and into the back of our panel truck two years before, scared but determined. Using her birth name now would be like renaming an object you see around the house every day; even if your mouth formed the word, it just wouldn't feel right to your brain.

She never wore makeup, cosmetics having been

laughably unnecessary in her hard-scrabble Coahuila youth. After we were together she still abstained, saying she found make up impractical. While six years my junior, she possessed a much older soul.

My upbringing had been simple, although nothing like hers. I knew the embarrassment of being sent home from school with lice and what it felt like to roll loose change to pay an electric bill. Growin' up, we hunted deer out of season for food, and when I was young I ate so many armadillos I still roll up into a ball when I hear a dog bark. Medicine was my first ever job that didn't make my muscles sore and my back hurt at the end of the day, and I was paying off educational loans for the better part of twenty-three years.

So all that made me appreciate the life I led as a physician. Through the twists and turns of karma, I've met all manner of accomplished people: CEOs, high-ranking military brass, two sitting governors, and a Nobel Prize winner. I had the privilege of sharing a meal once with Georgia O'Keeffe— incredibly kind, she was mostly blind from macular degeneration at the time, but that didn't stop us from discussing our mutual affection for Palo Duro Canyon over blue corn tamales and *calabacitas*. I had the good fortune to spend a month in medical school working with the great surgeon Robert McLelland, one of the doctors at Parkland Hospital who received JFK in the emergency room and who operated on Oswald a couple of days later.

Angelica's intellect would've held its own with any of them. In another time, she'd have walked the halls of power or lectured at universities. Born under a luckier star, I could have seen her sitting in a medical school lecture hall of her own, learning the craft. As it was, though, the universe decided to put her in a dusty village on the Mexican frontier with a mother who died during childbirth and a father whose mistakes led to hard men looking to cut off her and Miguel's heads in order to send a message. In escaping she'd covered their tracks well, but in '82 we still lived under the assumption those same hard men would enjoy finding them.

"I picked up *cerveza* at the grocery store."

"You're a mind-reader," I said, grabbing a can of Pearl. "Want one?"

"*Sí, por favor.*"

Setting hers within easy reach, I bent and sniffed the saucepan. "Chicken *molé* on a Tuesday? How come're you doin' that?"

"Oh, I'm sorry. Are you complaining?" she asked, acting offended.

"Hell no, just wondering what brought this on so I know to do it more regular."

"You know why."

"I 'spect I do." She was proud of my work with Chebo and the immigrants.

"*Mi madre* always said, 'If you're lucky enough to find a good man, keep him happy'."

Leaning back against the counter and crossing my ankles, I gave her a wink and said in a low voice, "And here I was hopin' you'd go doin' that 'bout ten o'clock tonight."

"Who says I can't do both?" she replied in a hush, one corner of her mouth turning up a smile.

"Hot damn. Well, since you're in such a charitable mood, how 'bout we kill the flame on that right now, and I take you in the back and fill you out like an application?"

She rolled her eyes. "Mister Romance."

"Miguel awake?"

"Yes, he's working in the study. Plus, I wouldn't

need to kill the flame since I'd only be gone for a minute and a half anyway," she added in a coy tone.

"Hell fire, woman, I'm not Superman."

"You can wait 'til tonight, I'll make it worth your while. Here, taste." She lifted a spoonful of the *molé* sauce and blew on it, then cupped a hand under as she held it to my lips.

I blew on it also, then sipped. The mild spiciness complimented the chocolate base in a way I've never had anywhere but in her kitchen. I closed my eyes and bumped a fist on the chopping board. "I say, goddamn."

She went back to stirring. "Plan on eating in about an hour."

"'Kay. I'm gonna shuck my duds and scrape off a layer of grime."

"Please." She wrinkled her nose playfully.

Beads of sweat collected on the beer can, so I put it in a coozy and went down the hallway to the study's transom-topped door.

I peeked inside. The previous owners had gone for opulence in that room, with silver brocade wallpaper and iron leaf wall sconces and ivory wainscotting. I was too lazy to redecorate it to my own tastes and had abdicated the space to Miguel who used it for his work.

As usual, he sat in a nylon-strapped lawn chair facing a card table. With a bad complexion and gangly frame, he looked younger than his fifteen years. As I watched, he stroked the downy whiskers shadowing his upper lip, deep in concentration.

A piece of plywood occupied most of the tabletop. Orderly perforations lined the wood, with three rows of evenly-spaced holes, ten holes to a row. Three disorganized piles of clear plastic cutlery lay jumbled in front of him: spoons to Miguel's left, forks to his right, knives in front.

Brow furrowed, Miguel picked up one spoon from the pile and assiduously placed it handle-first into a hole in the row of perforations that had a picture of a spoon taped out to the side. Methodically, he picked up another spoon and repeated the process. Then a third time. Over and over, he placed spoons in the perforations until the entire row was full. He then moved on to the plywood's middle row, repeating the process with forks. After finishing the bottom row of knives, he removed all thirty utensils and placed them in a ziploc bag. He sealed it with precision and placed the bag gently in a half-full cardboard box on the floor next to him. It bore the logo of the Amoret Community Center and School. Then he started over.

The Amoret Community Center and School was a residential home and community center for kids and adults whom we'd now describe as "special needs" or "developmentally delayed," but who in 1982-west-Texas were still just called "retarded." I know that word hurts the ear today, and I'm embarrassed to say it was a part of my vocabulary prior to having Miguel enter my life. But those were the times.

Until they're throwing dirt on my face, I'll remember the first time I laid eyes on Miguel. It'd been raining the day he and Angelica made the walk, and they clambered into the panel truck dripping and shivering.

Handing out dry towels and blankets, I managed to hide my surprise upon seeing Miguel among the group. With his wide-set eyes and prominent epicanthal folds, there was no mistaking Miguel had Down's Syndrome, and Chebo had an unofficial policy of turning down folks who had the potential to be trouble on the walk. That might sound harsh but put yourself in Chebo's position. Best case scenario, if someone has a behavioral issue on the trail in the middle of the night, it's inconvenient or frustrating. Worst case scenario, it could be downright dangerous. On that wet morning, I looked at Chebo, then back at Miguel, then back to Chebo and raised an eyebrow. He gave me a subtle palms-up shrug.

I leaned over and whispered, "I'm surprised to see that kid here."

Chebo answered in a voice so low only I could hear. "What can I say? I got a thing for lame dogs."

When I went over Miguel back at the motel, I found the magnitude of risk had been even higher than known. Angelica was exhausted from exertion and fear, and as I examined Miguel she huddled under a swaddle of blanket in their room, loose frizzy strands of dark hair hanging in her face and fighting to keep her eyes open.

I looked in his ears and eyes and listened with my stethoscope to his lungs after telling him, "*Respire profundo.*" She watched as I moved along, listening over his heart. She noticed my body language change as I lingered there, leaving the bell of the stethoscope in place, my eyes squinched shut in concentration. Wordlessly, I swiveled the end of the scope around to its other side, to a bell that allowed me to hear different, more resonant sounds. Her maternal sixth sense brought her out of her eyes-open nap, suddenly wide awake and asking, "Is everything all right?"

My eyes still closed, I held one finger up in the air, then put it to my lips, asking for a moment of silence as I strained to hear. Finally, I took the buds out of my ears and wrapped the stethoscope around my neck. I gamely patted Miguel on the back and smiled at him, then asked her, "Will he be okay here by himself for a minute while you and I step outside?"

She nodded weakly before putting on a brave smile. "Miggy, wait here. I'll just be right outside the door. Don't touch anything."

"Okay, mama," he said with a blank expression. I turned the television on and found a Bugs Bunny cartoon for him to watch, then held the door for her as he happily rubbed his nose and immersed himself in the cartoon.

Later she'd tell me that was the worst moment of the trip, the fear that came from only knowing something was wrong, but not what. She'd say her feet were only vague, numb aches as she followed me outside.

The rain was really coming down at that point, thrumming hard on the porch's corrugated tin overhang, like the sound of eggs frying. I had to raise my voice to be heard.

"Your English sounds pretty good, but if you'd prefer Spanish, I can go get Chebo to translate?"

"No, English is fine," she said, her face a mask of fear. She couldn't look at me, instead staring at rainwater sluicing down a drainpipe into a hooped barrel three feet away.

"Great. Like Chebo said, my name is Doctor Grady. Did you know Miguel has a hole in his heart?"

She shook her head slowly side-to-side.

"It's a condition we see sometimes in people with Down's Syndrome. You're lucky to have made that walk without it givin' him trouble. Does he get short-winded when he exerts himself?"

"No. He plays with other children with no problems. Is this serious?"

"Right now I don't know. I can hear blood passing from the left side of his heart through the hole and over to the right side of his heart. That's abnormal, but right now he looks pretty comfortable. He isn't having any chest pain; he isn't short of breath. So those are good signs. How old is he?"

She didn't answer, then I noticed her color had gone ivory white and she was about to pass out.

"Whoops, here, lay down for a minute." I controlled her descent onto the damp concrete, bundling her further with her blanket and squatting so I could prop her feet on my bent knee.

As she collected herself, I thought about what it must've taken for her to set out on that journey with her son, to launch into the unknown, and then, unmoored and in a strange country whose government viewed her actions as a crime, to receive news like that which I'd given her. I couldn't imagine how someone handles something like that. Still can't. Right there on that wet concrete outside of room seventeen is where I think I first started to fall in love with her.

I offered to sneak Miguel into my Amoret clinic after dark to do an ultrasound of his heart. Ultrasound was new technology back then, and the machine I'd bought for my clinic took up half the wall in one of the exam rooms. Funny, that same contraption fits in a backpack nowadays. I offered to pay for the two of them to stay at a motel in Amoret while I made all the arrangements, and she took me up on it.

Two nights later we stood in my darkened clinic, her watching me watch the screen. As I ran a jellied probe over Miguel's chest, she saw my face break into a smile, and I told her the hole was something doctors would need to keep an eye on as he got older, but for the moment that was all. She sagged with relief, and I suggested a big meal to celebrate.

I took them to my favorite place in town, a

barbecue joint with sawdust on the floor and a lady picking on a guitar. After we ate I asked her to dance, and she pressed her head against my chest as we slowly swayed to "I'm So Lonesome I Could Cry." At the end of the song, she looked up at me and stood on tip-toes to give me a soft kiss on the cheek and whispered something I missed.

"What was that?" I asked.

With a tenderness I'll never forget, she said, "I think God has answered two of my prayers today. Miguel is out of danger, and in our new land I have found a man with a good heart."

Right then I would've roped the moon for her, and I knew I would do whatever it took to make a future with that woman.

I snapped out of my reverie. Gently rapping twice on the door so as not to startle the boy, I entered saying, "Knock, knock." I clapped my hand on his shoulder and gave it a squeeze.

"Hey, superstar, you doin' all right?"

Without looking up he said, "Hey, Noah."

"You're making good progress here."

"Yeah."

"Anything you need my help with?"

"No. I'm almost through."

"Sounds good. Dinner be ready in 'bout an hour."

I tousled his hair then turned to leave but came back when he said, "Noah, can I ask you something?"

"Sure, buddy."

"Can I get a tattoo?"

"D'you ask mama?"

"Yes."

"And what'd she say?"

"She said it depends on what you said." He spoke slowly, still laser-focused on his task.

"What kind'a tattoo you lookin' to get?"

"One just like yours."

I was taken aback by that answer. I had a caduceus on my upper arm, a souvenir from a night of liquored-up assholery in medical school.

"Sure, buddy. But why do you want to get that?"

"Cause I want to be just like you." It came out matter-of-fact, like he was making small talk at a bus stop. The honesty of the statement made me feel warm to my core. It was no attempt to butter me up, no part of a scheme to get his way on something. Just the simple, straightforward truth. I felt tears prick my eyes.

I cleared my throat and said, "Sure, buddy. We'll get 'er done soon."

"You promise?"

"Indeed I do."

"'Kay."

I kissed the top of his head wondering how I'd gotten so lucky to have the two of them in my life.

It was dark outside, and with the lights on in my study, the window reflected our image back to us true as a mirror. The sight made a wave of affection and appreciation for what I had wash over me once again, and I paused to give Miguel one last squeeze.

In that moment, a flash I took to be lightning lit up the darkened window of my study as I turned to head to the shower. I remember thinking that strange as the sky'd been clear on the drive home, nor was it followed by a roll of thunder. I considered it for the briefest of moments, but in my fatigue I shrugged it off and went to clean up.

I've told myself the man I'd later come to find was outside watching us through the window was surely smart enough to have hidden himself, that I'd only have seen my empty backyard under the stars.

But a part of me still wonders, would things have turned out differently in the end had I taken a moment to check out that odd lightning flash, had I seen the man skulking in the shadows, waggling the Polaroid he'd just taken of us?

Chapter 5

The next morning brought a thick blanket of clouds. Outside the community center, Angelica licked her thumb and wiped a smudge off Miguel's face before hugging him and shooing him inside. Then together we headed to my clinic.

I'd started her off as office help, but when it became clear how quickly she picked things up, I'd moved her along. Soon, she was helping with my billing, then just doing it herself. By six months, I was introducing her as my practice manager.

She learned rudimentary medical skills, at first assisting me in little things like starting IVs and suturing, then showing enough proficiency that I let her start doing them independently. Of course, this was back in a time when you didn't need every piece of paper in the world just to touch a patient.

The day flew by as I ran back and forth between my two exam rooms while Angelica checked people in, restocked supplies, and pecked out correspondence. Meanwhile, I tweaked blood pressure medicines and swabbed sore throats, did pap smears and looked in fussy babies' ears. Unsurprisingly, the small talk that day centered around Blaine's disappearance, and the town rumor mill was cranking up.

"I got it on good authority that a car dealer in Fort Stockton identified Blaine from a picture the deputies showed him. Man said Blaine bought a clunker from him on Monday and paid extra to have the VIN removed," said Eloise Harkins, the town librarian, as I felt her thyroid for lumps.

"You didn't hear this from me," said Sheila Biggs, a diabetic who ran her own beauty shop out of her rec room. "I hear tell Blaine's got a gamblin' problem. He'd been tryin' to keep it secret, but finally he lit out for the territories instead of payin' off his debt," she said as I examined her feet.

"Truth be told, I don't get what all the fuss is about. Anybody with a lick of sense can see what's goin' on, seems to me. The man just had hisself a mid-life crisis," said Tiny Beaumont, an obese electrician with chronic diverticulitis. While I pressed on his prodigious belly, he said, "Seems as plain as the nose on yer face there, doc. He woke up one day in a town he don't care for and that don't care for him, and just decided life's too damn short of a ride to spend it in a situation like that."

Mmm, what's that? Lordy, I do apologize, I keep forgettin' you're coming at all this for the first time. You'll have to forgive me, but for forty years I've been chewing all this over in my mind. I haven't spoken of this business aloud to another soul in so long, and a stranger no less, I may need reminders from time to time that you don't know all the back stories. Just jump in like you did there if I say something you don't understand.

While Darla Beckett was a native Texan, Boston-raised Blaine never seemed to fit in despite living in Amoret twenty years. When I say he didn't fit in, it was more appropriate to call it— well, almost like a self-imposed exile. It's fair to say he earned the label "outsider," that it was a reaction to his treatment of neighbors and strangers alike as knuckle-dragging flat-earthers.

Blaine was a creature of the mind, you see, and I'll admit a first-rate intellect. Deeply religious, he'd chosen as his purpose in life the study of the church's greatest thinkers and the passing on of their intellectual heritage. Hearing that, you'd be forgiven for believing such a man would be contemplative and accepting, but he wasn't any such. Blaine's was a harsh and judgmental God, more fire and brimstone than suffer the children unto Him.

Once Blaine'd completed a doctorate in Divinity at Fordham, he was offered a job teaching theology at Saint Francis Assisi College here in town. You passed the school on your way here today, just outside the western city limits, big sprawling place. Back then, though, the school was brand new and smaller than your average east Texas high school. Its construction was the life's work of a group of benefactors, the most prominent of whom was Darla's father. These folks envisioned the college as an island, a bubble where dogmatic religious beliefs would be handed down generation to generation. I'm told they even chose the remote west Texas location to reinforce that image. Blaine was their star faculty recruit, and when they cut the ribbon on the college it was assumed he'd be groomed for greater things. So as newlyweds, he and Darla packed up and moved from the big city to Amoret, Texas.

Over the years, on the rare occasions I talked to Blaine I found he gave off a Jane-Goodall vibe about the town, like he was studying a herd of silver back gorillas for a science project. He was a snob, which led to his being a loner. I can say it wasn't an aversion to the landscape, though. To the contrary, despite growing up a city boy Blaine became a competent outdoorsman and hunter over his years out here in the desert, capable of taking down pronghorn with shots of over three hundred yards and going camping regularly at Big Bend National Park just south of here. But he always did it alone.

He set himself apart from the town in ways great and small. In the early days he turned down invitations to barbecues and social events without the courtesy of a response. Around town he'd yell at waiters, and if he wasn't lecturing his conversational partners he was likely opining on life in Boston. Sanctimonious and dismissive, patronizing and biting, he got a reputation as someone who'd argue with the wooden Indian in front of the feed store. He made no friends when his response to a nudie-booth joint opening in Fort Stockton was to camp out in a parking lot across the street and take pictures of the patrons' license plates, then pass them out in the back of church after services for a good old public shaming. Beyond his sanctimony, his refusal to support local businesses was another sticking point. For his fortieth birthday he'd wanted to buy a new rifle for hunting antelope, an antique .300 Savage that would have been a boon for our local gun dealer, Duane Sheehan. The commission on a rare caliber like that would have been the better part of a mortgage payment for Duane had he acted as middle man, but Blaine used a dealer in Chicago. I know that may sound like a little thing to big city folks, ma'am, but in a small town where everybody's just trying to make a living, that's the same as taking food off someone's table.

As I listened to the gossip fly through the day, my dread built for the last appointment on my schedule. When it finally came, I stood outside the closed door and reviewed the chart for a few minutes longer than it actually took, dawdling before taking a deep breath and rapping twice on the heavy oak door. I entered after hearing a soft, "Come in."

Francis Beckett sat quietly in an ornate chair, his legs crossed, one knee over the other, reading a dog-eared copy of *Horseman, Pass By*. Good-looking and soft-spoken, he had a demeanor that normally seemed— I don't know, lonely seems too harsh a word but it's the one I'll use. He was nineteen and a sophomore at Francis Assisi. He'd been coming to see me for about six months without his parents' knowledge, worried about a weight loss he was experiencing. I'd known him his whole life and understood his concern: always asthenic, his cheekbones seemed higher, more hollowed out, and getting worse by the passing week.

While Blaine cast himself as an outsider in Amoret, Francis, on the other hand, wanted to fit in, but could no more force himself to do so than keep his eyes open when he sneezed. He shared his father's intellectual rigor but lacked Blaine's convictions about the ends to which it should be applied. Although Blaine wanted to be a force in the religious intellectual world, his son was a rudderless English major. Francis was effete. Prissy even.

On that morning, he smiled wanly when I entered, closing the book and resting it in his lap. As I took a seat on a castered stool, I noticed he wore the only pair of penny loafers I'd seen on a patient all day, and his blue jeans were pressed.

"Afternoon, Francis." Pointing at the novel in his lap I said, "Great book."

"Hi, Doctor Grady. How are you?"

"Fine, but I should be asking you. How you

holding up?"

He shrugged. "Unfortunately, things are in such a state that you could be talking about a couple of things."

"I understand. Want to talk about your dad?"

He turned toward a curio cabinet next to him, the small brass key in the lock more for show than function and ran his finger over the grains in the wood. "If he ran off like people are saying, if I'm being perfectly honest it wouldn't break my heart."

"Your mom handling it OK?"

"She's upset. Say what you will, she still loves him."

"Okay. Well, anything I can do for y'all, just holler."

He pursed his lips and nodded grimly.

"'Nuff about that. Tell me how you're doing since I saw you last."

"I've tried exercising like you said. I run out of energy quickly, though."

Flipping the pages on my clipboard, I said, "I see your weight's down another two pounds from two weeks ago."

He shook his head. "I don't doubt it. I've quit checking. I just get full so quickly."

"Sleeping any better?"

"I'll get a few hours at a time."

"Any break in the night sweats?"

He shook his head.

"How 'bout the skin lesions? Hop on up here and let me take a look."

He sat on the exam table and unbuttoned his shirt. Scattered from his collar bones to his belly button were a dozen purple, raised bumps, each about the size of a pencil eraser.

I lifted the tails of his shirt. Several glistening

violet lesions had sprung up between his shoulder blades, sinister in their silence. I put the bell of my stethoscope over his lungs and said, "Gimme some deep breaths." I heard the normal roar of air coursing to and fro, in and out, like surf at the beach, but underneath the cacophony I heard something ominous. Barely perceptible, each breath was accompanied by a whisper of soft, subtle crackling, like someone pulling velcro apart.

Under his armpits, I rolled the small swollen lymph nodes I'd found two weeks before back and forth under my fingers, like marbles under the skin, making sure they were still untethered to any other structures. "That hurt?" I asked. He shook his head.

After finishing my exam, I shucked my latex gloves, then sat back on my stool and scribbled notes. Francis stared at me expectantly while I paused, staring off into space and whorling the pen in my hand, thinking, then finished scribbling my thoughts while they were fresh. Finally, I clicked the pen and put it away.

"I think you're still getting worse, Francis. I'm sorry."

Tears welled in his eyes and he nodded his head. He had a thickness in his throat when he asked, "How much longer do you think I'll be able to go to school?"

"No crystal ball, but at this rate I'll be surprised if you can return next semester."

He was silent, and I let it hang in the air. I was feeling him out, seeing how much he wanted to hear.

"Did you know you're still the only person I've told?" he asked.

"About your disease or that you're homosexual?"

"Both, actually."

"Look, Francis, you know I'm going to support

you all the way through this. But understand, your physical appearance is changing in a way that people are gonna start to ask. It's better if you've thought about what you're gonna say ahead of time so you don't get caught off guard."

"Have you read in your medical journals about anybody surviving this?"

I shook my head. "I'm so sorry to say, but no. Once I got your test results back telling me this wasn't lymphoma, I was afraid this was the direction it was gonna go."

"What did you say it's called again?"

"Doctors are even arguing about that now. We been calling it 'GRID,' 'Gay Related Immune Deficiency.' But about a month ago there was a report that they been seein' it in heterosexuals too, mostly hemophiliacs, so I suspect another name'll be coming down the pike."

"This is going to kill my parents," he said, forgetting for a moment his father had gone missing.

Now it was my turn to be silent.

"My Uncle Robert, one of my dad's brothers, came out when I was a child. I listened to my father go on and on to my mom about it. Kept calling him a 'sodomite.' Said if Uncle Robert insisted with that choice, he'd be going to hell because homosexuality was 'an affront in God's eyes.' It made an impression, as I'm sure you can imagine. It ended with him cutting all ties, telling Uncle Robert he was dead to the family."

"Pretty dogmatic guy, your dad."

"Hmph, yes. He named me after the school's figurehead, after all. Did you know that?"

I offered a conspiratorial smile and shook my head.

"Meanwhile, my grandfather disowned Uncle

Robert too. Grandpa Max's animosity isn't driven by religious beliefs the way dad's is, just old school hatred. I can remember as a little kid listening to him tell stories about going 'queer-stomping' in South Boston with his friends."

He stared at the floor, and I could see he was picturing a day in the not-too distant future when he would be in a sick room, alone.

"What about your mom? I know her pretty well. I have a hard time picturing her turning her back on her flesh and blood."

Before he could answer, there was a light tap on the door.

I raised a finger to Francis and turned my head. "Is it important?" I asked the closed door.

The heavy door muffled Angelica's voice. "I think so."

Francis buttoned his pants and shirt then nodded. "Come in," I said.

Angelica poked her head in and the anxiety on her face was immediately evident. I felt a knot in my stomach.

"Francis," she said, "they've found your father's car. Someone set it on fire."

Chapter 6

F rancis froze except for the rapid blinking of his eyes. Outside the window, three young girls played in the backyard of a house that backed onto the clinic's property, not twenty feet from where we stared at each other. The juxtaposition of their squeals with the somber young man before me were a harsh illustration of how fickle the universe could be in deciding which children get to experience the joyfulness they have coming to them by virtue of their birth, and which ones get the callous side.

After a beat, Francis' face clouded and he tilted his head back against the sheet rock with a soft *thunk*. In a shaky voice he asked, "What happened?"

"I do not know," she said. "Only that they found the vehicle on Mariano's ranch. I just got a call from the sheriff's deputy." She jutted her chin at me. "Noah, he was calling to ask if you would be willing to go out there in case someone needs medical assistance."

Francis cast his eyes down and stared intently at the penny in one loafer as he picked at it with a manicured thumbnail, trying to appear brave although whether for me or himself I couldn't say. He looked to be steeling himself, then coughed into his fist. Clearing his throat, he asked without looking up,

"Umm, did they say if there was a body inside?"

Angelica shook her head. "No, they did not, Francis, I am so sorry."

He released an audible breath, and wiped tears with the back of his hand. For a second I could swear I got a glimpse into his soul, groaning with the effort of bearing this new weight. I worried it might snap, like the spine of an overburdened mule.

I nodded my head, "Francis, tell your momma that I'll come by and talk once we've finished up out there."

By the time I got the deputy's directions from Angelica and walked out to my truck, the day's shadows had disappeared.

Jesus. As I look back on it now, ma'am, sitting here talking to you all these years later, this part of the story makes me cringe. I hate even to think about it, much less speak of it aloud. When I considered your invitation to discuss that awful autumn in '82, this topic made me hesitate, and of all the things I'm going to tell you, the one matter I fear most you and your readers will judge me for.

I'm a flawed man.

I know we all are, and that statement sounds like false humility, like I'm deflecting my blame. If so, I don't mean to do that. I'm not making excuses. But if you and I were to consider the seven deadly sins, when God was passing out the normal allotment of pride and wrath I must've gotten in line twice is all I can figure. So it's going to sound funny when I say the subject at hand has nothing to do with either of those flaws. And I'm pretty sure when I'm through you're not going to say I'm being hard on myself.

Darla Beckett and I had an affair that lasted for over twenty years.

It started off in college, the summer of '58 to be exact, when she and Blaine were only dating. She'd come back home to Texas for the break, and we were introduced by a mutual friend. And brother, did we fall hard for one another.

It kept on for years. Through their marriage, through their raising of a family. Early on, she talked of breaking things off with him, and I was fool enough to believe it. Actually, that's not fair. I think she believed it at the time she was saying those things to me. But it was always something. She lacked the courage to take action and coming from a religious tradition that venerated martyrdom didn't help. I'll never forget, she actually told me once, "I think some people just aren't meant to be happy." I mean, what do you say to that?

The situation was made more complicated by her family, the Studdards. Wealthy Galveston gentry, they'd adopted Darla from an Irish orphanage as an infant when her biological father, a member of the IRA, left her at a convent with instructions that if he didn't return for her in twenty-four hours, the nuns were to put her up for adoption. He didn't, and they did. Her alabaster skin, raven hair, and strong Catholic faith were the only vestiges of Irish life that she retained. The Studdards managed their wealth well and set Darla up for life.

Her adopted parents went on to separate, but her father's dogmatic Catholicism proscribed divorce. Her mother had no such qualms herself and went on to divorce him, a legal procedure only in his eyes, and one which he didn't recognize.

During our college years, Doctor Studdard was polite around me, honoring the "just friends" charade Darla and I put out to the world while she struggled with breaking things off with Blaine. He could read the situation, though, and once she confessed her true feelings for me, he'd weighed in with the opinion that Blaine was her best path to get to her heavenly reward. I came to find years later that he also added the caveat that if she felt otherwise, that was fine, but they might have to revisit the question of her trust fund if she chose me. That's the kind of man he was. So, that set us on a course of over twenty years of weekend getaways, stolen moments, and emotional pining while she went through the motions with a man whom she didn't love, a roommate for all practical purposes.

Believe me, ma'am, I know how sordid and melodramatic all this sounds from the outside, like a goddam soap opera. For my part, I thought she was the one for a lot of years and would have been happy keeping that arrangement up until I was looking at the wrong side of the grass. All that time I figured if I could have her in every way except the kind with a piece of paper that was good enough for me, and I walked away from getting serious with a lot of women over the years because of what I had with Darla.

All that changed when I began things with Angelica, though. I broke off the affair with Darla, and never looked back. I came clean about everything with Angelica— hell, she deserved to know—but she never doubted that I'd moved on. Angelica was my future, and I made sure both women knew it.

Darla hadn't been happy when I broke it off, but she didn't really have any choice than to accept it. We stayed friends, having been too much a part of each other's lives for that not to be the case anymore. She knew me better than any soul on the planet. There's history there, you know? And since we'd managed to get to that point with the town and her husband unaware of our indiscretions, we both thought we could just carry on with the appearance we'd projected for all those years of two old friends from back in the day.

Chapter 7

I've heard it said, "Coincidences are God's way of staying anonymous."

Wish I knew who it was said that, because I happen to believe that to be true, and the events surrounding the discovery of the burned-out husk of Blaine's ride did nothing to dissuade me.

What's that? No kidding. Was Einstein that said that? Well darlin', I have to say, I'm impressed as hell you knew that, young as you are.

Oh shit, really? That's too funny. I keep forgetting nowadays that kind of stuff is just sitting right there on your phone. Well, I got another one for you then, and this time I do know who said it. Isaac Asimov told some reporter, "Sufficiently advanced technology can't be distinguished from magic." That's how I think about those phones.

Anyway, coincidences.

Blaine's vehicle'd been found about ten miles south of town in the back country of a ranch belonging to one of Amoret's more prominent citizens, a man named Mariano Enriquez. Mariano had started off making good money as a directional driller for Gulf Oil in the seventies. He'd been sitting on a dozen acres of caldera east of town with no real plan as he tells it until one hot afternoon in July of

'76. There was a parade scheduled through downtown Amoret for the Bicentennial that day, and Main Street was full of families milling about, baking in that hot Texas sun.

Mariano said the high school band's belting out "Louie, Louie" gave him a headache, so he ducked into Skinny Dick's Tavern for a shot and a beer. Standing at the bar next to him was a stranger wearing shined boots and a three-piece suit, and as he nursed his Schlitz Mariano mentioned light-heartedly how out of place the visitor looked in a shithole icehouse like Skinny Dick's. The man laughed and said he was a lawyer for Texaco, in town to negotiate development of some gas leases on the land of a friend of ours, old Mordechai Runnels. Now normally, Mariano believed the fastest way to double your money was to fold it over and put it back in your pocket. I loved the son of a bitch, but he was so tight he squeaked when he walked. On that day, though, the two men got to talking more and Mariano started getting excited, so much so he missed the parade. He says he walked out of Skinny's three hours later with an idea, and when they struck oil on his property eight months later, Mariano found himself a rich man.

Mariano used that oil money to buy up more parcels of land in the region, and success begat success. While most of his purchases were for exploration, though, he set aside one piece of desert south of town, keeping it pristine in every way except for the construction necessary to build a homestead. I've seen aerial photos of it since, and his ranch house is a pinprick in the middle of a sea of desert. The tract of land on which he lived was massive, so much so in fact Mariano was technically my neighbor even though the property line on my much smaller ranch was a good five miles away from his ranch house.

Make a short story long, if you were looking to torch a vehicle and have nobody notice it for a while, you'd have been hard-pressed to pick a better place, surrounded as it was by thousands and thousands of acres of empty desert scrub. Blaine's Jeep had been found in a dry creek bed where it entered a short box canyon about three miles from the highway as the crow flies. Frankly, it seemed a small miracle anybody had found it at all.

My truck lurched over the broken ground as I cut my way through Mariano's property. The primitive road glowed a dull white in the purple gloam, just two parallel ruts, ragged and overgrown with candelilla grass that *tinked* off my front bumper like rapid-fire Morse code before scraping along under my chassis.

As the sky turned lead gray, my eyes swept the bajada, looking for I don't know what. I recognized the silliness of thinking I might stumble across some sign of what had occurred out there, some clue that a clever investigator would notice, saying, "Wait, what's this?" as happened in the mystery novellas Angelica loved. But I looked anyway. There was only the desert pan, though, dotted horizon to horizon with creosote brush and yucca and juniper stands.

Eventually, the plain sloped downward, and I could see where the road crossed a dry creek bed. The box canyon started at that point, running off to the left where the stream had eons ago carved a swath thirty feet deep and twenty feet wide through the sandstone for a distance of a few hundred yards. The canyon's steep walls petered out at the crossing of the road, and off to the right was just more open prairie. Parked single file where the trail crossed the creek bed were a big Ram Charger with a rack of roof lights and a Brewster County Sheriff's Department truck with a scatter gun propped between the seats.

Pulling up behind the deputy's truck, I had no more slammed my door than I heard another vehicle approaching, something big-engined. Moments later, a truck came laboring down the road, eating the dust I'd kicked up. Through the haze, I recognized the spiderwebbed windshield on Sheriff Lloyd McHenry's ancient pickup, and as it got closer I saw his bushy-browed shape belted in the driver's seat. We were friendly at first by dint of our positions in Amoret society, but with time came to be genuine *compadres*.

Once upon me, his window hummed down before he killed the engine. Staccato bursts squawked from the police radio he kept in his personal vehicle.

"Evenin', Doc. You better watch out, missin' dinner for something like this. That woman of yours is gonna wise up one day and trade your ass in."

"Evening, Sheriff. One of your deputy's asked if I'd head out here."

He waved it off with a nonchalance that made it clear I needn't explain. He got out and looked around, turning a slow circle.

"Funny thing, Doc. I knew this canyon a younger man. Right outta high school, me and my brother spent a summer diggin' a well and puttin' in a windmill out here for old man Lousteaux back when he owned all this. Makes my back hurt just thinkin' about it." He reached through the window to his center console for a long-handled Maglite. Its beam stabbed the dusk, sweeping the brushy flatland like a spotlight sweeping a prison yard. It centered on an approaching deputy, making him throw a long, skeletal shadow.

"Billy James, you got this all sorted out yet for

me?" the sheriff hollered.

Billy James clicked his own Maglite on and beckoned us to follow him back. "Gettin' there, Sheriff."

We followed Billy James over the rubbled caliche, our gazes following his arm as he pointed off to the flat plain on our right. A rectangular box seemed to hover several feet above the scrub a few hundred yards away, the precision of its angles marking it as man-made. Once illuminated, we could see the familiar weathered plywood and black tar paper of a deer blind.

"Mariano gave that truck's owner"— he swept the beam over the Ram Charger— "permission to come back here and hunt pronghorn out of that stand, young feller named Gutierrez. Gutierrez said he first got an inkling something was wrong when he found the padlock on the gate from the road'd been cut. Said whoever did it looped the lock's shackle back through two links on the chain so's from the road you couldn't tell the gate was unlocked, you had to be right up on it to see. Gutierrez come down the road and parked about a quarter mile out so's he wouldn't spook nothing, plannin' to hunt 'til dark-thirty. Said he climbed up in that deer stand yonder, but soon's he checked his line of sight down the crick he saw this."

We stopped at the mouth of the short canyon. Some fifty yards away in the direction that would have been upstream had there been water, a hardtop Jeep sat at a forty-five-degree angle in the creek bed on flat tires. The windows had exploded outward, presumably from the heat generated by the fire. Carbon scorches marked where tongues of flame had licked the roof and central frame down to the chassis. The back hatch was open, and the front of the vehicle looked to be relatively spared, with some of its dark green paint still intact. Hearing the rounded river stones clack with each step of the sheriff's Mayhans, I felt a sense of déjà vu come over me.

"Them's Blaine's plates, I'm guessin'?" the sheriff asked.

"Yessir."

"Any sign of him?"

"Nosir."

The sheriff nodded slowly, then turned his back to us and took a few steps away in the direction of the vertical canyon wall. He tucked the Maglite under one armpit before unzipping his pants and began to urinate against the crumbling earth. Mid-stream, he asked over his shoulder, "What d'you know about this feller Gutierrez?"

"Works at State Farm, knows Mariano from church," the deputy said. "Says they're in the Knights of Columbus together. Apparently, Mariano's sort of a grandfather to the boy."

McHenry zipped up and turned back to me. "Mariano got any grandkids of his own?"

I said, "Just the one, up in Chicago. Kid was on dope pretty bad from what I hear. Died of an overdose a year come June."

The sheriff puckered his lips and nodded as we headed toward the vehicle. He stopped me short saying, "Doc, stay here for a minute if you would." I obeyed while he made his way to the Jeep, first sweeping his beam back and forth across the smooth river stones along his path. "No chance of gettin' footprints out here," he called out.

At the vehicle, he pulled a red bandana from his back pocket and set it on the roof's warped metal. He tapped it with his fingertips, first quickly, then let them sit.

"Metal's cold. This happened more'n twenty-four hours ago."

Making his way around the chassis, he stepped onto a small heap of rocks by the burst passenger window. Several glass shards had fallen there, and now they picked up glints from the beam. Like a diamond plinth, they sparkled while he stood atop the mound to better survey the interior.

"Case you hadn't noticed, Sheriff, I saw a chunk of melted plastic in the front floorboard," Billy James called out.

"Bet it was a jerry can of diesel somebody used to speed this along," McHenry said. He swung his light between the hood and the popped rear door. "Would explain why the interior got it so bad, but not the front."

"Sheriff, you think we might could get some latents from those spots?"

"As long as thinkin' don't cost nothin', yes I do."

As McHenry made his way back, Billy James asked, "What are the chances Blaine could'a done this hisself?"

Without looking at the younger man, the sheriff asked, "Makes you say that?"

"Well sir, I mean, if somebody stepped to Blaine intent on doin' him bodily harm, don't seem to me like this is how they'd go 'bout it. Ask me, this looks more like a feller don't want his car found for long enough to buy him time to do somethin' else."

McHenry sucked his teeth. "Well, there's fuckery afoot without a doubt. I'll swear to that and that only." Looking around the car's surroundings, he asked, "How come you're so slow to string it up, hot shot?"

Billy James looked down at the ground and shifted his weight from foot to foot. "I run outta yellow tape last week. Keep meanin' to get me a new roll."

The sheriff gave him a pained look. "Goddammit, boy. I got a roll in m' toolbox. Go on an' get it." He tossed his key ring to Billy James who caught it cleanly.

As Billy James jogged back to the sheriff's truck, McHenry shook his head. With a half-hearted wave in Billy James' direction, he said to me, "Round the office we call him 'Blister'."

"How come's that?"

"'Cause generally he don't show up 'til after the work is done."

"You think there's anything to what he was saying? About Blaine doin' this himself, I mean?"

"You really wanna know what I think?" the sheriff said, looking disconsolate.

I nodded.

"I 'spect some technician at the county morgue'll be stuffin' gauze up Blaine's asshole this time next week. That's what I think."

We were quiet for a long time after that, chatter feeling out of place after that sentiment. I can't speak for the lawman, but I was worried at the direction things might go as folks around town started clamoring for a resolution to all this. Two of the strongest elements of human nature are the need to feel safe, and a mistrust of folks who're different, "them" and "us." Unpopular as Blaine was, his disappearance and that burned out ride pricked the bubble in which most folks prefer to live, a bubble that was as illusory as it was understandable. If a howl started up for someone's head, there were lots of vulnerable people around who could make a good target. I liked to think McHenry was a good enough man to avoid turning to a scapegoat, but as I studied the man while he jotted notes in a small spiral book, I had to admit it was more a wish than a certainty.

In the peacefulness of the purple twilight, I wandered a short distance away and scanned the landscape. Nothing moved, but as the shapes in the approaching darkness played with my imagination, something made me stop short.

A sense of foreboding hit me, suddenly and hard. At first, I tried to be rational about it. After all, the vehicle of a man I'd cuckolded for two decades had been found burned out and hidden, and as a separate matter I still didn't know if there would be consequences for involving myself with the mule and his pack. I had plenty of reasons to feel anxious. But if I was being honest with myself, the suddenness of this wave of paranoia was something else, something that came from my gut, not my brain.

As the early moon's shadows closed in on all sides, I couldn't shake the feeling that someone was up in those rocks, watching us.

Chapter 8

As I walked up a lamp-lined curving sidewalk to Darla's gabled house later that evening, the place was bigger than I'd remembered, with its square balconies and sleek columns and life-size angel statues flanking the front door. Flames guttered in old gas lamps above the massive oak door and glinted off the discolored brass of the heavy knocker. I rapped it twice. I recalled her once saying the door came from some church in Scotland.

Every town has a moneyed section, and the Becketts were the anchor for Amoret's. Oil and gas were behind most of the rock-walled estates and manicured lawns on the bluffs north of town, and not knowing any better one would assume being a theology professor at a fledgling religious college must pay pretty well for the Becketts to be rubbing elbows with that set. In actuality, it was all Darla's family money that kept 'em out there.

You'd have thought I'd been to the Beckett house more often than I had. But truth be told, when I left the canyon to keep my promise to Francis, I had to look up Darla's address first because, it'd been nine years since I'd set foot on the property. For the years she and I carried on, I'd avoided their house like it was radioactive. On the couple of occasions when I'd gone there for a fundraiser, I felt like a stranger, an interloper. I never had any squishiness about feeling like a home wrecker because I knew she was never going to leave Blaine. But being around that house reminded me she and I weren't sharing the life both of us thought we were meant to have together.

The door swung silently on well-oiled hinges, just a few inches, revealing one green eye. Then she threw it open wide and crossed the threshold to draw me into a warm embrace. It caught me off-guard, and I flinched for the briefest of moments before relaxing. Even then, I returned it partially out of obligation, but mostly out of sentimentality.

"Thank you so much for coming, Noah." She broke the hug and gestured toward the slate-lined foyer. "Please, please, do come in."

Despite her casual clothes she still gave off a patrician air, like using a paper bag to store diamonds. Busts set in niches stared back at me as I followed her in her socked feet toward the living room with its broad, oiled boards and recessed lighting. They'd changed the decor since my last visit. Gilt figurines occupied the mantel over a five-foot wide fireplace, and a stained-glass window overlooked the backyard facing east, the better to get the morning sun I assumed. In the backyard, rose bushes surrounded a pergola and marble bird bath. Fifty yards from the main house and hunkered under a large oak was an apartment I knew to be Max's, where a low light flashed in ebbs on the curtains, the glow of a TV set.

Darla glided behind the wet bar. Tucking a loose strand of hair behind her ear, she asked, "Want some wine?"

"I'm good, thanks."

Glass in hand, she came to the couch and tucked

her feet up under her, gesturing for me to sit.

I quickly relayed the details of what we'd found at the canyon. When I finished, she sighed, and stared at me without saying anything, holding the glass in both hands and tapping one finger on the rim. I matched her silence.

Then she said, "Noah, all the times I rehearsed this in my head after Francis called to say you'd be coming over, I never settled on a way to ask. So, I'm just going to come out and say it. Did you have anything to do with Blaine's disappearance?"

I hadn't been expecting that. "What do you mean?"

Her demeanor softened, and she set the wine glass down before moving closer. Placing both hands on my thigh, she leaned in close, looking me in the eyes. I saw the old Darla in her gaze, the woman with whom I'd walked on sandy beaches and held hands in the darkness, with whom I'd made love wrapped in blankets on the desert floor at sunrise and cooked meals and shared books and planned a life. She opened her mouth to speak, paused to collect her thoughts, then continued.

"I've gone through a lot of emotions in the last few days, as you can imagine. I'm concerned for Blaine, obviously. I want him to be safe. But I'm worried for him as the father of my children, not as the love of my life."

Her cheeks flushed and she dropped her chin to her chest. "When you settled down with Angelica— that was hard. I'd always labored under the delusion that one day we'd be together, and for the first time— I know I have no right to say this, but I felt betrayed. I know, I know, that's stupid, but feelings are feelings. The last two years have been among the most difficult in my life, watching from afar as you two play house. Angelica seems like a good woman, but putting myself in your place, I can see that there are obstacles to long-term happiness for the two of you."

"If you're talking about Miguel—" I began angrily, but she looked up and cut me off.

"Since I realized that Blaine was missing, a million thoughts have gone through my head for what may have happened. But there's one possibility I keep circling back to.

"Noah, did you orchestrate Blaine's disappearance so that you and I could be together, at long last after all these years?"

"That's what this is about?"

"I have to ask. Because if the answer is yes, I want you to know that whatever you may have done, if you'd done for the purpose of our being together, I could forgive you."

"You could?" I asked, looking at her hands on my knee.

She squeezed as she said, "For years, I was too weak willed to walk away from a failed marriage. You, on the other hand, you're one of the strongest people I've ever known. Everything you have, you've earned. Growing up in a world of trust fund babies as I did, your individualism and faith in yourself is just— well, it's refreshing. And that's led me to ask myself, could you, under the right circumstances, have done something, committed some act, made some arrangement that's led to the present situation so that we could finally, after all these years, have the life together we both want?"

Her shoulders loosened as the tension ebbed, then she said, "I think you could."

Too late, I realized the intensity of the hug at the door hadn't been based in grief as I'd first assumed, but yearning. In light of that, it shouldn't have surprised me that she wanted to rekindle our relationship now that she thought she was newly single. It did surprise me, though, that she thought I was capable of making Blaine disappear so that she and I could start a life together.

An unseen wind chime tinkled, the only sound. I was quiet for a moment, then lifted her hands from my thigh and placed them in her lap.

"I've moved on, Darla. I can see why you might think what you think, and I'd be lying if I said that in years past I didn't hope to get a phone call that something had happened to the man. A car wreck, a tumor; hell, a meteor coming through this here ceiling and striking him down. But— and I need you to hear me on this— those days are gone. I've got a beautiful woman sitting on a couch six miles from here, reading a book while she waits for me to come home from talkin' to an old flame. I'd never do anything that might mess that up. My life is better with you in it, but only under the right terms."

I stood up. "I mean this, I hope they find your man safe and sound. I'll show myself out."

I took three steps, then looked back where she still sat on the couch with a forlorn expression. I said, "You and me, we were destined to come to this, to a sad end."

Chapter 9

Iwas almost to my truck when a wash of
headlights swept across the front of the house.
Heralded by the growl of a big V-8, a restored
'71 Thunderbird with a vinyl top and suicide doors
climbed the circular driveway and pulled up behind
me. Francis emerged from the sedan, a morose look
on his face and beer on his breath.

"Evening, Doctor Grady. What did you find out
at the canyon?" he asked with an edge of anxiety.

I gave him a quick rundown as I climbed behind
the wheel, omitting the deputy's speculation about
whether Blaine might have done it himself and the
sheriff's guess that Blaine was dead.

He looked pensive. "Thanks for taking the time. I
decided to spend the night over here instead of my
dorm just so the house doesn't seem as empty. I
appreciate your coming by and looking out for my
mom."

"My pleasure," I said as I cranked the engine, but
Francis hadn't moved. He stood watching me, then
put one foot up on the running board.

"Doctor Grady, can you hold on one moment
before you take off?"

Surprised, I killed the engine and sat patiently.

He clasped his hands on top of his head and brought his elbows in tight. "I've got a confession to make."

"Sounds serious."

"I don't know if it is or not," he said with sad eyes. "I'm worried that I may know something about what happened to my dad."

I felt myself tense up. "I'm listening."

He looked at the ground self-consciously and drew half-moons in the crushed gravel with the toe of his loafer. "I've been seeing someone for a while now." He paused.

"Mm-hmm."

"This is new for us, and we're just kind of feeling our way along, but I could see this getting serious. We talk about a lot of things, about the future. About getting out of this place, maybe running off to San Francisco for a life together."

"Sounds nice."

"Yeah, it is. Even if it turns out to just be talk, it feels good to have someone, you know?"

"I do, but what's this got to do with your dad, Francis?"

He hesitated before answering, "This person, he's got— well, he's got a lot of anger in him. At this town, at God. At the whole world it seems like sometimes."

"Is this about your health problems?"

"No. Well, yes, I guess, in a way. But that's not where I'm going with this. He knows the kind of man my father is, and what my dad believes about people who are gay. All the, 'It's a mental sickness,' 'they choose to be that way,' 'they're all going to hell,' stuff. Once, I made the mistake of telling him my dad is wanting to invest some of our money in a chain of those camps that convert gay kids back to being straight again. This man, he got so angry he punched a plate glass window. It cut his forearm up pretty badly, and I had to take him to the ER for them to sew him back up."

"Let me guess. He drinks too much, and his temper gets worse when he's shit-housed?"

Francis nodded. "Sometimes something'll just set him off, and he flies into a rage. I've seen it a couple of times, and his loss of control— well, it scares me if I'm being honest. He told me about this one time in Piedras Negras when he got in a fight with some poor Mexican who didn't know what he was dealing with. Left him battered and broken in some dirty alley and just walked away. Over an insult in a bar. Can you believe it?

"Here's the thing, Doctor Grady. When he drinks, when he gets that way, he says things about my father that are hurtful, sure. But I always assumed it was just whiskey-talk. He says things like, anybody who thinks the things my father believes doesn't deserve to live, or that he'll do whatever it takes for us to be together."

Francis' breath hitched, and his voice cracked. "And now, I don't know where he was all weekend during the time my father went missing."

I got out of the truck and held my arms apart. Francis collapsed into my chest and the dam broke. He began to sob, his shoulders heaving, and I gave him a bear hug, gently clapping his back.

His voice muffled by my shirt, he said, "I swear to God, Doctor Grady, I don't know how much more of this I can take. My sexuality, my disease, and now this. I can't go keeping all these secrets from the world. I think I might be going crazy."

When his sobs trailed off to sniffles, I released

him. Looking at his red-rimmed eyes, I tried to lighten the mood. "Shit, you got snot all over the front of my perfectly good shirt. Goddamn thing looks like a Rorschach test now."

He snorted and dabbed at my shirt with a handkerchief, then wiped his nose. I noticed it was monogrammed and appeared to be linen. His mood turned serious again after a moment. "So, what do you think?"

"I think your man's got enough issues that you may want to watch out for yourself. Life's too short to spend it scared of the person you're with." As soon as I said it, I regretted my reference to short lives and moved on quickly. "As far as telling the sheriff's office 'bout this, though, listen here, no bullshit; do you really think it's possible your man had something to do with your daddy disappearin'?"

"You'd have had to see his face when he was talking about my father, Doc. There was a kind of hate in his eyes that makes me think he's capable of anything."

I felt intrigued, as though looking at the pieces of a puzzle on a tabletop and getting the earliest sense of how they might come together. Trying to sound casual I asked, "This town's already had one Beckett man come up missing. If suddenly you disappeared it occurs to me I'd have nothing to tell McHenry. Call me crazy but I feel like I gotta ask, you comfortable telling me who this mystery man is?"

He wiped his eyes with his palms. "That's not as crazy as why I feel like I should say no." He blew out a long breath, then shook his hands hard at the end of his limp arms, letting it go. "I feel like I need to protect him. And thank you for your concern, but he hasn't raised a hand in anger towards me."

Yet, you mean. I left that thought unspoken and

pursed my lips, then slowly nodded my head. "Why don't you try to pin him down on where he was over the weekend when your daddy disappeared? Might be, turns out he's got an alibi?"

Francis untucked the tail of his shirt and used it to polish his glasses. "I'm just worried that he won't."

Chapter 10

After I got home from the Beckett house, I was quieter than usual, distracted and distant. I sensed menace in the air. It felt like with Blaine's disappearance some dark, malevolent entity had been released from its cage, or better yet, birthed. Yes ma'am, birthed. That was the way to think of it. Because this thing, this force had started off small but grew bigger and stronger by the day, running amok, indifferent to the destruction it was causing. It threatened everything in its path, and now through my actions past and present I felt like I'd put my family in its crosshairs. I felt the need to step up and protect them, to stand in harm's way. I had to elevate them from the rising water before it whisked us into a current that was too strong to fight.

Angelica sensed my preoccupation. As she prepared for bed, she hummed with the radio. Suddenly, she turned to face me with a dramatic pose and threw one hand in the air, singing into her hairbrush with her eyes closed, trying to bring me back with her silliness. Later, in the dark, she came to me, her breath soft on my chest, and whispered she would make all my worries melt away.

Afterward when she was asleep, though, restlessness still tugged at me. Rope Tail could tell I was awake and came to my side of the bed, a ghostly black-on-black outline, tail swinging through an arc where it made a soft thump against my nightstand. When I heard the living room clock chime two in the morning, I surrendered. Sitting up, I looked at Angelica's naked back, the spill of her hair over the pillow, the slow, even rise of her chest. I pulled the duvet over her bare shoulder and went to the dark living room in my boxers and t-shirt with Rope Tail padding behind.

I sunk into my recliner and draped one leg over the armrest, picking up at the halfway point of *The Good, the Bad, and the Ugly*. The TV's lighting threw shadows on the living room's everyday objects, giving them a spooky, unfamiliar feel. I thought about the rest of the audience also watching old movies at that time of night and wondered at the origins of their insomnia. It's strange to say, but even though they were anonymous I felt a kinship toward them.

As Lee Van Cleef stroked his holster with a hand missing a fingertip, I found my mind drifting back to Francis' mystery lover. Francis mentioned the man had punched a window and given himself a laceration deep enough that he needed to go the ER to have it stitched up. The likeliest place for that would have been Big Bend Regional ER, Amoret's tiny twelve-bed hospital. Frankly, the only thing "big" about the place was the word in the sign. I covered that ER from time to time, and in fact was scheduled to do so the following night. And that gave me an idea.

What's that? Oh no indeed, working the Big Bend ER was nothing like the television shows you see now with the craziness of big-city emergency rooms, although it could have its moments. I always took pride in the fact that I did everything in my practice. Frankly, you can't agree to take a job like that and not be okay with working at the edges of your comfort zone. Back then, every specialist in the world wasn't a phone call away like it is now, some other doctor who could swoop in and save the day if you didn't know what to do. Big Bend Regional had no operating room, no CT scanner, and only one ventilator that I used to joke was woodburning. Seriously, that respirator was so primitive I'm pretty sure its first version was attached to a little bicycle seat someone had to pedal to keep it powered. We didn't even have access to a medivac helicopter until Junior Rayburn became County Commissioner in '91.

A handful of doctors cobbled together by the hospital kept the ER covered in those days. Besides myself, there were three internists, each of whom would make the sixty-five-mile drive down from their practices in Fort Stockton, young physicians starting out who needed the money. Plus, for a brief period – and I do mean brief – there was a fifth, a big city pediatrics doc named Elvis Harjemone. Man was pushing sixty and had come to the hospital saying he wanted to give up the bright lights and power medicine of serious academia to come work in our small west Texas town, and he was willing to do it for a song. I didn't know the man – a name like that's hard to forget once you've heard it, after all – but I mentioned to the hospital administrators that I thought the offer odd. Well, they hired him anyway at a bargain basement rate, and champagne corks were popping in the C-suite. At least they were until three months later when ol' Elvis got caught playing I'll-show-you-mine-if-you-show-me-yours with a twelve-year old Little Leaguer in the men's room at the baseball park, and just like that we were back down to four.

Things were generally slow enough you could count on getting some sleep, which meant that you could work the ER for two or three days in a row if you were so inclined. They kept a lab technician and a nurse in the ER twenty-four/seven, but the radiology tech lived around the corner, so you'd have to call her in from home if you wanted to get an x-ray on somebody. It was about one step above *Little House on the Prairie*, medically speaking, but the money was good, and they fed you well. Between the four of us, the hospital managed to keep the ER's doors open.

After no sleep followed by a full day of clinic, I was running on bloody stumps when I walked into the ER's central charting area the following evening. I hadn't bothered to shave that morning, and my eyes were bloodshot when I looked in a chrome paper towel dispenser on my way in. At a squared-off, Formica-countered space the nurses called "the pit," I found the doctor I was relieving scribbling in a chart. Deuce Loury was a good man, always wearing a starched white coat buttoned all the way up to a neatly Windsor-knotted tie. He looked straight out of central casting for an egg-headed, Ivy-League intellectual, at least until he opened his mouth. Then he was pure west Texas. He died about two years later from a lung cancer he unknowingly had as we spoke that night.

He chuckled when he saw me enter. "Goddamn *primo*. You look like you been shot at and missed, then shit at and hit."

"Hello to you too." I dropped my overnight bag and leaned on the counter. The ER charge nurse handed me a six-inch high stack of charts from my previous shift that still needed my signatures. While I flipped through the manila folders, she took stock of my rumpled chambray shirt, Levis, and dusty boots.

"Doctor Grady, you even own a white coat?" she asked with a disapproving expression, like she found a Playboy beneath her son's mattress.

"Now what would I want to do that for?" I asked, flipping through pages.

"Well, I'll say this, the ladies like that professional look that Doctor Loury gives off."

I scrawled my signature over and over without looking up. "Do they now?"

"Yes, indeed."

"Well,"—I glanced quickly at her name badge—"Jenny, do you know the difference between my woman and Doctor Loury's lady friends?"

"What's that?"

"My woman has *fake* diamonds and *real* orgasms."

Loury wore a bemused smile. "I been meanin' to ask. You got any nekkid pictures of that woman of yours?"

"What? No, 'course not."

"Hmm." After a beat, "You want some?"

I chuckled and set the charts aside. "Okay, what you got?"

Loury said, "Nothin' too bad. Fella in bed two had chest pain coupl'a hours ago, went away on its own but still came in to get checked out. Diabetic and a smoker. Waitin' on his EKG to come back. Other one's a wetback workin' the drill floor on Sonora Pete's place, threadin' pipe and let his mind wander at the wrong time. Hard hat took most of the blow, didn't even knock him out. But the joint caught him just right and nipped his left ear clean off." Loury snapped his fingers. "One in a million it didn't hurt him worse. He come in pressin' a bunch of paper towels to the side of his head with one hand, and holding his ear in the other, whole side of his head a goddamn bloody mess."

Jenny tsk'ed disapprovingly and raised one eyebrow. "Poor sumbitch hands his ear to Doctor Loury and says to him, he says, 'Doctor, can you save my ear?' Go on, tell him what you said."

"I told him, 'Sure I can save your ear. Where do you want me to send it?'"

I shook my head. "And they call *me* a smartass."

"Anyway, did an auricular block for you already. Just need to debride the macerated tissue. Shouldn't take twenty minutes."

"No epi in the lidocaine, right?" I asked.

He snorted. "My momma raised an ugly child, not a stupid one."

"I still need an order for his tetanus," Jenny said, holding out the patient's chart.

I darted my hand out to beam him to it. "Here, I got that. You get out while the gettin's good."

"Don't mind if I do," he said, capping his Mont Blanc pen and returning it to his monogrammed pocket. Yawning so widely I could see his silver fillings, he headed toward the exit, but not before he threw two fingers in the air and called over his shoulder in an awful accent, "*Hasta luego, mis amigos.*"

Writing the order for the immunization, I tried to sound nonchalant as I said to Jenny, "I got a call from the CEO of the hospital in Fort Stockton. Sounds like they're trying to recruit some big shot hand surgeon out there and he was asking me how many bad forearm lacerations we might could send them in a year if this fella was to come on board. How many you think we see here?"

"Bad forearm lacs? I don't know, one a month?"

"Any chance you could pull the charts going back, say, one year so I could take a look and see how many might have been candidates for transfer?"

She tapped her pen against her pursed lips. "Yeah, that shouldn't be too hard. I can look by the diagnosis codes. Going back one year, you say?"

Francis had made it sound like the relationship was fairly new, and I'd gotten the sense the event had happened during the time they'd been together. "Yeah, sure, one year should be fine. Thanks."

I left her to go remove the last of the ragged tissue where the oil rig worker's ear had been. When that was done, I read the EKG of the man whose chest pain had gone away on its own. I was just finishing writing in his chart when Jenny returned with a stack of manila folders that she set next to me with a thump.

"Here you go. Eleven patients over the last twelve months."

"You're the best, Jenny, thanks. Here, trade you." I handed her the two charts of the patients now ready for discharge and slid over the stack she'd collected.

A quick perusal of the face sheets revealed two of the patients were females, so that narrowed the pool to nine. Two more were pediatric, narrowing it further to seven. One patient was miscategorized when his hand had been crushed in a machine press at work. Crushing trauma was classified separately from lacerations which were considered sharp injuries, so six. Of those six, three had sustained their injuries by punching windows.

Francis said it'd been an argument about his father's homophobic comments that had sparked his lover into lashing out, so I was realistic about the fact that even if the mystery man was one of those three patients, he'd likely lied to the ER doc about the circumstances of his injury. I still checked, nevertheless.

Of the three window-punchers, two were nondescript kids in their early twenties, an oil field hand named Christian Hidalgo, and Gustavo Benitez, a car wash attendant, names that meant nothing to me. Both said they'd been drunk and arguing at the times of their injuries, Christian at a bar, Gustavo at a family reunion. Christian had been the more severely injured of the two, with a transection of one of the arteries in the forearm. He'd required transfer to Fort Stockton where they'd taken him to surgery. Gustavo had been so intoxicated he insulted the ER doctor, calling him "*gabacho*" over and over. To return the favor, the ER doc stapled the wound closed, and judging by the dose of lidocaine he documented, had done so with minimal local anesthetic.

The final patient was twenty-two-year-old Wallace Gorman, a muscular kid with winsome eyes whom I knew fairly well as his family owned the town's single-screen movie theater. He'd given the story that while working the projection booth he'd become frustrated with a piece of malfunctioning equipment. Frustration turned into rage and he punched the booth's glass pane, winding up elbow-deep in the shattered window.

After jotting down their names and addresses, I closed the charts and returned them to the wire basket labelled "FOR RE-FILING." Honestly, ma'am, I was unsure what I'd even do with the information. I mean, it wasn't like I was going to take the names to Francis and ask if his new love was on that list. I think I went looking more just to have a starting point in the event something happened to Francis like had happened to his father. Knowing I'd have information I could share with McHenry in that case made me rest easier, but only a little.

I rapped my knuckles on the counter and said to Jenny, "I'm gonna grab a nap."

"Page or a knock?" she asked.

"Page'll be fine."

I walked down the hall to the spartan call room. Pulling off my boots, I emptied my pockets on the nightstand, and was asleep before my head hit the pillow.

I had no idea how long I slept, but the shrill alert of my pager jolted me awake. I pawed through the darkness in the direction of the sound without lifting my head from the pillow and blindly pressed the second button from the left with a dexterity that suggested the hundreds of times I'd done it before. I lay in blissful silence for a few moments, and without realizing it coasted back to sleep.

When the second page came, the screeching was about three inches in front of my nose. I'd never let go of the pager, which now lay on the pillow in front of my face. I flipped the beeper back onto the nightstand where it slid across the smooth cut glass surface and fell off the far side. Squinting like a pirate, I sat up and scratched my scalp with fingers curled like rakes and ran my tongue over my teeth. My cotton socks were bunched at my ankles.

As I cut through the cobwebs, I became aware of a heavy chugging, the low growl of a diesel engine, barely above an idle. Out the call room window, a pair of headlights approached through the fog, the blurry shape around them congealing into an ambulance. It crawled up the shallow ramp leading to the ER's sliding double doors and stopped under the porte cochere, the neon lights of the overhead hospital sign reflecting off its hood in distorted, fun house waves. It ran no-lights, but the siren blatted once, a courtesy announcement. The leisurely pace with which the driver went around back to tend the rig's doors told me I had time to brush my teeth, that whoever was in the back of the rig wasn't trying to die.

When I sauntered to the bedside in exam room two a few minutes later, I found a thin teenager shackled to the stretcher at the left wrist, wearing an orange jumpsuit and writhing in pain. A crude cross tattoo marked his cheek, and his slipper-clad feet stuck out over the end of the stretcher, rotating like windshield wipers in a hard rain. Jenny squatted, starting an IV in the crease of the boy's right elbow while his left hand and wrist lay wrapped in a white towel cradled across his abdomen. One EMT completed paperwork on a chrome tray while a second spun his baseball cap on his index finger, a bored look on his face.

I recognized Beau Alexander from behind, standing in the doorway with his fingers tucked in the small of his back, watching the proceedings. I slapped the deputy on the shoulder, making him jump.

"Goddamn, Doc. 'Bout give me a heart attack."

"Well, you're in the right place for it, then. You doin' okay this evening?"

"Can't complain. I'll take prisoner escort over sittin' at the jail any day of the week."

"What happened?"

The second EMT put his cap back on and spoke up. "Efraim here found himself on the wrong end of a pot of prison napalm."

"Jenny, how you comin' with that IV?"

"Just finished." Her knees cracked as she stood

up.

"*Hola, amigo, me llamo Doctor Grady. ¿Prefere español* or is English okay?"

His breath hitched as he said, "*Español.*"

I smiled. "*Disculpe, mi español es muy malo. ¿Tiene alergias a alguna medicina?*"

He shook his head. A rivulet of snot ran from his nose, and his lower lip began to suck in and out with his sobs, childlike.

"Okay, let's let Efraim here have five of morphine. *Efraim, le voy a dar medicina para su dolor. Relájese. No se preocupe, lo vamos a cuidar bien. Se lo prometo.*"

Once he'd gotten his pain medicine I pulled on rubber gloves and gently took down the towel. The boiling sugar-water concoction thrown at him by his assailant had badly burned his hand and forearm, the stickiness of the solution causing it to adhere to the skin and deepen the injury just like the jellied gasoline from which it got its name.

Beau spat his gum in the trash can. "How bad's it look?"

"Third degree. That hand's gonna be jacked up once it's all said and done."

"Poor guy. There's gonna be hell to pay when the sheriff finds out 'bout this in the morning."

"I expect so," I said as I gathered wound cleaning supplies from the glass-faced cabinet in the back of the room.

"Yeah, Efraim here and Lloyd Cooper'd been arguin' all day. They shouldn't never have been allowed back in the kitchen together, no way no how. Willie Lofton was supposed to be tendin' to 'em, and he said it went off in the blink of an eye."

More to make conversation than anything, as I cleaned the wound I asked, "Willie Lofton? Don't think I know him."

"He's new, still on his thirty-day probationary period. Sheriff let me hire three deputies. Other two're workin' out fine but Willie might not make it into good stead. If we got to let him go, Sheriff's gonna have my ass in a sling."

"Well, don't beat yourself up. Even Jesus Christ couldn't pick out twelve good men." I washed the wound with soap and water, gently scrubbing off the dead blistered skin. "*Necesito limpiar su herida.*"

Beau shook his head. "Takin' on that peckerwood Lloyd. Kid's got gumption, I'll give him that. Anybody could'a told they was comin' to a fracas from the way they was arguin' about Mr. Beckett."

That made my ears perk up. "How's that?"

"Yeah, you know Lloyd. Mister 'white power', swastika tats. All day long he'd been givin' Efraim an earful 'bout wetbacks, sayin' they're to blame for Mr. Beckett disappearin', this is what happens when the races mix, all that nonsense."

I sighed. "I been hearin' more of that than I care to around town. Granted not with things ending up like this, but still."

Beau leaned over my shoulder, watching me work with prurient interest, close enough I could smell the Copenhagen on his breath. "I suppose it's gonna get worse too, what with the news come out this afternoon."

"What news is that?"

"Shit, Doc, you ain't heard? What, you been under a rock all day?"

"Goddammit, boy, you make it sound like I missed out on a whole World War. What're you talkin' about?"

The nurse said, "Hell, Doc, I slept all day since I was on tonight, and even I heard about it. It's a sorry piece of business, that."

Beau said, "We was able to lift some prints off the trunk of Blaine's car. ID on 'em come back around lunch time."

I froze.

"No question about it. They come from Jesús Barrera."

Chapter 11

A cold front moved in overnight, so once I'd been relieved I sipped coffee in the ER's lounge while I watched my truck idle 'til the cab was warm. My mind glided back to the mystery of Blaine's disappearance, turning things over, probing and testing. I still believed deep down the whole affair would fade away, that Blaine would never turn up and people would just eventually move on. Or maybe I just hoped that to be the case. It seemed a real possibility that if the truth of the mystery was ever known it could cause lots of collateral damage to lives and reputations.

I came home to find Angelica still in bed with the duvet pulled up to her chin. I knitted my fingers in hers and kissed her gently, ignoring her morning breath.

"I'm going to head out to the ranch for the morning, get some work done. Probably home a little after lunch time."

Without waking up completely, she mumbled, "Tell Gilberto hello for me."

"Will do. And do me a favor. If you and Miguel go out to town— I don't know, just be careful. I love you."

"I love you too." She snuggled deeper in the

sheets and was asleep again.

In the living room, Miguel watched Saturday morning cartoons cross-legged on the carpet, a bowl of cereal in front of him, guffawing at Scooby Doo.

"Shh, shh, shh. Your momma's still trying to sleep buddy," I cautioned him. "I should be back later this afternoon, okay? Love you."

"I love you too, Noah," he responded automatically as he poured more cereal.

The early Saturday dawn was crisp and clean, and my breath plumed as I loaded up Maybelline and Rope Tail. The two hounds bounded out to my truck, zigzagging back and forth, pacing in eager anticipation then nimbly skipping onto the bench seat in one clean stride. I handed each of them a hard-boiled egg from a Ziploc bag, then had two more myself.

Bouncing down the road through my property a short time later, I saw Gilberto's truck parked in its usual spot outside my white barn. The steep angles of the corrugated tin roof created a high ceiling, and the double doors were open wide, showing the machine shop where Gilberto and his grandson Hector worked on one of my two utility vehicles. I pulled my truck in next to his.

Gilberto waddled over to shake my hand and greeted me with a warm smile.

"*¿Qué pasó, mi jefe?*"

"*Muy bien.* Y'all doin' all right this morning?"

"*Sí, sí, mucho trabajo.*" Gilberto noticed his grandson still leaned under the propped hood, watching us. "*Ay*, Hector, come say hello." Turning to me, he said apologetically, "Not only do I have to teach him engines, but manners too."

Grinning, I extended my hand to Hector. The young man shook it half-heartedly but didn't return the smile. "Good to see you again, son. Listen to your granddaddy. When it comes to engines, he's slicker than a boiled onion." Hector turned back to the utility vehicle wiping his hands on a small red rag, and I watched him for a moment before mentioning to Gilberto, "I'm goin' out to the back of the property for a while this morning checkin' fences."

Gilberto pointed at the second utility vehicle sitting on the far side of the machine shop. "*Sí, sí, sí.* We finished changing her oil. You want to take that one, you are set."

"Naw. Think I'll take the mare out." The previous winter I'd picked up a magnificent pair of Duns, a mare and colt tandem I named Bonnie and Clyde.

"Very good. Hector, *ándele.* Saddle the horse with the white blaze."

I waved the young man off. "I appreciate it, Hector, but the day I don't saddle my own horse is the day I want you to put a pillow over my head and put me out of my misery."

"As you wish," Gilberto said, and gave me a final wave before ambling back to Hector and the engine repair.

Once saddled, I nudged the strong mare past the paddock and down the road, the dogs trotting behind. After a hundred yards, I stopped at my small, two-room ranch house and tied Bonnie off at the hitching post by the eastern wall, a wall Darla had hated whenever we'd gone out there for a rendezvous because of the skulled antlers that hung of the twenty-plus pronghorn I'd taken out of the place over the years. She said it made the place look like a white-trash graveyard. I always told her I took that as a compliment.

The porch was simple, just two rocking chairs and a small, battered table not much bigger than a dinner plate. I clomped across the sturdy boards and noticed a new wasp nest in the corner I'd have to do something about later, but right then I had more pressing matters on my mind.

A musty smell greeted me inside the cabin, but I didn't plan on being there long enough to air it out. I took my grandpa's old twelve-gauge down from the wall, a gun the old-timers called a thumb-buster from the effort it took to pull back the hammers. He'd often say that gun was just like him—old but capable, with good stories.

I broke the breech and paused, looking at two boxes of shells on the shelf beneath where the gun hung, one filled with heavy buck shot, the other with punier bird shot. After a moment's consideration, I grabbed the buck shot, figuring if it came to it I didn't want to make the mistake of shooting a large caliber man with a small caliber shell. I dropped two casings in the gun and snapped my wrist. The gun's barrels swiveled up and locked with a satisfying metallic *clack*, then I dropped a half dozen more shells in my front coat pocket. I hoped I wouldn't need the gun, but I figured it was like a parachute. Better to have it and not need it than the other way around.

I dropped the shotgun into a bootleg scabbard. The saddle creaked as I climbed back on Bonnie, then nudged her into a trot as I pointed her in the direction of the property line I shared with Mariano Enriquez. I figured that was the best place to start my morning's work: hunting down Jesús Barrera.

Ma'am, could I trouble you to reach into that cabinet behind you and get out the bottle of Jamison's? Gonna Irish up my coffee here. Feel free to grab a tumbler for yourself while you're in there if you like. Much obliged. We're getting to the point in things that a stiff one'll make telling this easier.

Depending who you asked, Jesús Barrera was either a bogeyman or a *bandido*, a free loader or a free spirit. For sure you could call him a nomad, an outdoorsman who knew the sun-baked landscape around Amoret like few others. He had the unique ability to disappear like smoke, to just melt into the desert pan like a ghost. He'd come out of the desert into town every few weeks and work odd jobs for a while before getting restless and disappearing again. His mistrust of people in general and whites in particular fueled— oh, what's the word I'm looking for? What's that? Yes ma'am, a misanthropy, exactly. That's why you get paid the big bucks. It fueled a misanthropy that years before had stripped him of any desire to be in the company of his fellow man, preferring instead to skulk across the landscape. I think much of it came from the fact he had one milky eye and a jagged scar that ran from his bushy brow to his jowl. Like a grotesque Halloween mask, it was the kind of look that made mothers pull their children closer when he passed on the sidewalk.

I came to know Jesús through Gilberto. The old man asked me one day if I'd mind his hiring Jesús for some help in building a fence, and when that went well, for additional labor over the coming months. He did good work, but more than that I was happy to keep having him back because, against all odds, he seemed to click with Miguel.

They were an odd couple, those two. They'd spend whole afternoons together barely talking, Jesús whittling little wooden figurines for the boy, while Miguel brought him insects or plants of which he asked a litany of questions. Sometimes while he played in the dirt, Miguel would ask more personal questions in that unabashed way children will do, and

Jesús would permit the boy to run his finger over his scar's bumpy length. It was touching, their relationship. Just two of the world's misfits enjoying judgement-free moments.

Based on all that, I had a soft spot for the man and had given him free use of my property. Now, though, I worried about both what it meant that his prints had been found on Blaine's Jeep and the law's clear thought that he had something to do with the man's disappearance. Even if there was a benign explanation, I feared his lack of sophistication could make him an easy target for a witch hunt and I wanted to let him know what was afoot. I took the thumb-buster along as a precaution because in his conversations with Miguel I'd overheard Jesús tell stories of time spent in 'Nam. This was back before we had a name for post-traumatic stress disorder, and if he was out there in the back country, possibly jumpy and maybe not in his right mind – well, let's just say I wanted to be prepared for all contingencies.

The sheriff knew Jesús' skill at living off the land, which is why he had the good sense to put out an APB on the man, but not to try an all-out manhunt. Fact was, if Jesús didn't want to be found, the sheriff's department would have had better luck standing in the town square, holding hands and praying for God to miracle Barrera's ass down to them.

Ten minutes past the cabin, my eyes wet from the wind, I spooked a covey of quail where the landscape morphed into rolling hills, a sea of creosote bushes and spiky lechuguilla where islands of limestone and shale stair stepped from their low peaks to the desert floor. I slowed Bonnie down because of the dangers posed by prairie dog holes. Plus, I wasn't in a hurry, enjoying the isolation and the opportunity to gather my thoughts. The dry creek bed where Blaine's car had been found eventually crossed my property line a few miles downstream, and it was to that spot that I pointed the mare.

The dogs explored ahead, noses to the ground, Rope Tail marking territory as he went. They'd periodically raise their heads to check on my location, content to just keep me in sight as Bonnie and I plodded along. They jumped two javelina at one point, little black lightning bolts squealing in fear as they darted through the harsh underbrush. Maybelline knew better than to give chase, but Rope Tail crashed through the thicket after them, baying, until the thorns that scraped painlessly at the small hogs' thick hides became too much for him to bear. Giving them one last warning bark, he trotted back to our line and kept moving west with us.

Eventually, I found the fence line dividing my property from Mariano's and followed it north a short distance until we came upon the dry creek. I cast an eye down its length as it wandered deeper into my property, and, seeing nothing unusual, guided Bonnie down the crumbly four-foot earthen bank, easing her past gnarled creosote roots that jutted into the air like zombie fingers, clawing their way out of the grave.

Once we'd made the smooth-stoned creek bed, I turned Bonnie to follow its path deeper into my property, her shoes clacking, a sound like cobblestones.

We'd gone about a mile when in the distance I saw my destination. The creek's chest-high dirt walls briefly gave way to a short stretch of limestone that sloped upward. Set into that wall was a scooped out spot with an overhang that extended outward about three feet, forming a sharp C-shape, like God had taken an ice cream scoop to the soft rock in that spot. I was enchanted by that place ever since I'd first discovered it shortly after buying the property. The divot in the stone provided shelter from both wind and rain, while not so deep that it could hide a rattlesnake. The shelf was flat enough to permit fire-building, and high enough that only the worst flash flood would reach it. Arrowheads and a softball-sized depression drilled into the soft stone to hold water testified to the Comanches' opinion about its suitability as shelter.

That was why I'd offered its open-ended use to Jesús Barrera many months before, and it was where I thought it most likely that I'd find him on that crisp fall morning.

Chapter 12

Still twenty yards short of the stony alcove, I stood in my stirrups and scanned the desolate terrain. The empty bajada glared back at me, like it was— I don't know, contemptuous? Resentful? I had days back then when it would feel like that history-filled land was disdainful of my claims to ownership, like it scoffed at the idea that a mere piece of paper was all it took to be the master of that rough country.

Bonnie's bobbing head and the circling dogs were the only movements from horizon to horizon. Still, I withdrew the shotgun from its saddle scabbard and laid it across my lap.

I bellowed at the empty countryside, "Jesús! It's Noah! I'm comin' in to your camp!" No hint of an echo as a desert breeze kicked up, whisking my words away. "Once I see you're alone I'll put the scatter gun away so we can talk!" Again, no response as the light wind whispered over the rocks and soil.

Giving a nudge to Bonnie's flanks, I urged her forward. The dogs froze at my shouts, but seeing my mount move again, resumed exploring. The sun broke through the overcast and for the first time I threw a long shadow, brightening the prairie but not my mood.

I stopped Bonnie and dismounted. I'd learned the hard way she could be skittish, so I hobbled her where she stood before sauntering toward the hollow in the rock.

The remains of a fire smoldered on the stone floor. A scorched, blue steel coffee pot sat on the coals' margin, and as I stood there the percolator burped. Atop rumpled bedding at the back of the alcove lay a pipe, a tobacco pouch, and a battered Spanish-language paperback. On the cover, a gambler held his cards with a lurid smile while a busty woman stood behind him with one hand on his shoulder, looking away. Jesús' bulging pack lay at the head, a poor man's pillow.

A glint of chrome in the bed's ticking caught my eye. Leaning closer, I saw it was an ornate Zippo lighter engraved with the initials "BB."

"Morning, Doc."

I yipped, smacking my head on the alcove's ceiling as I turned.

Jesús stood atop the creek's far bank. The sun perched on his shoulder, shining in my eyes and making him hard to see. No accident, that. One hand leaned his shotgun against his shoulder, the barrel pointed at the sky. In his other a dead rabbit dangled by the hind legs, a long strand of clotted blood hanging from its mouth and swaying in the light breeze.

"Morning, Jesús. You got any company out here with you?"

"Nope."

I jutted my chin at the rabbit. "I didn't hear you shoot."

"Snared it."

I nodded. "Well, I don't want to keep you from your breakfast. I'm gonna put my gun away now, okay? Why don't you come on down here so we can talk. We got serious business to discuss."

"I suppose we do." He took the steep crumbling bank in three nimble steps, his momentum carrying him into a short trot at the bottom. As we passed, he smelled pungent, all man sweat and campfire smoke. While I replaced my shotgun in its scabbard, he tossed the rabbit next to the fire, and pulled a battered army surplus cup from his pack. "Coffee?"

"Don't mind if I do."

"I only got the one cup, so we gotta share." He bit the middle finger of his glove and pulled it off with his teeth, then poured a cup and handed it to me. Grounds swam in the brew, and the sip I took was gritty with a harsh taste I didn't recognize.

"That's good," I lied. "Got somethin' else in it?"

"I grind up some agave to mix in with the grounds. Gives it a nice flavor."

His one good eye opened wide when he spoke, while the scarred contracture around his milky eye gave his gaze a squint. With his tendency to speak out of the corner of his mouth, he resembled a pirate when he talked. When deep in thought, he'd stroke the thick scar that notched his eyebrow and cheek with his index finger. A ponytail snaked from under his wool cap, hanging down to the middle of his back, and in thermals and flannel he looked comfortable against the chill.

My knees popped as I stood. "Might as well make myself useful." I scrambled up the bank and was gone ten minutes, reappearing with enough kindling and wood to cook the rabbit as well as a long, sturdy branch that'd make a good spit. He'd skinned the rabbit in my absence.

"It's green, so it'll smoke, but it'll get the job done," I said as I dumped the wood next to the fire.

"*Chido,*" he grunted. Skewering the carcass, he blew gently on the coals, coaxing the flames back to life with the kindling and within a few minutes the rabbit roasted at the edge of the fire. The work done for the moment, we could talk.

"How much you know about all the business going on in town?" I asked.

He shrugged. "I been out here 'bout two weeks."

"Well, the long and short of it is Blaine Beckett disappeared sometime over the weekend. Lotta rumors about what might've happened."

"That's too bad. Can't say I cared for him much, but I like Miss Darla." His manner seemed guarded.

"Why 'cared'?"

"Come again?"

"Can't help notice you said 'cared', not 'care'."

He shrugged a second time, then casually lifted the spit to his good eye and inspected the rabbit. "You come all the way out here just to tell me about that?"

"No, you know me better 'n that. Sheriff found Blaine's car burned out way back in Mariano's property. You know, where this creek bed here runs through that little box canyon of his, 'bout a mile past the property line?"

"I know that place."

"When was the last time you were there?"

"Couple days ago. I was watching you and the sheriff from up in the rocks. You two looking at the burned car."

I remembered back to that evening in the box canyon with McHenry, and the sense I'd had that we were being watched. "Yeah, well, they found your fingerprints on the hood of Blaine's Jeep."

He looked sideways at me. "So let me guess, they're saying the Mexican must have killed him then?"

"I know you're not the man-killin' type, Jesús. Problem is, lotta folks who don't know you like I do are howlin' for your head down in town."

"I dunno what happened to Mister Blaine."

"I believe you. But I need you to tell me, what do you know about all this?"

"What does it matter? Sounds to me like they already made up their minds."

Grease dripped from the rabbit onto the hot coals, sputtering and sizzling.

"I gotta say, it makes me nervous when you won't tell me what you know 'bout all this."

"I didn't do nothing."

"And I'm not sayin' you did, but you gotta work with me here. Tell me your story."

I let the silence hang. Ten seconds, then twenty. Finally, he spoke.

"I can't tell you the night exactly, but I been out here about a week at the time. You know, the days, they run together after a while. Mister Mariano, he doesn't know I go back up in his land sometimes. I just take a few rabbits, maybe a javelina, don't leave nothing behind.

"I was camped up by a little hole he got, holds water sometimes. Lotta small game. Good place. I stay up there a good bit, far back enough nobody mess with me. Figure people leave me alone.

"Real late one night, I get woke up by a car engine, maybe quarter mile off. I figure good idea to see what was going on, see if Mister Mariano or one of his workers coming. Might need to move my camp.

"There's a deer stand out there, so I climbed up on top to see good. I seen a car coming down Mister Mariano's road, a jeep, but coming too fast for this country. I thought, '*¿Qué carajo?* If this *pendejo* don't got a winch, he's gonna get stuck way out here, middle of the night'. Then, I saw when the jeep got to the creek, the driver turned left, go into the canyon, up the *arroyo.* Car bouncing hard over the rocks, made a lotta noise. I hear one tire pop on the rocks, but he just kept going. Now I'm thinking, this guy *no es un pendejo*, he *loco o borracho*, you know? Crazy or drunk.

"The driver, he took the car as far as it could go 'til it finally got stuck, then he turn the car off, he get out. I see he take something out of the car, splash it all over the insides, then throw something at it. Whole inside of car, just, *boom.*" He mushroomed his hands and puffed his cheeks. "Big fire. He watched it for a minute, then he start walking away."

"Did you see his face? What'd he look like?"

"Hard to say. It was real dark, I was far away. People ask, I gotta say I'm not sure.

"The car, she burn hot for a while, but I just sit and watch. Later, when the man long gone, I go down and look 'round, see if there is anything I can use. I find this," he reached over and picked up the Zippo. He clinked it open and struck the flint. As he stared at the flame in silence, I would have given anything to know his thoughts at that moment.

"And got your fingerprints on the hood in the process," I finished.

He closed the lighter and tossed it back on his bedding, then went back to rotating the rabbit on its spit.

"After this man lit the car on fire, did you see where he went?"

Jesús nodded, still staring at the rabbit. "Along the *arroyo.*"

"He followed the creek bed? Which way?"

At this, he looked over and for the first time met my gaze. "Like he was going toward your land."

Chapter 13

I'm not going to lie, that news shook me.

I said, "Listen, we're friends, you know that. And friends look out for one another. I can tell you, right now, things in town are nasty. If you get picked up and give the sheriff that story, I worry for you."

"What you mean?"

"I mean, there's a possibility you'd still get blamed for this. That for a lotta folks, they're gonna hear what they believe, not believe what they hear. You understand what I'm sayin'?"

"Sounds like you're telling me don't go down into town."

"You'd be smart to stay away until this blows over, that's true. I'm not telling you to lie to anybody. Sheriff finds you, you tell him that story exactly like you told it to me. But meantime, I think the safest thing for you is to just clear out. If you wanna talk 'bout doin' that, you know I can help. You grew up here in town, that much I know, but you got people someplace else? Somebody who'd take you in while this all blows over?"

He thought about this for a moment. "I got a brother in Laredo."

"What do you think about goin' to stay with him for a while? I could even help you get there, lickety-split."

He pulled the rabbit from the fire and propped it

in the air to cool. He was difficult to read, his face impassive.

I lingered, wanting this decided one way or the other. I believed him when he said he had nothing to do with Blaine's disappearance, that he'd just been in the wrong place at the wrong time to get his prints on that trunk, but I also knew Texas prisons were full of indigent men with similar stories. Injustice is the default human condition, and human nature was going to have a lot of people in town ready to blame a poor Mexican who looked like an ogre.

Finally, as he quartered the rabbit, he said, "Okay."

I sagged with relief. "I think you're doing the right thing. This is where I'll come find you in the next couple, three days. We'll have you outta here most ricky-tick."

I dawdled on the ride back to the cabin, my mind at peace for the first time since hearing of Jesús prints on Blaine's vehicle. I rested easier knowing he'd made a decision that would protect him from the sweep of events, events that threatened to suck him in like a whirlpool. I didn't have a moment's guilt that people in town, had they known, would see this as abetting a fugitive. I felt like— I don't know, like I was serving cosmic justice or something, trying to get him away from an investigation that was picking up steam. With no dead body, they wouldn't be able to get him on a murder charge, but I also knew in the face of a public outcry for vengeance, Johnny Law could get creative enough with charges to land Jesús in prison. I couldn't have lived with myself if I'd stood by doing nothing while he wound up behind bars.

My ranch house hove into view, and I was

surprised to see McHenry's pickup parked in front. The lawman sat on the porch rocking easily in one of my chairs, hands in his jacket pockets, legs crossed, seeming to enjoy the morning sun. He gave a polite wave, and I returned the gesture.

The dogs ran ahead to drink from my trough, then flopped exhausted on the patchy dirt next to his truck. Maybelline's tail rhythmically *whumped* the ground, the whites of her eyes showing as she tracked my movements without lifting her head.

"Catch any desperadoes with that ol' thumb-buster?" McHenry asked with a wan smile as I withdrew the shotgun and broke the breech.

"I do, you'll be the first to know. To what do I owe the pleasure?"

"I swung by your house a little while ago, and Angelica told me I'd find you out here. Listen, Doc. Somethin's come up. We need to talk." He dug at gouges in the wooden armrest with his thumbnail, frowning.

I tried to appear casual but concern knotted my gut. "M'all right. C'mon in, I'll make coffee."

Inside, he took a seat at my battered kitchen table, fingering the brim of his cowboy hat and staring at the sweat-stain ring as if he'd discovered something interesting there. I put a few pieces of split wood and a half cup of kerosene in the pot belly stove to get a fire going, then shook some grounds into the percolator. In the silence, the cabin creaked and settled while the pot brewed.

While I waited for the percolator to burp, I said, "Call me crazy, you look like a man who's carryin' a heavy load."

He snorted. "Brother, you don't know the half of it."

"Anythin' I can do to lighten it for you?"

He didn't look at me, but rather out my window at Bonnie as she swished flies with her tail.

"I checked your record and saw where you ain't never been arrested. Mind if I ask if you ever came close?"

"What?"

"Came close. To gettin' arrested."

I laughed. "You come all the way out here to swap stories about the old days?"

He smiled but didn't speak as he waited patiently for my answer.

"Well, I got into a little scrape once."

"What happened?"

"I'd just got home from 'Nam. Been back in the world all of seven hours, still in my dress uniform. I come out of a restaurant by the bus station in Modesto, Californ-eye-ay when some hippie and his girlfriend started in on me, callin' me a baby killer and whatnot."

He shook his head in revulsion. "I mean to tell you, sometimes it feels like the world's tryin' to break my spirit. It's gotten so's my wife, she won't hardly open up the newspaper no more."

"Thye kept following me, jibber-jabberin'. I only wanted to climb up into that bus, find my seat, and start puttin' miles between me and them, but they kept on, one on each side of me. Then the fella— only way I knew he was a man was the beard what with both their long hair and hippy clothes— he spit on me. And well, sir, there's just so much a man can take."

"You didn't touch her did you? I can't see you hittin' a woman."

"No sir, I was raised better than that. But I took him to the woodshed pretty good."

"Touched him up, huh?"

"And then some. When an off-duty cop pulled me off him, I had aholt of the back of his head, smackin' his face into a fire hydrant. Busted all his front teeth out. Cop said later they were scattered on the concrete like Chiclets."

"How'd it come out?"

"Bus station manager called the *po*-lice, but the off duty cop said he'd swear the hippie took the first swing. They called it self-defense, let it drop."

"Hmph. Good for them." McHenry accepted the steaming cup I set before him. "Much obliged." He blew on it and took a sip. Then he asked off-handed, "Can I ask where you were last weekend, who you was with?"

My stomach clenched and I involuntarily drew in a sharp breath. The last thing I wanted to be doing was discussing last weekend's activities with a lawman, friendly or no. And now not only was I forced to do so, but on the fly as well. I cursed myself for not having taken the time to craft a cover story prior to now, but only for an instant as I commanded my brain to slow my thoughts down, to get my story straight lest I blurt out some inconvenient details that would stick to me later like glue.

"The weekend's a long time. What part?"

"Whole thing if you don't mind. From Friday close of business to Monday mornin'."

I searched his face, but his expression was inscrutable. "What's this about, Sheriff?"

"In due time."

I stared off into space as I edited the story in real time, right behind my tongue. "Well, Friday I was at home with Angelica and Miguel all night. Saturday morning I came out here to the ranch and did some work. I had Shy Mike with me most of the day, and we finished up late so I spent the night out here by m'self. I got up early Sunday and finished up the job from the day before, that time with both Shy Mike and Jimmy Wayne. Took most all of the morning, then back home that afternoon and spent the rest of Sunday with my family at the house. Then to work Monday mornin'." I omitted the facts that the work I'd been doing with the boys all weekend was MIG-welding the handles into the cargo bay and the Monday work consisted of our run to the river.

"So the only time you was by yourself was Saturday night, and you was out here?"

I thought about it, counting back. "I believe so."

His eyes grew pinched." You got a map of your property? A good one?"

"Show me a landowner who don't."

"Mind if I take a look?" he continued.

On shaky legs, I crossed to a cabinet where I kept cooking oil and spices and fetched a battered topo map. I handed it to McHenry then jammed my hands in my pockets for fear they may start trembling. The sheriff unfolded it on the table with care, its fatigued creases fragile and crumbling from age and use.

McHenry oriented himself with calculating eyes, quickly identifying the highway and my fence lines, then placed one gnarled finger on the blue-inked circle that marked my cabin. "OK, we're here." I watched as his nicotine-stained finger wandered, his eyes surveying the contoured, brown topography lines with expertise. After a few moments, he plunked his thick yellowed fingernail down several inches to the left on the map, indicating a spot to the northeast.

"Less'n I'm wrong, that's the box canyon where we found Blaine's car?"

I checked. "Looks like it."

Keeping his finger on the spot, he gauged the

distance from that spot to my cabin. "Looks to be about, what? Four, maybe five miles as the crow flies?"

"Where you goin' with this, Sheriff?"

He reached into the inner pocket of his jacket and pulled out a small zip-locked evidence bag and blindly handed it to me while he continued studying the map. "I got this in the mail yesterday. No return address, no fingerprints."

Inside the see-through bag was a standard white business envelope with the address typed and an Amoret postmark, now smudged with a fine dusting of fingerprint powder. Floating around loose in the evidence bag along with the envelope was a white piece of paper the size of an index card.

On the note was typed a single, simple, anonymous line, all lower case:

saturday night the doctor killed blaine beckett

Chapter 14

R andall Bingham was running behind, as usual. I sipped my coffee at the counter, my nerves on edge as I stared into space and thought about the interview to come. The runner squeaked rhythmically from the restless bobbing of my legs, sounding like a honking flock of geese. Sunday morning church services meant a lull in the usual crowd at Penny's, and I had the diner to myself.

After showing me the anonymous note, McHenry had said we needed to talk on the record. He graciously agreed to do it on a Sunday morning both to accommodate my clinic schedule as well as to starve the gossip mill, but it was like a child bailing the rising tide to protect a sandcastle. From Skinny Dicks to the beauty parlor to the bail bondsman's shop, Blaine's disappearance and the anonymous note implicating me seemed to be the only thing anyone in our small town was talking about. Rumors flew, many of them outlandish.

Blaine and I intended to run for the same political office and I needed him out of the way. Blaine caught me in the nudie booth at a Fort Stockton adult theater and I killed him to keep him quiet. I'd bumped him off when he reported me to the state board for a missed diagnosis. It seemed the further removed folks were from the events, the more likely they were to speak of them like experts. If the situation hadn't been so deadly serious, it would've made me laugh.

I'd replayed my cabin conversation with McHenry over and over and hadn't found any obvious problems that I'd created for myself. Since then, I had time to create an alibi, one that was serviceable if not airtight. Prepping myself, I tried not to think about all the people who depended on my getting this right.

I was about to ask for a refill when the bell over the door jingled. A six-year-old boy scooted into the diner squeezing the front of his pants in a death grip, his face contorted in a grimace.

"Mister, where's the bathroom?"

I nodded around the corner of the counter and the boy Charlie-Chaplin'ed his way in that direction. A pot-bellied man wearing jeans and a satin softball jacket trailed him, holding up an index finger to me as he passed.

When they returned from the restroom, I said to the man, "You'll be late to your own funeral."

"You think this just happens?" he circled his hand in front of his clean-shaven face. Then, "Church league's got a tournament today if these showers'll hold off. His momma's meeting me here to pick him up and I'm goin' straight there from the interview."

Bingham was a good man and the sharpest lawyer around, with an easygoing demeanor that opponents underestimated at their peril. His aw-shucks persona was for effect, cultivated over time and perfect for a west Texas clientele. Behind the mask was a trenchant intellect that could be charming one moment and withering the next. When I'd called him and explained the situation, he took the case without hesitation.

"Don't sit down, we haven't got time," I said.

"Wasn't gonna." Pointing at my coffee cup he asked, "Darlin', can I get one to go?"

The coffee and the boy's mother arrived simultaneously. She wore a clear plastic hair cover because it looked like rain, and once she'd corralled their son, Bingham and I walked to the sheriff's office where it faced the courthouse on the town square.

Approaching the front door, we were stopped short by the sound of a raised voice inside, a shouting accompanied by loud snaps of noise, like the crack of a bullwhip.

Bingham and I exchanged worried glances, and cracked the door a few inches without going in.

"Well, son of a bitch," Bingham whispered.

Maxwell Beckett stood over Beau Alexander's desk, red-faced and veins bulging. The hapless deputy tried to calm the old man, soothing him with palms up. Beckett was having none of it, punctuating his invective by smacking Beau's desk with the curl of his cane on the last word of each sentence.

"It's been a gawddamn week!" the old man roared in his thick Boston accent, spittle flecking his lips.

"Mister Beckett, like I said, we're makin' progress on figurin' out what happened to your boy, but I'm gonna have to ask you to--"

"Don't you 'Mistah Beckett' me, I want some gawddamn answers! You buncha inbred hillbilly fucks are *useless*!" *Smack.*

Beau persisted. "Mister Beckett, I know you're worried 'bout Blaine, and I promise you as soon as we—"

"The piece of shit who's responsible for my boy being missing is wahnderin' the streets of this shit-burg, and the bunch of you ah sitting around heah without a care in the world, feet up and eating donuts!" *Smack.* "Now you heah me on this, if I don't staht getting—"

"Maxwell, that'll do." McHenry emerged from his office to sneak up behind the old man. With his hands in his rear pockets, he said, "You made your point."

Beckett's hands shook with fury. "I haven't even stahted—"

"I said, 'Enough'." McHenry kept his voice even and his manner calm as he grabbed the old man's upper arm in a vise-like grip and walked him toward the front door. "We're workin' on it, and soon's we have somethin' to say, we'll say it. But shit shows like this don't help nobody. We clear on that?"

He glared at the sheriff as the lawman escorted him outside without releasing his clutch. I stepped aside to allow Maxwell to pass, and for a moment his eyes locked on mine. In his fury he'd not noticed me, but now his eyes narrowed in recognition and he tried to stop, but the sheriff kept his feet moving. McHenry put the old man out on the sidewalk like he was setting out a garbage can for pick up.

"Now go on 'way from 'round here and let us do our job," the lawman said before motioning Bingham and me inside.

Just before the door closed I could hear the old man muttering, "Should'a had my gawddamn head examined for agreeing to move heah. They should call it the Mason-Dumbass line."

"Mornin' Doc. Randall. Appreciate y'all comin' down. Follow me." The office air was filled with the sounds of routine, phones ringing and the clack of manual typewriter keys as we trailed him through a pebbled glass door that bore his stenciled name.

He gestured to two ornate chairs across his desk and said to his secretary, "Eunice, could you bring me a coffee when you get a chance? Gents, how 'bout y'all?" We shook our heads. "Just the one then."

As he took his seat, I noticed the tape recorder on his desk.

McHenry pointed at the device. "You okay with that? I never could take notes worth a damn."

I looked at Bingham who nodded. "I got nothing to hide."

Eunice brought his mug, steaming and strong-smelling, and gave me a brief, polite smile before closing the door behind her.

He took a sip and winced. "Lord, I can tell Beau made that. Swear, you gotta carve it outta the pot. Okay, you ready?" I took a deep breath and nodded. He pushed the record button and positioned the microphone between us.

Glancing at the clock, he said, "This is Sheriff Lloyd McHenry interviewing Doctor Noah Grady, zero-eight fifteen on Sunday, October tenth, the year of our Lord nineteen eighty-two. Doctor Grady is accompanied by his counsel, Mister Randall Bingham.

"Doc, could you walk me through your activities last Saturday, October second?"

I cleared my throat nervously, self-conscious at the situation's formality. "I woke up early, like I normally do. Had breakfast with my family, then headed out to my ranch late morning. I met up with Shy Mike Culverson, and we spent the morning and afternoon working on a vehicle in my barn's machine shop."

"Anybody else out there with y'all?" the sheriff asked.

"My ranch foreman, Gilberto Moreno. I got a windmill, feeds into my stock tank on the south side of my property. Blades needed repairs. Gilberto's scared of heights so he brought his grandson, boy named Hector, to help him. The two of 'em spent the day comin' and goin' while Shy Mike and I worked on our project."

"And what was the nature of that project again?"

"Hold on," Randall interrupted. I'd previously apprised him of everything, and he knew not to allow McHenry to go down that path lest it lead to questions that would terminate at our work with Chebo and the immigrants. "My client said they were working on a vehicle together. Beyond confirming the fact of their presence at the ranch witnessed in each other's company, the nature of the work he was doing with Mister Culverson isn't relevant to the matter at hand."

McHenry leaned back in his chair and crossed his arms. "Fair enough. What time did y'all finish this irrelevant vehicular project?"

"Sundown, thereabouts."

"Then what?"

"Shy Mike went on home. I decided to spend the night at the cabin, so I went inside to make some supper."

"Were you alone for the rest of the night?"

"Yes— no. Gilberto and Hector came down to the cabin when they saw the lights on from the barn, just wantin' to give an update on the windmill repairs. I asked if they wanted to stay for dinner. They said no, they were gonna get cleaned up and go into town to get something to eat, then maybe go out for a couple of drinks."

"Time would you say that was? Think hard, this's important."

"Call it six-thirty."

The sheriff sat looking at a point over my shoulder, far off in the distance. Then he said, "Did they go straight into town?"

"No. When they left the cabin, I saw them drive to my barn. I finished off a room at the rear of the place a while back. It's got running water and gennie power, a couple of bunk beds. Gilberto mostly lives there year-round. That's where they parked, went inside for about an hour or so, 'bout as long as it takes two grown men to clean up from a hard day. Then I saw their truck leave, heading down my ranch road toward the main gate and the highway. By then it was full dark."

"Is that the last you saw of 'em that night?"

"Yep. When I woke up in the mornin', I went out on the front porch to take a piss—excuse me," I said, looking at the microphone, "—relieve m'self. I could see their truck was back, parked in that same spot in front of the barn, but I don't know what time the two of 'em got in."

"Okay. Let's shift gears a little bit. How well d'you know Blaine?"

I watched the wheels spinning on the tape recorder as my mind raced ahead. Where was McHenry going with this new line of questioning?

Again I cleared my throat and fought to bring my emotions under control. "Sorry, what was the question again?"

"How well do you know Blaine?"

I tried to sound casual. "Better than some, not as good as others."

"How would you describe your relationship with him?"

"I'm old friends with Darla. Blaine not so much."

"After Blaine went missin', we took a look at Blaine's office. You ever seen it, Doc? Where he works when he's at home?"

I could feel my heart thumping in my chest. "Can't say as I have."

"Books and papers everywhere. Top of his desk. Stacked on the floor. You gotta wind your way between 'em when you walk through the goddamn room," McHenry said, apparently having no qualms about cursing on the record. "I didn't think a man could read and write that much if he spent all day every day doin' nothin' else.

"Anyway, what with all that, took us a while to make our way through all them papers. Been doin' it in shifts, lotta time and a half gettin' charged to the city. Yesterday mornin' we come across this."

He reached into the bottom drawer of his desk and gently retrieved an evidence bag filled with perhaps thirty yellowed envelopes, all stamped and postmarked and opened neatly along their top edge as though with a letter opener. "Look familiar?"

I stayed quiet. There was nothing left to say.

McHenry tossed the bag in the air a few inches before allowing it to smack down on his desk with a dull thump to emphasize its weight. He paused, and if he hadn't been such a serious man, I would have sworn it was for dramatic effect. "Found these takin' up a couple of good-sized boxes. Love letters, from you to Darla, goin' back more'n twenty years from the look of it. The story I got from the sample I seen is the two of you had quite a thing goin' for a long, long time.

In my peripheral vision, I saw a muscle in Bingham's jaw twitch.

"I talked to Darla first, as you can imagine. She tried to deny it at the outset, said they wasn't real, but it don't take Scotland Yard to see they are. Pretty soon she come clean, once the shock wore off and she realized she was talkin' to law enforcement and not her sewin' circle.

"She said she kept 'em for all these years, hidden

up in boxes in their attic." He got a wistful look, placing his coarse palm on the bag. "Told me she'd go up and re-read 'em from time to time when she was feelin' down or lonely. Was actually kind'a sweet.

"She said the whole time the two of you were carryin' on, Blaine acted every now and then like he had suspicions, but he never knew for sure. Well, now that we found these in Blaine's office, it stands to reason he found 'em, brought 'em down, was reading 'em himself. And then with him goin' missin' not long after, I gotta say, that starts lookin' a lot like a motive." He let the thought trail off.

Bingham's chair squealed as he stood up. "That's it. This interview's over."

Chapter 15

The phone ringing woke me up. The glowing hands on the nightstand's clock showed two-thirty.

"Hello?"

"We need to talk." Pablo's voice. Curt. All-business.

I snapped awake. "M'kay. When?"

"I will pick you up in ten minutes."

Angelica stirred, clutching the sheet to her bare chest. As I set the hand piece back in the cradle, she mumbled, "What is it? Is everything okay?"

"Pablo wants to talk."

"So ...?"

"So that means we talk. He's pickin' me up in a couple minutes." I heard the harshness in my reply and instantly regretted it. "Sorry, I didn't mean it like that."

She stroked my arm. "Be careful."

"Don't worry. I 'spect he heard about the interview today with McHenry. I was him, I'd want to talk to me too. Go back to sleep, I shouldn't be long. I love you."

Despite my assurances, I still worried as I dressed in the dark. While I'd been telling her the truth when I assumed Pablo wanted to discuss the interview with the sheriff, I was far less confident that he'd accept the results with equanimity than my tone implied. I tried to imagine Pablo's thought processes, to anticipate his reaction now that the law was poking around. I quickly shut that line of thinking down, though. There was a degree of darkness at the end of some of those rabbit trails that I didn't want to contemplate.

Nine minutes later, heat tumbled out and hit me in the face as I stepped up into Pablo's cab. The radio announcer relayed the day's news in Spanish, and I rubbed my hands in front of the warm air vents. Pablo sat with one wrist draped over the wheel while the other idly stroked his bushy moustache with hairy-knuckled fingers. His burly physique belied a taste for fancier things, but on this night his normally bright face was grim.

I knew next to nothing about who was above Pablo in his organization's hierarchy, and it dawned on me that he could be lying, that "the people he represented" actually didn't exist and he ran the show. I wondered, if true, how that would benefit him. Hell, it was academic. Whether he was middle management or *el jefe*, he was the one in the cab with me now and that's what I needed to concentrate on.

"Evening. Or rather, mornin' I guess." I stifled a yawn.

"For me, it is the end of a long night. For you, it looks like the start of a long day, eh, *amigo*?" He pointed the truck toward the highway.

"Where we goin'?"

"To talk."

"'Bout what?"

"Things have gotten complicated."

I snorted. "No shit."

"Is there anything you need to tell me?"

"Yeah, I 'spect there is." Over the next fifteen minutes, as the lights of town fell away behind us I told him about the interview with McHenry, the warrants, the search, the letters. I told him about Darla. Every few miles, the headlights of a passing vehicle lit our faces, but he never looked at me, just listening quietly as his eyes stayed fixed on the road. All the while we drove east.

I felt rumblings of alarm in my gut. Normally chatty and upbeat, Pablo looked worried. In none of my meetings with him had I ever felt like I might be in any physical danger, but as I continued telling my story, a small part of my brain began to realize that many of Pablo's problems would disappear if I did too.

Thirty miles outside town, he slowed the truck and pulled off the highway's smooth asphalt onto the grit of a gravel lot. A row of vapor lights illuminated the front of a solitary medium-sized warehouse, the lone structure for miles. Its façade faced the highway, but we idled around behind the building.

Thick clouds obscured the moon, and Pablo idled around back of the main structure. Some twenty yards behind the warehouse, a sheet metal shed emerged from the darkness, a yellow bulb casting a dim pool of jaundiced light onto its doorway. Pablo pulled up to the shed's thick slab and killed the engine, then approached the shed's door, beckoning me to follow. Off to my right and just beyond the edge of the shed's illumination, I could barely make out the silhouette of a second truck squatting in the darkness.

"Where are we?" I said through the window.

"This is one of my businesses. *Venga.*"

"I'm not goin' anywhere 'til you tell me what the fuck is goin' on."

"I already told you, we are going to talk."

"I been talkin'."

"Yes, and now it is my turn."

"We can talk right here."

"No, it is better if we talk inside."

"What else we got to talk about?"

"Consequences."

"The fuck you mean 'consequences'?"

"Come, *amigo*, I grow tired of this. You are an educated man, but there are still lessons we all must learn the hard way. This is one. *Venga*," he repeated.

I shook my head. "Mmm-mmm. Fuck that." I resisted the urge to just open my door and bolt, sprinting off into the black night, taking my chances in the open desert.

For a moment, the only movement came from the helical cloud of insects circling the bulb over the doorway. Then Pablo abruptly rapped his knuckles twice on his truck's hood, the sound reverberating through the silence like a clap of thunder.

From the darkness, I heard car doors click open, then slam shut, and two men emerged from the shadows. Bundled against the chill, one clasped his hands casually behind his back while the other had his wrist in a cast. They walked with the confident gaits of men accustomed to violence. Faces impassive, they stood by my door like coiled snakes, silent as statues.

"Relax, my friend. If I wanted you dead, you would already be dead," Pablo said and turned to key the shed's door.

I followed him, taking each step with care, like walking through a minefield. My senses were focused, hypervigilant. The copper taste of fear coated my tongue as Pablo disappeared into the shed's interior.

As I crossed the threshold, I noticed the lock on the door frame was bent and twisted with fresh scrapes in the metal, the unmistakable signs of a crowbar's recent work. A small rectangle of outside light fell on the concrete slab by the door. The rest of the interior was dark as the air in a coffin.

I barely had time to register layers of smells, the biting scent of solvents and gasoline mixed with a heavier odor, salty and familiar, before Pablo flipped on the lights. The single fluorescent tube snapped on with a low hum, illuminating a body dangling from the rafters, it's feet less than six inches off the ground.

The man's jeans were wadded around his ankles, leaving the tops of his cowboy boots peeking out above the loose waist. Blood coated his bare inner thighs and pooled in his jockey shorts, forming a thick clot like grape jelly. More blood trickled onto the concrete in a large puddle, with smaller stains dripping off at angles, like a crimson map of Hawaii. An ornate belt buckle drooped at the end of his worn leather belt, pointing to the scarlet puddle as though it was a divining rod searching for gore instead of water.

His groin bore a ragged wound shaped like an upside-down valentine, the source of the bleeding. His penis and testicles protruded from his mouth, stuffed there in what I hoped was a post-mortem desecration, but I couldn't be sure.

I winced. "Jesus Christ."

"Christ had nothing to do with this my friend." Pablo looked at the dangling corpse with a blasé expression suggesting he cared less about the man's death than the ramifications it brought.

"Who is it?"

Pablo jerked his head for me to approach. I stepped forward, minding the blood spatters on the concrete, and squinted upward to examine the dead man's face more closely.

"Does he look familiar?" Pablo asked.

The face, suffused with an anoxic purple, bore little resemblance to the man I'd known in life. His eyes bulged, their whites now a dull red from burst capillaries, the tiny vessels rupturing in the final stages of his struggle to breathe. In the dim light, I'd never have been able to recognize him if not for the spider web tattoo on the side of his shaved head.

"The kid with the dope," I said.

Pablo said, "My night foreman, he came out here to get some equipment and found this." He appeared to be having difficulty controlling his anger. In frustration, he pushed the corpse's hip. The rope creaked as the body swayed like a pendulum, the shadow on the concrete beneath him shrinking and elongating in turns as his remains swung through an arc.

"So why's he in your storage shed?"

"Let me tell you why, *cabrón*. This man worked for one of our competitors as we suspected, purely lower level. I am told he was unreliable, insubordinate, spoke before he thought. He became frustrated at his lack of progress in their organization and decided to make a better future for himself by stealing that backpack and going on the run."

"Oh, shit."

"'Oh, shit,' indeed. Catching someone with a backpack full of their stolen product has a tendency to make our competitors irritable. So tonight they caught this *pendejo* in Lajitas, trying to arrange a sale. As though anyone in the region would buy that much tainted product from a *culero* like this."

"I still don't see what this has to do with you. Or me."

"I am getting to that. When he was on his knees, begging for his life, they said they would let him go if he simply told them who else was involved. It was nonsense, of course, but they wanted to sniff out whether anyone else had a hand in this. He told them that the theft had been *your* idea, that he was only following *your* orders. So instead of putting him in a hole in the desert, they brought him here. As a message to me."

"*What?* Come on now, Pablo, you can't really think—"

"No, of course I do not think that what he said was true. A man looking into the face of death will say anything. The problem, though, *amigo*, is not what I think. It is what my *competitors* think."

"We gotta go find—"

"*Relájese, amigo.* I have already spoken with them tonight, before even I came to pick you up. How do you think I know all of these things? You are under my protection and moving on you would be moving against my people. They are telling me they have their doubts about what he said, and that they have no plans at this time to harm you and yours."

"What does 'At this time' mean?"

"That at the moment, they have enough questions about your involvement that they are not willing to undertake an all-out war over one backpack of product."

"Why do I get the feeling there's a 'but' coming at the end of this?"

Pablo put out a hand and stopped the swaying corpse. Its inertia rotated the torso at the last moment and smeared his palm with blood, making him wince. He wiped it on a nearby bag of horse feed before continuing. "What we must worry about, my friend, are people who would harm you— what is the saying— 'on speculation'?"

"'On spec', yeah."

"Men who would seek to ingratiate themselves with our competitors, who would curry favor with them by harming you, while giving our rivals a cover of deniability."

"So what're you plannin' to do to keep that from happenin'?" I asked.

"First thing in the morning, we will begin to put the word out that anything looking like a reprisal against you will be dealt with swiftly and with the worst kind of cruelty the imagination can conjure."

"Only issuing threats? That's not very reassuring."

Pablo's face grew stern. "I understand. But do not forget for a moment, *guey*, that but for your actions we would not be in this position."

"So now what?"

Pablo spit in disgust at the slowly rotating body, hitting the lower back. "Now, *mis compañeros* will cut down this trouble-making *ladrón* and disappear him."

"No, I mean now what for me?"

"Now, you return to your bed."

"So there's nothing I can do 'bout this situation?"

Pablo shrugged. "You can pray that God considers this matter closed."

Arthur Herbert

Chapter 16

Well, ma'am, it turned out McHenry's well-intentioned desire to tamp down gossip by conducting the interview on a Sunday morning was pointless, like catching raindrops to keep the ground dry. All that next week around town, I caught people staring, nudging each other when I passed. In my clinic, over and over again, I'd be sitting in an exam room talking to someone about, say, their blood pressure medicine, and I'd notice I lost them, that they were no longer listening. Rather, they'd be looking at me with— I'd call it appraisal. They'd cock their head, eyes darting down to scrutinize my hands, like they were wondering what those hands might've done, if I was capable of the things the rumors were saying.

It's funny, you might have a hard time understanding this coming from a modern perspective, where keyboard activists spend all day signaling their virtue by denouncing anything that stinks of injustice on social media. But despite the gossip I didn't see any drop off in my appointments. There were no unexplained cancellations, no angry letters, no announcements of plans to drive into the big city for future care. In fact if anything, my days were busier than usual. I guess that shouldn't have

- 136 -

surprised me. There's an old saying that all actions come down to three basic motivations: money, power, and/or sex, and the Beckett story had a little bit of everything: old money getting its comeuppance, clandestine infidelity, foul play. Life is slow in a town like Amoret, after all, and for a lot of folks back then speculating on a titillating mystery was a way to pass the time.

I took the rumors and gossip in stride as those were beyond my control. My worries all pertained to my legal jeopardy, and frankly I didn't have the time or energy to think about what people were saying. I knew who I was— what I was— and that it was ephemera for most of those folks.

All small towns out in this part of west Texas have some little salacious bits of history. Hell, about ten years before Beckett disappeared, a few towns over in Sanderson, the mayor was caught changing out license plates in a dark corner of a truck stop parking lot at two in the morning, bug-eyed with fear and covered head to toe in blood. He offered up some bullshit excuse for the blood about hitting a javelina with his car, but never did say why that would make him need to switch plates with those of an out-of-towner passing through on his way home to New Mexico. In the end, he apologized to the vehicle's owner, the Sanderson police dropped the charges, and it all just disappeared like black smoke. He even won re-election about six months later, despite all the rumors about what he'd left in a shallow grave out in the desert that night.

The revelations were harder on Angelica. Not that they caught her by surprise, mind you. I'd told her about the affair long before with the thought that in her position I would want to know. Through our years together, she never seemed to waver in her belief that my involvement with Darla was a thing of the past, ancient history from which I'd learned a lesson and moved on. No, when I say it was harder on Angelica I mean that the buzz around town didn't stop with folks talking about me. In the interests of decency, ma'am, I won't share the worst of the gossip. All I'll say is once you injected the facts that she was Mexican and here illegally into the already lurid details, the talk went to some pretty dark places quickly. While the folks who whispered about me had an interest that was prurient, the ones who talked about her were cruel. One night not long after my interview with the sheriff, I addressed it as we lay in bed.

"You know that I'd never do anything to endanger what we have? That I'd do anything and everything in my power to protect you and Miguel, right?"

"I know, *mi amor*."

"I worry sometimes, is all."

"I have faced far worse in my life than a bunch of *entrometidas*."

I wrinkled my brow, not knowing that word. "*No entiendo*."

She thought hard for a moment. "How do you say, 'busybodies'?"

All these years later, I can still picture her laying there on her side looking at me, the window's blue moonlight falling on her face, the strap of her nightgown loose on her exposed shoulder. She smiled and placed one delicate hand on my stubbled cheek, stroking it with her thumb.

"Do you know how much I love you?" she asked.

"I worry that in the comin' days we're gonna have to find out," I whispered.

"Do not be afraid. We are in this together."

"Us against the world," I murmured.
"Us against the world," she echoed.

The day after my interview with the sheriff, I decided to make some house calls on patients I treated through my Presidio clinic. Back in '82, Presidio was a little hiccup of a town on the Rio Grande about sixty miles upstream from the pick up point for Chebo and our clientele. Across a span of chipped concrete sat her sister city, Ojinaga, Mexico. In those days, you could just walk it, checking in at a booth like you were buying movie theater tickets instead of entering another country. A simpler time.

Together, both towns might have been twenty thousand people. I know that doesn't sound like much now, but for west Texas in the early eighties, that was a goddamn metropolis. Pablo's people set us up on the river road a couple of miles south of Presidio outside a ghost town called Cardencita.

The set up was a joy to behold. Not the clinic itself, mind you, which was just an old Airstream trailer that I bought on Shy Mike's recommendation. I'm talking about the spirit of the endeavor. I gave my time, and Pablo's people kept it stocked with basic supplies and equipment as well as samples of some common medications. I kept an eye on the bottom line for them, making sure expenditures stayed reasonable, and they made sure nobody messed with the place. Once, when somebody broke in and stole the generator, I called Pablo and told him I needed a new one as it got too goddamn hot during the summertime not to at least have a window unit. He asked a few questions, and once I explained what happened, he said he'd look into it. Three days later, the gennie was back, dropped off by two sheepish looking teenagers with black eyes, no questions asked. That was the first and last time we had to deal with a burglary.

Some of our clients established a small enclave in Cardencita. The settlement arose organically, picking up steadily in parallel to our business until if I had to guess there were in excess of twenty families calling the place home. They checked in on each other, helped watch each others' kids, fixed each others' cars, and sent money back to Mexico. They gave each other rides and dug each others' graves. They'd even been there long enough to intermarry.

Most gratifying of all, the *gringos* in Cardencita welcomed the immigrants with open arms in the view that any neighbors pitching in to stave off the town's death rattles were a blessing. The sign at the edge of town read, "Cardencita, Texas, population 211," a number that'd been declining steadily for twenty years since the Southern Pacific moved the rail stop. The town had no stop light, no grocery store, no gas station. The only things to be found in abundance were rumors the government planned to shutter the post office. The world had given up on Cardencita, even if those two hundred plus people hadn't.

So you can see why the townsfolk had no problem with our former clients coming in to call the place home. Who wouldn't want neighbors that worked hard, who valued family and community, who didn't cause trouble? Now, if you were cynical— or an asshole, or both— you could argue that view was transactional, sure. But I preferred to see the positive in it. That's just me.

I was specifically going there to see a woman named Fatima Rivera, the mother in a large family Chebo and I'd gotten across a year before. The Riveras had come over with five children ages twelve to nineteen for the promise of a better life, and up to that point they'd landed on their feet. The father, Victor, caught on with a landscaping crew at a small company in Fort Davis, and Fatima found work as a house keeper at a motel in Presidio. The kids were going to a public school where they didn't have to worry about gunfire in the hallways, and their English grew by leaps. Like the saying goes, they may not have had much, but they had each other.

But the last time I'd seen Fatima in my Presidio clinic, she'd had a new onset of dizziness. She'd tried to work through it, poor lady— bills don't stop coming in just because you're not feeling right— but she took a spill while on the job and sprained her wrist. The motel was a little family-owned shop with no workman's comp or any such, and they told her if she agreed not to talk about a lawsuit they'd hold her job for her while she got right. When I examined her, I thought it was a type of vertigo that's relatively common, caused by little crystals in the middle ear breaking loose and causing trouble. The good news was that the condition usually responded to letting your head dangle off the back side of the mattress, and she promised to give it a try. She'd weighed on my mind since then, though, as her income helped keep that family afloat.

On the drive, my only companion was the SoPac railroad tracks on my left. Eventually, I found my turn off the highway at a flat intersection with two crumbling stucco buildings and took it without signaling. The near one had a hand-painted sign on the highway-facing wall, but desert winds had sand-blasted the lettering to illegibility. The second structure had a charred hole in the roof, and I couldn't help but wonder. Lightning strike? Bad wiring? A few splashes of diesel in a half-ass attempt at insurance fraud? Regardless, the desert appeared bent on reclaiming that stretch of ground.

Clustered a mile off the main road, the community had started off as a rough semi-circle of trailers. It'd sprouted outward from there, like a grain of sand growing into a pearl. Goat pens and chicken coops and generators materialized, and the desert breeze made for easy windmill water sucked from the edges of the Ogalalla Aquifer. If folks complained about the austerity, it wasn't to me. Two of the town's white homesteaders tried to make a go of dry land farming within walking distance of the little community, and I'd heard from others work could be found in their bean and pumpkin fields.

I stopped to ask directions to the Rivera's trailer from an older woman feeding chickens. One hand held the edge of her apron in a scoop, while the other tossed the feed out in arcs to the birds busily pecking the ground. A do-rag held her hair back, and her lined face looked familiar.

Before I could say anything, her expression lit up. She dropped her grip on the apron causing the chicken feed to puddle at her feet, and the birds rushed forward in a bustling frenzy. She reached across the chicken wire and gave me a hug, then kissed my cheek before yelling over her shoulder toward the open screen door, "*¡Ven! ¡Mira! ¡Es el doctor!*"

I stammered, "*¿Como estás? Qué gusto verte.*"

She released me and wiped her hands on her apron, still sporting a grin with a missing lower tooth. "*Y tú, y tú. ¿Qué haces aquí?*"

"*Estoy buscando a la señora Rivera. ¿Dónde vive?*"

A lithe man in flannel and overalls, unshaven with a touch of grey at his temples appeared at the door of the trailer. He, too, looked vaguely familiar and grinned as he came forward to shake my hand. We all exchanged pleasantries as they caught me up on life since coming over. He'd found work in the oil fields outside Presidio, making good money as a roustabout. She said the trailer seemed empty now that their daughter had married one of the boys in the community. The young couple hoped to start on a family soon, would I mind stopping in on them to say hello and give her advice?

I told her of course, and after she pointed out their mobile home, she also pointed out that of the Riveras, an old Fleetwood with laundry hanging over the balcony rails. As I approached, Mrs. Rivera emerged and slung a pan of dirty dishwater into the packed dirt.

She greeted me with similar enthusiasm, inviting me in and moving gracefully around their living room with no hint of a wobble. She updated me on her progress even as she disappeared to an adjacent room while raising her voice to still be heard, saying she felt better and had returned to work without a recurrence of dizziness. She reappeared after a few moments pushing an old woman in a wheelchair with a blanket across her knees and a smoldering cheroot between her thin lips.

"Look who is here, mama," Mrs. Rivera said. At the sight of me, the *abuela's* face broke into a toothless grin. She reached her arms into the air for a hug, the cigar clutched between two arthritic fingers and gave me a cheek-touching air kiss. The three of us visited and laughed, told jokes and exchanged updates on families. Finally, I stood to leave and had just given them one last hug when a tentative knock came from the door.

A child who couldn't have been more than ten years old stood in the doorway and said in embarrassed English that his mother heard I was at the Riveras and told him to ask that I follow him back. I smiled my goodbyes, then trailed the child to his squat home.

It turned out the young mother was anxious about a tender lump she'd found in her breast a few days before. The mass looked and felt like a routine fibroadenoma, and as she was only twenty-eight years old with no family history of breast cancer, I told her to just watch it through one menstrual cycle. If it didn't disappear then come see me in clinic. She looked relieved and thanked me profusely.

I went to see the newlywed daughter, and while discussing prenatal vitamins another messenger tapped at the door requesting my presence when I finished.

For the rest of the afternoon, I examined rashes and sore throats, arthritic knees and painful ears. I saw crying babies and demented grandparents. Word spreads fast in a community that small, and I moved from trailer to trailer, helping some, reassuring others, visiting with them all. No paperwork, no fuss, no muss. Wherever I went, they greeted me with smiles and gratitude. I tell you, a day like that reminded me why I went into medicine to begin with.

Finally, when the last visit drew to a close, it was pushing five o'clock. I rubbed a kink out of my back and said good bye, then gathered my bag and headed toward my truck.

I found the hood covered with food. Tupperware containers with hogs' head tamales and fried chicken, *birria* brimming with chunky meat and *verde* enchiladas. I won't lie, I actually got misty-eyed. Hell, I'm getting a little choked up talking about it even now, nearly forty years later. Just salt of the earth people.

It's mankind's evil that gets the headlines. Sometimes we need a reminder that God sprinkles the goodhearted among us too.

Chapter 17

I'd just gotten home from Cardencita and we were settling in to watch the Cowboys on Monday Night Football when headlights washed across the living room The sound of a serious motor growled in from our driveway, and as I got up to answer the doorbell I recognized the heavy lope of the cam as Gilberto's.

When I opened the front door, I found him disheveled, which wasn't unusual, and with a swollen face and black eye, which was. That puzzled me. I'd heard Gilberto was a happy drunk, that even when he howled at the moon he never instigated anything that might lead to a brawl.

"Goddam Gilberto, what happened to you? You all right?"

"Meester Noah, I come in?" His swollen jaw made it come out "meefter," like he'd stuffed his cheek with cotton balls. Drool trickled from the corner of his mouth and hung suspended, oscillating with his speech. From the transom I could diagnose a fractured jaw.

"Sure, sure, sure. Come on." His legs wobbled as I led him to the living room.

Angelica's smile vanished at the sight of Gilberto's face. She leaped off the couch to take his other arm. "*¡Ay, qué susto! Ven, ven.*" He collapsed into his seat, and she disappeared into the kitchen where I heard the freezer door open, then the crunching of ice cube trays.

"What the hell happened to you?" I asked again as she brought him a twisted towel, a poor man's cold compress. He nodded his gratitude and held it gingerly to his swollen face. She sat next to him, rubbing his back with a knitted brow.

Angelica turned to Miguel, who squatted nearby on the carpet staring wide-eyed, one finger hooked in the corner of his mouth. "Miggy, go to your room."

"I don't want to," he mumbled, fascinated.

"*Miggy!*" she barked, clapping her hands once with a loud smack and pointing to his room with a glare. He obeyed, kicking his feet out in a petulant snit as he shuffled away. Once we heard his door slam, we turned our attention back to Gilberto.

He said, "I so sorry, meester Noah. I no mean for this to happen." He struggled to control his emotions, sounding distraught and ashamed.

"For what to happen? Who did this to you?"

"I don' know where to start."

He and Angelica spoke rapid Spanish, too fast for me to follow. In his angst, his words garbled and I could only catch bits and pieces, something about a betrayal. Her expression stayed soothing and calm.

"*Respira hondo,*" she said. He complied, taking a deep breath, in through his nose and out his mouth, then again, slowing himself down, calming himself.

I poured him a splash of brandy from the wet bar. Holding it in two shaking hands, some of the amber liquid slopped as he held it to his lips but he downed the rest at a gulp, wiping his lips with the back of his wrist.

"Now. Whatever it is, it will be fine, okay? Tell

Noah and me what happened."

He exhaled, long and slow, but his voice quivered as he spoke. "On the day you and Meester Mike work on the truck, and I work on the fences with Hector. Do you remember?"

"You mean Saturday before last? When we welded the handles in the cargo bay of the truck? Yeah, I know the day you're talkin' about. Go on."

"You remember that night, me and Hector, how we stop at you cabin? You ask us if we want to eat supper wit' you? We tell you, no thank you, we going in to town?"

I nodded. "Yeah. I saw y'all go into town about an hour later after you cleaned up at the barn."

Gilberto shook his head. "No. After we get back to the barn, me and Hector, we have big argument. We both get mad, very mad. When we make fighting, he tell me he no want to go to town with me, he want to stay at the barn. I tell him, '*¡Pues, vete a la chingada!*'" He looked down momentarily, embarrassed at repeating the vulgarity in front of Angelica, but she paid it no mind.

I asked, "What were y'all arguing about, you don't mind my asking?" Disquiet began squeezing my gut.

Gilberto looked even more uncomfortable. "He no like you, Meester Noah. I tell him many times, you a good man, you help *Mejicanos*, do much good for our people." He turned to Angelica for affirmation, and she nodded sympathetically while caressing his shoulder.

He turned back to me. "But he say, you think you better than us, only want us to make work. You treat us like servants, like dogs. I tell him, you give us good money, make for good life here. Give us place to live, safe place. But he no listen to me."

He drew himself up, mimicking his resolve in the argument. "So that night, I go to town and leave him at the barn. I tell him, he stay back and think about things that he say. I go to *Cantina Mayahuel* until it closes. Then when I drive back to the barn, Hector, he already asleep. I think no more of it."

"I do not understand," Angelica said. "How did that lead to this tonight?"

"*La policía*, they come today to the ranch, asking me about that night. I explain everything to them I just tell you. I tell them I see you that night when you ask if we want to eat with you, then again in the morning. I tell them I know nothing else, I see nothing else.

"But Hector, he quiet the whole time I talking to them. Then, when I am finish, he tell them he have something to say.

"Meester Noah, he tell them that when he there at the ranch by himself that night, after I go to town and leave him at the barn, he hear a car coming down the road of the ranch. He say he look outside, think it will be me coming back. But he tell the police he see that the car is the jeep that Mister Blaine drive, that the jeep go past him toward you cabin. He say a long time later, he see the jeep drive back past the barn out to the highway. They ask him, why he no say anything before? He tell them, no one ask."

Gilberto's voice rose, cracking in distress. "Meester Noah, he no is telling the truth! He tell the police these lies because he no like you! I tell *la policía*, he only know what the car look like because it say so in newspaper! I even show them, newspaper sitting right there on the table, wave it in front of they face! But they no care. It was like they *want* to believe what he say, *happy* to believe it.

"After the police, they leave, I tell Hector that

you get in real trouble. He say he no care, that you deserve it for the things you do. I try to get him to go back to the police, say he make it all up, he make a mistake. He say he hope they arrest you, put you in jail. I tell him I make him go, he push me, I grab him, and, *pues*—." He gestured to his swollen face, his eyes brimming with tears.

Angelica turned him and held his bony frame close, gently rocking the old man as he sobbed. Even as she cooed Spanish in his ear, her eyes locked on mine. The fates were conspiring to convince the world I'd killed Blaine Beckett, that motivated by my love for his wife, I'd removed him as an obstacle in service of a future with Darla.

I thought about how this looked to an outsider. Blaine was the cuckolded husband of a woman with whom I'd had a deep emotional connection for over twenty years. My love letters to her had been found on his desk right before he went missing. His car had been found burned out on a property adjacent to mine, and the arsonist had been witnessed setting off in the direction of my land. And now, a young man with an axe to grind and access to a newspaper story picturing Blaine's car told law enforcement he'd seen the missing man's ride at my cabin a few hours prior to its getting torched. All this occurred during a window for which I had no alibi, and an anonymous note had implicated me as the perpetrator.

Absurd as the idea that I was trying to reclaim a life with Darla may have been, I was stuck arguing these were coincidences. I put myself in the place of a reasonable man hearing all of these facts back to back to back, and I realized I probably wouldn't believe it was coincidence either. That was the moment the uneasiness in my gut morphed into outright fear.

The Bones of Amoret

Chapter 18

Bingham looked worried as he smoothed his tie. "I'm not gonna sugarcoat it. Hector's allegations are tough for us. Plus, 'bout an hour ago I got word through the grapevine of one more problem. Late last night, deputies picked up Jesús Barrera in the ER. 'Parently he cut his hand real bad, bad enough that he needed medical attention. Walked himself to the hospital where a deputy there with another prisoner recognized him and cuffed him. Jesús told 'em 'bout the little chat you two had out in the back country. Says you told him to clear out to Laredo, and that you'd help him do it."

I cursed inwardly. What were the odds that Jesús would be picked up in the short period of time before I'd been able to get him out of town? That this most competent of outdoorsmen would injure himself? That there would happen to be a deputy nearby at the hospital after hours, and the man was paying attention rather than dozing in a corner? Random strings of unlucky events were lining up against me like holes in Swiss cheese. My inability to catch a break was making me feel punchy.

I couldn't blame Jesús for telling the law about my offer to clear him out of town, though. The instinct for self-preservation is a powerful thing, and he was a smart enough man to recognize how quickly he could become a scapegoat in the whole mess. The stakes were high for him too, what with his fingerprints at the scene and his possession of Blaine's Zippo lighter. He and I were in a plane with engine trouble and only one parachute.

Upon hearing that news, Angelica reached down from her seat on the armrest of the overstuffed chair and took my hand in both of hers. Seeing Bingham nervous shook me, like watching your flight attendants' hands tremble when strapping themselves in amid turbulence. Bingham's office suddenly felt claustrophobic.

"The circumstantial evidence against you is significant. They got a motive which they pretty clearly feel good about. Now they got a witness in Hector who can put you'n Blaine together around the time of his disappearance, and another in Jesús who saw the arsonist heading in the direction of your ranch after the deed was done. The letters are gonna hurt us too. Expect to have to read from yours on the stand, so the jury hears the contents in your own words. Between what Hector and Jesús got to say, I've seen cases lost on less.

"Now, it's not all bad," he continued. "Fact is, they ain't got a body, which means that technically there's no evidence of an actual crime other than somebody torchin' the vehicle. Along that line, they still ain't got any physical evidence tying you to anythin'. Now, that doesn't mean they can't prosecute you or anybody else, but barring something changin', they're gonna have to build a circumstantial case. That's a lot tougher to do.

"I'm hearin' the sheriff's gonna get bloodhounds out to your ranch and to that box canyon on Mariano's place with the hope of tracking Blaine's carcass down, but the dog's handler told him it's been too much rock and sand for too long to expect much chance of success with that.

"The other thing that's huge for us—and I can't stress this enough— is your reputation in the community. People here like you, Noah, and generally speaking aren't as pissed off 'bout this as you'd think. If it comes to it, I plan to impanel as many Mexicans on a jury as I can squeeze in. Hector notwithstanding, generally that community is very loyal to you. It also doesn't hurt, frankly, that so many people think Blaine was an asshole.

"Bottom line, based on where things stand at this moment in time, if it comes to a courtroom, I'd give us an even-money shot at an acquittal."

Driving home, it seemed shocking to me that only nine days had passed since Blaine had gone missing. Nine days. Before then, my biggest legal worry was that my clandestine smuggling efforts might come to light causing some problems with my medical license. Those worries now seemed minor, almost quaint. Now I'd just been told by my lawyer that I was the prime suspect in the disappearance of a town luminary, and if it came to a courtroom, I had at best a fifty-fifty shot at acquittal. What with the revelation of the affair with Darla, it was likely the charges would be murder one which meant in turn that a conviction was likely to have me headed for Huntsville and death row. You're too young to remember this, ma'am, but that was the year Texas started putting inmates down with lethal injection. As I drove, I caught myself staring at my forearms wondering which vein they'd select.

Despite the noose tightening around my neck, Angelica and I tried to maintain a sense of normalcy for Miguel, insulating him from the drama. We'd caught him eavesdropping on us, so he had a vague sense that something was going on, but we kept his routines up to minimize his anxiety. His birthday was coming up, and we planned to throw a party at the state school with cake and ice cream and his friends. There'd be dancing— man, did those kids love to dance back then. Bringing up the party never failed to distract him. What's more, he hadn't let go of the idea of getting a tattoo, either.

"*Mijo*, are you sure about this? After all, you will be sixteen years old, and that is too big to cry when it hurts," Angelica teased at dinner the night of our meeting with Bingham.

Miguel scooped rice with his fork, staring intently at the plate, then nodded vigorously.

I said, "It's okay to change your mind. Like, how 'bout if we were to get you, let's see, Joe Theismann's jersey number, inked in real big right here on your arm where everybody can see it?" The suggestion of anything relating to the Washington Redskins' quarterback would get under his skin. His two favorite teams were the Dallas Cowboys and whomever was playing against the Redskins.

"No," his mouth bent into a toothy grin.

"Then what, *mijo*?" she said.

"I told you," he said, and pointed at my upper arm below the cuff of my t-shirt. The bottom inch of the dark blue caduceus tattoo peeked out, the tails of the intertwined snakes just visible.

Angelica pursed her lips, exasperated. "*Ay de mi.*" Then to me, "I still think you put him up to this."

I threw my hands up in a gesture of innocence. "Hey, don't look at me. My name's Bennet and I wasn't in it."

She cocked her head. "Then, how do you say"— she squeezed her eyes shut to remember the phrase, then said with an impish grin—"'My name's Paul and this is between y'all'?"

I laughed at her use of the idiom, then shrugged my shoulders. "Meh. I was sixteen when I got my first tattoo. I can't say anything."

"So it's okay, mama?"

"Fine, you win."

Miguel threw his fists in the air in momentary triumph, then began to shoulder dance in his chair.

Turning back to him, she said, "Miggy, you know they put the tattoo on with a needle? It feels like getting many, many shots in your arm. Over and over. It is like a sewing machine." She plucked a toothpick from the holder on the table and playfully dotted the tip across his arm. "*Deet, deet, deet, deet.*"

Miguel hated shots. When his expression became wide-eyed, she laughed and tossed the toothpick on her plate. "If I had to bet," she told me as she stood to clear her setting, "you will never make it past them turning on the ink pen."

We hand-washed dishes and spoke further of the tattoo, handing scraps to Maybelline and Rope Tail and wrapping leftovers in cellophane. At one point, I paused, worried that family nights like this might be drawing to an end.

The future was about to show me I was right.

Chapter 19

Clouds roiled the sky two days later as I prepared to head to work. I remember the first norther of the season was closing in, the big wall of cobalt-blue clouds on the horizon rolling ahead like an advancing army. I'd just scooped my keys off the counter when the phone rang. It was Bingham.

"I need you to cancel your clinic this mornin'. You're goin' with me to the sheriff's office."

I felt light-headed and reached out to a chair to steady myself. This was it. I was going to be arrested.

I croaked, "What's goin' on?"

"Not sure. I just got a call from McHenry sayin' you and me should meet him at his office. He wouldn't say for what except that it wasn't to arrest you. I tried to pin him down but he won't budge. Just kept sayin, 'Get your client down here.' I'm not gonna lie, anybody else but McHenry give me that phone call I'd tell 'em to go fuck themselves, but McHenry's all right. If he says we should come down, then we probably oughtta be headin' in that direction. I'll pick you up in five."

When we arrived at the sheriff's office, Beau Alexander escorted us to an interview room and brought us two black coffees.

My nerves were on edge by that point, wanting to get things decided, whatever the outcome. The anticipation was killing me. I consider myself a resilient man, but, Lord. Between the possibility of being arrested on murder charges, the threat to me and mine from faceless cartel members looking to avenge stolen dope, the threat to my license if my smuggling activities came to light—I'll just say that every person has their limits and I felt like I was coming dangerously close to finding exactly where mine lay.

I drummed my fingers on the tabletop, then after five minutes of waiting, got up and paced loops around the small room.

If my nervous energy annoyed Bingham, he didn't show it. He just sat patiently reading loose papers from his briefcase and jotting notes on a yellow legal pad.

Five minutes turned into fifteen, and fifteen turned into thirty. I peeked through the door's inset window where the only activity in my view was Beau typing on a battered Underwood, filling out reports. I tried the door handle. It was locked from the outside, so I rapped on the glass. When Beau glanced up, I raised my hands and eyebrows, the universal sign for, "What the hell?"

He came over and keyed the door, propping it with a wooden wedge. "Sorry, gents. Sheriff'll be with you soon as he can. Left instructions he shouldn't be bothered less'n it's life and death. Don't know how much longer he'll be, so here you go meantime. Bathroom's over there, and coffee pot's to the right."

To Bingham I said, "I'm gettin' another cup. You want me to get you one?"

He didn't look up from his scribbling. "I'm

coffee'd out. Didn't need the one I had."

Crossing the deputy's work area, I stared at McHenry's glass-walled office at the rear of the station while I poured a cup, trying to see through the closed venetian blinds. Plaques filled the wall adjacent to his office, and I pretended to read them while I edged closer to his door, eavesdropping.

Inside, I heard two muffled voices. One I could identify as McHenry's gruff tone. The other was higher and squeaky, but familiar. The words were low and indistinct, so I leaned toward a meritorious commendation of some deputy from the sixties and concentrated. The words were still too faint to make out, so I shot a glance at Beau. The deputy paid me no attention as he two-finger hunt-and-pecked through the form, a pained expression on his face, like he was giving birth.

I edged closer to the door, straining to hear. By that point I could see through the half-inch gap between the edge of the blinds and the window frame. A shape wearing a blue shirt occupied the chair in front of McHenry's desk.

Suddenly, the door swung inward quickly enough that the blinds knocked into the glass with a clatter. McHenry came up short, startled by my presence.

My eyes darted past him. In the chair, tears streaming down his cheeks and wiping his runny nose with a tissue, sat Francis Beckett.

The sheriff closed the door behind him. "Beau, you wanna wrap this up while I go talk to the Doc?"

A look of relief crossed Beau's face at being excused from his battle against the typewriter. "Sure thing, Sheriff."

"Come on." McHenry led me back to the interview room.

Bingham made his annoyance clear the moment we entered. "Goddammit, Sheriff, I don't know what kind of bullshit mind fuck you're trying to pull making us wait for over a half hour, but if you think--"

"Simmer down, counselor. You're gonna want to hear this."

I took a seat, but McHenry leaned against the closed door and put his hands in his pockets, jingling his keys as he spoke. "This morning, 'bout a half hour after I got to work, Francis Beckett showed up. Said he wanted to talk. And hoo boy, did he ever talk."

Bingham gave me a puzzled look. I held my tongue, waiting to see how this unfolded.

"He's corroborating Gilberto Moreno's story that Hector is trying to set you up, Doc. That the man's got some kind of beef with you, and he thinks Hector took advantage of the situation when we went to go question him, that he saw an opportunity to throw you under the bus by talkin' 'bout seeing Blaine's car out at your ranch. He says Hector's been obsessed with all the talk of Blaine's disappearin', that he must'a read that story in the paper 'bout it a hunnert times."

"No shit," Bingham said in a low voice.

"Wait, I ain't even got to the interestin' part yet." The sheriff now took a seat and leaned the chair back on two legs. "Seems Francis and Hector been carryin' on for a while. Doc, he tells me you knew 'bout this?"

My face must have showed my surprise. "I know he's involved with somebody, a somebody who has a pretty bad temper. I didn't know who, though."

"What else did he tell you 'bout him?"

"Well, when I told Francis I was worried for his safety and pressed him to tell me who the man was, he said he couldn't because the fella was still in the closet. Francis was tryin' to respect that."

The sheriff *thunked* the chair down on all four legs. "What can you tell me 'bout this problem Hector's got with you?"

"When I've been around the boy, he's chilly towards me, stand-offish. Doesn't make much eye contact, then takes the first excuse he can to leave me alone. But we never had words or anythin' like that."

Bingham set his pen down and laced his fingers behind his head. "What's this mean for my client, Sheriff? You callin' off the dogs now or what?"

"I'll answer that if he'll answer somethin' for me first, counselor." McHenry turned back to me. "Why'd you talk to Jesús about runnin' to Mexico, and helpin' him get there?"

I looked at Bingham, who gave me a silent nod. "I like the man, and when I heard about his fingerprints bein' on Blaine's ride, I was worried there might be a—well, I'll just call it a rush to judgement. I knew in my heart he didn't have nothin' to do with Blaine's disappearin'. But an unsophisticated Mexican can make a hell of a scapegoat. People—I'm not sayin' you, Lloyd, but people— might start howling for his head. So I did what I thought was the right thing."

"Yeah, well, you picked a hell of a time to grow a conscience," the sheriff said.

I flashed back to the corpse of the dead drug runner and all of the separate trouble that was causing. "Sad to say, you're not the first person to tell me that this week."

Bingham spoke up. "Back to my question, then. Where does that leave us?"

The sheriff spun a pencil that lay on the table as he spoke. "Don't be goin' nowhere, Doc, but, yes, we're takin' this in a different direction. I got to check with Mariano whether there's any reason Hector would know that short canyon where we found the car. Jesús already told me that he's not clear of the exact night he saw the car burn, but that it could'a been Friday. Since you got an alibi for Friday night, that's why we been so focused on Saturday up 'til now. But if Hector did something to Blaine on Friday night instead of Saturday, it'd explain why Jesús saw the feller who torched the car head down the creek bed in the direction of your ranch."

Bingham raised his eyebrows and pursed his lips, slowly nodding in satisfaction. "Anything else?"

The sheriff said, "We're lookin' for Hector now, gonna bring him in for questioning now that all this come to light. I'll be in touch with y'all once we've had that conversation."

I felt relief wash over me, like the first dip into a warm bath. Finally, I'd caught a break. I had to caution myself against getting my hopes up, but for the first time I thought it possible that I might get out of this with my life intact, with the only price to pay being the public revelation of my long-finished affair with Darla. "Sheriff, I got to ask. What else did Francis tell you 'bout him and Hector? I've wondered so often about this, now I'm dyin' to know."

It seemed even McHenry wasn't immune to taking part in the small town chatter mill. We were done with the legal side. Now, this was pure gossip.

"Seems Francis and Hector met back around a year ago in Ojinaga at some bar there, caters to that sort of thing, and the two of 'em been sneakin' around since. Apparently, wouldn't neither of their families have approved. Be honest, I can see that. I don't know Gilberto all that good, Doc, but I know Blaine would'a absolutely lost his shit at the thought of his boy turnin' queer.

"Francis says they talked about runnin' off together, but he knew it was mostly just talk. Kinda talk, he says, that, well— sort of makes you feel better for a minute, like a sugar high." McHenry sounded melancholy, then he came back to the moment.

"Anyways, he says Hector started talkin' like Blaine was the reason they couldn't be together, that in his mind Blaine became sort of, I guess you'd say larger than life. Way he said it struck me." McHenry pulled a small notepad from his breast pocket and read from it. "He told me that to Hector, Blaine 'embodied everything about the world that was against them.' Wrote it down so I wouldn't forget it." The pad's metal curly-cue propped his shirt pocket open when he replaced it.

"Francis told us Hector has a tendency towards violence. Said one night he instigated a bar brawl at the place where they met in Ojinaga and got himself banned. And I personally know he's spent at least two nights in that cell right there"— he jerked a thumb over his shoulder— "for the same shit here in town."

Bingham asked, "Just between us, Lloyd, what do you know about Hector's whereabouts Friday night, then?"

I half-expected the sheriff to tell us that was none of our business but it turned out he had no such compunction. "Francis says that on the Friday night of the weekend Blaine disappeared, him and Hector'd been drinkin' pretty hard. Apparently, Doc, they used that finished room you got at your barn for a lotta their little get togethers if Gilberto was stayin' in town somewheres. He says that on that night, they got to arguin' about Blaine, which wasn't that unusual, but Hector got so pissed off that he threw a mason jar at Francis' car window, broke it good, and then lit out in his own truck for parts unknown in a spray of gravel. Francis said after that he just taped a garbage bag over the busted window and went back to his dorm room for the weekend. Right now, we can't account for Hector's movements for the rest of Friday night."

Chapter 20

After McHenry gave the news that the investigation had shifted to Hector, all at once I felt light, like a child climbed off after a piggyback ride. I slept twelve hours that night, so deeply I joked with Angelica in the morning she needed to check me for bed sores. The relief also meant it was easier to turn my attentions back to things that'd been neglected during the worst of my worry. Life doesn't stop, after all.

The morning after Francis spoke with the sheriff's office, I called the boys to discuss our next run to the river and once my clinic wrapped up that evening, we convened at the diner. Word had spread quickly about the previous day's events—apparently Bingham and I weren't the only ones with whom McHenry had been loose-lipped— and a few folks gave me congratulatory back slaps as I made my way through the crowd.

In a booth set back from the crowd, I caught the trio up to speed on everything. I told them about the encounter with the drug thief's body in Pablo's shed and the gangster's plan to prevent reprisals, his opinion that our biggest fear should be low level soldiers looking to curry favor with our competitors, and I emphasized to them that the only known identity was my own.

Jimmy Wayne murmured, "First things first. Let's talk about the sheriff's office. You sure we're all right to be makin' a run?" He played with his coffee mug, rotating the thick porcelain in slow circles, the napkin stuck to its underside. The memory of his interview with the sheriff had left him on edge. "Mean to say, normal times, we all know Johnny Law's probably content to look the other way with what we're doin' down by the river. But if they got a hard-on for you—."

"Then this'd make fer a good excuse to pick you up." Shy Mike finished the thought.

Chebo chewed his coffee's red straw into a jagged shepherd's crook. Holding it up, he studied it closely, brow krinkled while he listened.

I said, "McHenry's sayin' the heat's off me. I don't think we got to worry 'bout them followin' me if that's what you're askin'."

"That's what I'm askin'," Jimmy Wayne said.

"We just got to be careful like normal, but I think that's as far as it goes."

"Okay. Then tell me more 'bout these cartel boys, might be wantin' to do you on spec," Jimmy Wayne said.

"I'm not gonna lie, I've lost more'n a little sleep over it. But here's the thing. They could touch me anywhere. The river, my clinic, here in town. Hell, they could come at me on the way out to my truck when we leave here. There isn't anythin' I can do 'bout that, so I decided I'm just gonna live my life. Remember, I'm the one whose face and name they know, not y'alls. Well, maybe you, Chebo, but you two should be in the clear."

Shy Mike said, "You oughtta be more worried, Doc, is all I'm sayin'."

I shrugged. "Trust me, I've done enough worryin' in the last couple weeks to last me a lifetime."

Jimmy Wayne and Shy Mike looked at each other with skeptical expressions.

"I will say I could use the money," Shy Mike said.

Jimmy Wayne shook his head in frustration, then said, "Sons of bitches'll probably shoot at you and hit me. But all right, I'm in."

That settled, we started making concrete plans, going over particulars. We decided to make another run the following weekend, on Saturday. That would give us eight days to pull everything together, more than enough time. Responsibilities were assigned, the mood at the table lightening as we talked.

Once finished I said, "Well, Chebo, since you're gonna be in town a little while, you interested in picking up a day's work meantime? Shy Mike and Jimmy Wayne, y'all listen up, same offer goes for you."

"Sure, always," Shy Mike said. He flicked ash into his empty cup and blew a plume of smoke to the ceiling. Chebo nodded. Jimmy Wayne waited to hear the offer.

"Teddy Scofield came into the clinic yesterday."

"That the younger Teddy?" Jimmy Wayne asked.

"Nope, his old man. Gout's been flaring up again. Poor bastard's gimpier than you right now, Shy Mike. Got him walkin' like a cripple."

"Him and my daddy used to run together back in the day," Shy Mike said. "You gotta keep an eye on him. My daddy said he knew more ways to take your money than a room full of lawyers."

"Me and him got to talking and he told me he bought four of the houses on that stretch of tear downs on the north side, ones other side of the Texaco. Turns out they're all full of the original copper pipes and wiring. He can't rip it out himself 'tween his foot and his age, so he asked me if Miguel wanted the work. I said yes, but it's sounding like he wants this done quicker'n me and Miguel can do by ourselves."

"Rippin' out copper? *Shiiiit*. Hard pass," Jimmy Wayne said with a laugh and shook his head emphatically.

"Fair enough. How 'bout you two? Either of you ladies afraid of breakin' a sweat?"

"When are you thinking about doing this?" Chebo asked.

"How 'bout tomorrow early? That work for y'all?"

Both men nodded.

The next day, we gathered at dawn-thirty on the curb outside an eyesore, a blighted one-story house with a weed-choked yard and a history of squatters. When some homeless guy started a camp fire in it that got out of control, the AFD had to respond and, frankly, I'm surprised they hadn't just let it burn. Now, the left-hand side of the roof was gone, leaving scorched rafters exposed, like blackened ribs. Inside, the house smelled of smoke and mildew. Afterward, the city council had leaned on the absentee owner to sell, and Teddy'd scapped it up.

Lots of folks would rather wrestle a sweaty chinaman than spend a beautiful Saturday inside a rundown shack stripping copper. I didn't mind, though. It gave Miguel and the boys a chance to earn some extra money, and me an opportunity to clear my mind in a way only sustained physical exertion ever could. It was hard work, no doubt, but we set up a sort of conveyor belt. While Shy Mike's transistor played in the background, we set to busting up drywall and tearing out the floors, working the pipe cutter or snipping the circuits. We'd cut it all free, then toss it in a heap for stripping and sanding. Back then, Sonny was paying seventy-two cents a pound for clean and bright. I saw in the paper the other day it's over three dollars now.

Miguel barely weighed a hundred and twenty pounds dripping wet. His hands, small and soft and delicate, swam loose in the heavy work gloves I gave him but he worked his sledge with the cadence of a piston. The blue bandana he wore tight and low soaked through with sweat, but despite his small size, he never slowed. Watching him pour himself into the job, I felt pride well up at his effort.

A few hours into the job Teddy dropped by, looking to socialize. Teddy Scofield was an interesting man. Shrewd and serious, but with a penchant for gossip that'd gotten stronger with age until by that time in his late sixties he could've given a ladies' sewing circle a run. Not that the same couldn't be said for half of Amoret.

Taking a seat, he propped his gout-ravaged foot up. He rested his hands on the head of his walking stick, then his chin on his hands. He whistled as he admired Miguel's pace. "Boy, I'm gettin' tired just watching you. I'm gonna keep you on retainer. I got a row of post holes need diggin' out at my ranch, got your name all over 'em."

I mopped my brow. "One job at a time there, cap'n." Taking off my work glove, I paused from yanking on a piece of pipe to shake.

"Boys are makin' good progress, looks like."

"Yeah, we're winnin'. Late-afternoon, should be done."

Teddy lowered his voice. "You hear the latest? 'Bout Hector?"

"Nuh-uh. Anything new?"

"Still no sign of him. I run into Scotty Muschka down at the feed store. Says Gilberto's tellin' the police no money went missing when Hector disappeared, and the boy ain't got no credit card. Hard to see what he's been livin' on."

I shrugged. "Lord willin', everything'll be all right."

"I'm hearin' he made it out to the truck stop on the highway and hooked up with some long-haul trucker, just lit out." He leaned in and stage whispered, "If what folks are sayin' 'bout him and that Beckett boy are true, he's one of them shouldn't have a hard time doin' what it takes to make money to live on, know what I mean? But you didn't hear that from me." He brought up his hand and with his pinkie finger extended pantomimed turning a key at his lips.

"Hmph," I grunted as I pulled my glove back on. "Well, Teddy, this pipe isn't gonna cut itself."

"Yeah, and here I am runnin' my mouth." He raised his voice so Shy Mike and Chebo could hear him in the other room. "You real workin' men keep givin' it whatfer." Then to me, "Just let's settle up next few days."

"Sounds good. Give Mary Margaret my best."

The sun was just setting when the four of us finished loading the last of the bird's nest of copper onto the bed of my old three-axle panel truck. It was a tangle of wiring and thin pipes, like when you spill a new box of toothpicks. By my guess, we had a ton, maybe more.

I checked my watch. "Scrapyard's closed. You boys all right with me and Miguel cashing out in the morning?"

"Works for me," Culverson said.

"*Mismo*," Chebo agreed.

We all four shook, Miguel mimicking me, and parted ways.

Twenty minutes later I kept my promise. I watched as Miguel, shirt sleeve wadded up over his shoulder, got his upper arm inked. Amid the backdrop of the rotary tattoo pen's mosquito-buzz and the smell of disinfectant, the tattoo artist worked free hand. Her bracelets rattled against one another as she made the twin snakes of the caduceus wind around the staff like a helix. Underneath her seven facial piercings—I counted— she was pretty, with fetching eyes. As she concentrated on her canvas, Miguel took it well, squinching his eyes shut and turning his head away, but never telling her to stop.

When she was done, as she wiped antibiotic ointment and taped gauze over her creation, he looked at me and for the first time that day his face lit up with a big, slobbering grin I'll always remember. I could feel my heart swell, and my instinct to protect him from the world never felt stronger.

As she washed her hands, she asked, "How 'bout you? Thinkin' of gettin' anything yourself this evenin'?"

I hadn't even considered it to that point, but an impulse came over me.

"You know what? Think I will."

Come again, ma'am? I don't know, I guess I'm— I think I'm just dragging my feet, not wanting to talk about this next part. That awful day that changed things forever, the day we could never come back from.

Chapter 21

"I like it," Angelica said the next morning, admiring Miguel's tattoo before taping the gauze back in place. The skin was still red and scabby, but he grinned as he shrugged his shirt back on. "How sore is it? Are you going to be able to help Noah unload all that copper this morning? It's going to take longer if you're working one-handed." She set our breakfast plates down on the nook's table.

"It's fine," he said in his simple way.

"Did you cry, *mijo*?" she teased.

He shook his head vigorously, brow furrowed.

"I don't know. Is he telling the truth, Noah?"

"Shoot. He never batted an eye." I rumpled his hair before spooning salsa on my *migas*. "And as far as loading the copper up today, a one-handed Miguel could probably still get it done quicker than I can using both. You should'a seen him work yesterday. Boy's got the makin's of a hand."

"Hmm. Show me your muscles," she said. Reflexively, he brought his spindly arms up and flexed, fists by his ears, and held the pose. "Ooh, I see what you mean." She squeezed one bicep playfully then kissed the top of his head.

Turning to me, she stroked my cheek with the back of her fingers, my stubble rasping. "I like yours, too," she whispered.

"I just decided on it spur of the moment." I held up my left hand so she could once again examine the wedding band tattoo I'd had the girl ink onto my ring finger.

"I think I will get one like that myself." She kissed me lightly on the lips before sitting down to her own plate.

As we pulled up to the gates of Sonny Fitzgerald's scrap yard, Miguel simply said, "Oh my God." For a kid like him, it may as well have been an amusement park.

The open-air facility was massive, a sprawling sea of skeletonized vehicles, dented and degraded appliances, and twisted pieces of unidentifiable metal alloy arranged in mounds, some as high as fifteen feet. Dirt paths lined with crane claw and bulldozer tread marks snaked among the stacks and rows like a maze, a graveyard for iron and steel that stretched several acres. A twelve-foot chain link fence surrounded the entire property, angling outward at the top with three rows of barbed wire to keep out anyone considering some after-hours shopping in the spacious outdoor market.

Sonny didn't normally open on Sundays until nine, but when I told him the volume of copper we had on hand and my desire to be finished in time to make Sunday services by eleven, he'd agreed to come in early.

I pulled up to the trundle gate and twirled in the combination Sonny gave me for the padlock securing the entrance's heavy chain. While I worked the gate, Miguel pressed his nose and hands against the passenger window, making his nose into a pig snout as his breath fogged the glass. His wide eyes darted around in anticipation at that wondrous landscape, full of exciting potential.

The truck idling, I approached the squat one-story structure which functioned as both a front office and workshop. Overhead, a plywood sign on the pre-fab roof announced "Sonny's Scrap" in simple black lettering with a phone number. Just like its owner, the sign was no-nonsense, all business.

Sonny's truck was nowhere to be seen, and through the plexiglass doors the interior's fluorescents were dark. I rapped loudly next to the cursive-script "Sorry, we're closed" sign, and Sonny appeared from the inky darkness with a wave. With eyes like an owl and the body of Icabod Crane, he looked born to run a scrapyard.

He stooped to unlock one side of the double doors, but only cracked it a foot. "Morning, Doc. Why don't you pull around back to my big scales? Make both our lives easier. Plus, keeps the lot clear of vehicles. I don't want folks pulling up thinkin' I'm open just yet."

I steered the truck through stacks of junked vehicles that'd already undergone their turn in the compactor. Hundreds of metal cubes stacked in neat metal cairns dotted the packed dirt, guiding me like guardrails toward a high-roofed corrugated tin building at the rear of the property. I turned the truck around and backed up slowly, the rhythmic beep alerting only the empty air, until the rear tires edged up to a twenty by twenty-five- foot metal plate set flush with the packed dirt. The industrial scale's chrome surface was scratched and tarnished. I tested its resistance with a foot, putting my weight on it while I waited for Sonny to catch up.

Nearby, Sonny's scrap magnet dangled from its boom like a massive chandelier, supported by a pyramid-shaped trio of chains, each thick as my thigh. Miguel craned his neck to stare up at the rig, awestruck.

"What does this do?"

"It's a magnet. Magnets attract metal to them, like the ones we put on the refrigerator to hold papers."

"Is he going to use this one today?"

"Nope. Magnets don't work on copper."

He looked disappointed at the inconvenient science, more at missing the spectacle than for the increase in our work. The morning grew warmer, and we stowed our jackets in the cab.

Sonny appeared, and we shook. Miguel had moved on, discovering the nearby husk of a Chevy Vega, doors missing but frame intact. In the driver's seat, he sat spinning the wheel and making racing noises.

Sonny caught me smiling at him. "Kids're somethin', ain't they?"

"Hope you don't mind, he's just having--."

"Aww, that's fine, he ain't hurtin' nothin'. When mine were little, me and my old lady let 'em run 'round out here all day. They used to love it, said it reminded 'em of the *Fat Albert* cartoons." He pressed a finger against one nostril and blew a snot rocket, then turned his attention to the truck's payload, giving an impressed *humph* as he appraised the shiny metal pile with an expert eye.

"Weren't kidding were you?" He crossed to a waist-high fencepost adjacent to the scale. Bolted to the top was a small white box with a display screen. He fumbled in the breast pocket of his yoked work shirt for a pair of half-moon reading glasses, then pressed and held a button on the screen. "Okay, you're zeroed out."

"Think we got a ton?"

He pushed the reading glasses up onto his freckled scalp. "More'n that, I reckon. I make it twenty-two, maybe twenty-three hunnert pounds all said and done."

"Think so?"

"Not a doubt in my mind." He reached over the tailgate and pulled a single pipe out of the jumble like a pixie stick, inspecting it closely before tossing it onto the metal weighing plate. It clattered with a tinny *whang*, then rolled a few feet.

He checked the screen and nodded his head. "I'll be doin' some work up at the office, just come find me when you're through and we'll settle up." With that he left, following the old dozer tracks back.

I pulled on my work gloves and scanned the area, looking to call Miguel over. I spotted him wandering further into the yard, peering deep into an old toaster oven, puzzling over its viscera, poking and pulling at its coils. He grew bored with it after a minute, carelessly tossing it back onto the pile where he'd found it and moving on. A few paces away, he squatted on his haunches to inspect a transmission poking out from the bottom of a stack of debris. After jabbing at the output shaft with his heel, he found it rusted and unmoving. His face bore an expression of pure wonder, his body language all curiosity.

With a sigh, I said out loud, "Aw, hell with it. Let the boy have his fun." I pulled the pins out of the chains that secured the tailgate and let it drop with a *clang*, then hoisted myself into the back of the truck atop the pile.

I started pulling at pipes and tossing them onto the plate. Edges sharp as razors were scattered throughout the mess, making me mindful of my forearms and legs. I bent, pulled, and threw, over and over.

If not for the growing pile on the scale, I wouldn't have known I was making progress as the pile didn't seem to shrink. All the same, I didn't mind the work. I've always found repetitive physical labor clears my mind, calms me down even. In fact, you could say in a way it was better not having Miguel up there with me. It gave me time to think, to ponder the events of the last few weeks in a healthier way than staring at my ceiling in the middle of the night, unable to turn off my brain, the darkness of our bedroom magnifying my anxieties about the threats to our world.

Eventually, the work became easier as the pile shrunk, the pipes and wiring coming clear with an easy tug instead of a back-breaking pull. I caught myself slowing, enjoying the cathartic effect of the labor under a cloudy sky. Something about that moment, with the way the light breeze carried the smells of rust and far-off rain, the screaming in my muscled back and arms— it felt purgative, I guess would be the right word. Made me feel alive. It's fair to say I didn't want to see it end.

But like all good things, it did. With a heave, I tossed the last clump of shiny wire onto the stack below and took a long pull of water.

"*¡Miguel, vámonos!*" I shouted. I crawled out of the bed to the ground, not trusting my exhausted legs enough to jump. Checking my watch, I'd been at it for over two hours.

I hobbled over to the display. Black LED numbers on the dull screen showed two-four-two-one. Twenty-four hundred pounds. I did some quick math: about seventeen hundred dollars, split evenly between Miguel and the boys. I'd decided to forgo my share, the better to keep morale up in our party. For me the money would be nice. For them it would be food on their families' tables. They did good work, and I wanted to keep them happy.

"Miguel, let's go!" I shouted again. I walked back in the direction of the office but didn't hear his response. I paused, then sighed. The lot was easily big enough that he could be out of earshot, and it wasn't hard to picture him wandering afar without realizing it, following a path from one interesting discovery to the next.

I walked in the direction I'd last seen him meandering, deeper into the guts of the scrapyard, continuing to call to him. After a hundred yards, I gave up and went back to the truck. I slowly drove the maze of trails at random, leaning out my open window and shouting his name at the debris piles, periodically blaring the horn. After fifteen minutes with no success, I drove up to the office.

Sonny sat behind his desk, reading glasses still perched as they'd been when he left me. Seeing me approach, he pulled them down to the end of his nose before tapping his ballpoint pen against a display screen identical to the one on the scale's post.

"Twenty-four hundred plus. Nice day's work." He swiveled and pulled a large leatherette checkbook from a bottom drawer.

"Miguel come up here while I was working?"

"I thought he was helping you?"

"No, he was having so much fun, I just let him go on and did it myself."

"Well, he didn't come up this a'way. Got me a camera on the front gate." He pointed at the wall behind me. Above a thumbtacked Budweiser poster with the Cowboys' schedule and a tattered pinup of a topless woman reclining on a hay bale, a monitor displayed a fuzzy black and white image of the closed trundle gate. Two Mexican Jays hopped across the dirt just inside, pecking at bugs in the packed earth. "I should'a already opened 'er up, but I was busy and ain't nobody pulled up yet, so I was gonna finish m' books first."

He saw my look of concern and stood. "Don't worry, he can't have gone far. Whole place is fenced with barb wire."

"I drove around the lot already. He isn't answering when I call."

Sonny's brow furrowed. "Tell you what. When I check the property I use a three-wheeler. It can get in and out of places your truck cain't. C'mon." I followed him through the building onto a crude loading dock in the rear.

With a grunt of effort, he slid the rolling door up. It roared on its tracks, then drab sunlight spilled into the sheet metal warehouse onto a pair of utility vehicles parked on the oil-stained concrete. Straddling them, we fired up and headed out to the scrapyard.

I let Sonny lead the way. He idled his bike along at ten miles an hour, periodically goosing it as he followed the perimeter fencing. He'd been right, of course. The smaller, more agile three-wheelers were able to get all the way up to the fence line to follow a path I hadn't even been able to see from the cab of my truck. We continued to shout Miguel's name.

I judged we'd made it about a quarter of the way around the perimeter when Sonny stopped so short I almost ran into the back of him. He removed his cap and smacked it on his handlebars in irritation. Looking ahead, I saw the object of his anger. Someone had cut a four-foot long slit in the chain-link fence, all the way to the ground. The bottom edges of the fence curled outward, like the points of a collar missing its stays.

"Son of a bitch," he muttered as we walked up to the hole. "Goddamn kids. I get this couple times a year. I'd dearly love to get my hands on the little bent-dick cocksuckers did this."

Hands on his hips, he seemed embarrassed, unsure how to ask his next question. Delicately, he said, "Umm, so you know Miguel. Are kids with his— condition— likely to go out through a hole like this?"

Beyond the fence, desert scrub hunkered low as far as the eye could see. "I doubt it," I said. "I mean, why go out there when he sees desert all the time? Whole reason he wasn't working with me was he looked to be havin' so much fun in the yard here."

Sonny nodded. Then, looking closer at the fence, he frowned. He walked over to the hole and pulled one of the pig-tailed cut ends of chain link toward himself and put on his cheaters again.

He said, "Me or one of my boys checks this fence every couple days just like we're doing now. You know, a hole like this costs me money. Last time we checked was, let's see, probably three days ago. Everythin' was fine then. Now take a look at this."

He pulled the fence edge out for me to see. The cut ends of the metal links were shiny and clean. "These are fresh cut, last couple hours or so."

I pushed my way through the gap in the fence and looked around. A trail ran around the outside of the perimeter, big enough to accommodate a vehicle. Beyond it, the landscape was flat and thick with spiny ocotillo bushes to the horizon. I pushed my way through those thorny brambles for fifty feet.

The prickly barbs clawed at my thighs and chest, making it a miserable slog. I stopped and scanned the area, but the only movement was the sea of bushy branches, swaying in ripples from the desert wind. As

I turned back to the scrapyard, I knew without a doubt Miguel hadn't voluntarily gone in that direction.

That was when I first realized this was going to end badly.

Chapter 22

I called the house from Sonny's office and got the answering machine. I hesitated, unsure what to say, then tried to keep the alarm out of my voice.

"Hon, Miggy's gone missing here at the scrapyard. I need you to come on down as soon as you get this. Try not to worry, okay? I love you." As I hung up, I caught a glimpse through the plexiglass doors of the sheriff's cruiser crawling through the gate, McHenry behind the wheel and a deputy riding shotgun. Sonny's oldest boy had made it to work by that point in the morning, and I left him with instructions to bring Angelica to us if she should show, then set off toward the gap in the fence on foot. By the time I caught up with the cruiser, the sheriff was already examining the hole.

McHenry's body language appeared subdued, as though awaiting the biopsy results from a suspicious lump. "Y'all check the rest of the perimeter already? Nothin' hinky?"

"Yup, before we called you. Just this," Sonny said.

It felt surreal to be depending on the man who until recently might have been my ticket to death row. That said, it also felt good to be with him on the same side for a change. I'd always liked Lloyd, trusted him for all the years we'd known each other leading up to this mess. And frankly, his competence was one of the things that'd scared me when it looked like I was his quarry.

McHenry approached the hole indirectly, from along the adjacent intact fence line. Hunched over with his hands on his knees, he peered at the dirt for a full minute, as though giving the ground time to speak. "Best I can tell, looks like three different sets of footprints 'round the hole. Couple pairs of boots, probably you two from what y'all are tellin' me. Then a third pair looks like sneakers. Doc, what was Miguel's footwear?"

That was easy. "Desert boots. He lives in 'em.""

"M'kay. Y'all are sure, ain't nobody else been down here but you boys?"

"Nope, just us."

"And Doc, how tall's Miguel? He's on the small side, am I right?"

"Five-four."

"Well, I don't see no small prints, desert boot or otherwise, heading through the hole to outside. All these look like they come from grown men."

Without looking up, McHenry said to his deputy, "Do me a favor. Run get Scooter and tell him bring Arabella out here, would you?"

We retreated back to the scale, the pile of twisted copper as I'd left it. After twenty minutes, an old pickup rattled toward us, mashing the dried dozer tracks.

Scooter Gatson, thirty-something and stocky with an artificial leg from the war, climbed out holding a half-eaten sandwich. Behind him, a bloodhound sat in the cab, her tail thumping eagerly on the vinyl bench seat. On his command she jumped down to the packed earth and sat at attention. Scooter took another bite, then held the remainder of the ham and cheese chest-high. The dog froze, eyes locked on him. He flipped the sandwich toward her and she caught it cleanly before wolfing it down in two large bites. Scooter wiped his fingers on his bib overalls and scratched her head, then shook the sheriff's hand.

"Been keepin' busy?" Beau asked.

"You called jest the right time, we's finishin' up," Scooter replied. "Shady Acres had 'nother one of their Alzheimer's patients wander off. Second one in three months."

"Mmm. People who run that place don't know their ass from a hole in the ground. We put my grandpa there."

"You're tellin' me. I told 'em me and Emily's talkin' about what to do with momma, and after seein' how they do business--"

The sheriff interrupted. "Thanks for coming out, Scooter. Doc, you wanna grab the boy's jacket? Let's get after it."

Scooter put on the dog's harness as she hopped side to side. When he held the jacket before her face, she snuffled and snorted, head jerking around. He tossed the jacket back to me, then gave her the search command. "'Bella, hunt!"

The dog trotted in the direction of the Chevy Vega, pulling hard at her thirty-foot leash, nose glued to the ground. Periodically she'd lift her head, nostrils wrinkling and flaring as she sampled the breeze, then back down to the ground, searching. She located the toaster oven Miguel handled and discarded, then moved deeper into the bowels of the yard.

We lost sight of the weighing plate as we followed Miguel's path through the maze. The hound would dally here and there, presumably on objects Miguel touched, objects I could tell would have distracted him. Engine parts always seemed to fascinate the boy. He could spend an entire afternoon in the barn's machine shop at my ranch, sitting in silence on the high worktable, legs swinging as he watched Gilberto repair equipment. Miguel's broken brain had a unique ability to focus in a manner that was light-years beyond yours and mine, absorbed to the point of obsession, tuning out the world while devoting his entire conscious mind to an object in his hands. I'd seen him turn a carburetor over and over in his hands for five minutes straight, like a Rubik's cube, just slowly rotating it with an expression of fascination.

The bloodhound moved from stack to stack, locking onto a compressor here or a muffler there. At one tall mound of parts, she tried to climb the pile of twisted metal, but couldn't find purchase among the loops and pockets of scrap. The pile was high, twenty feet at least, and she pulled anxiously, whining as she grew frustrated at her inability to ascend with Miguel's scent.

The iron grip of panic suddenly seized me like a fist. An old refrigerator with a self-latching door lay at an angle atop the pile. As the dog danced from paw to paw, I heard Sonny mumble a slack-jawed, "Oh, shit." I broke into a sprint, past the dog and toward the dingy white icebox.

I scrambled up the heap of jagged debris. My feet kept finding momentary purchase which would give way under my weight, my boots disappearing up to the knee into the serrated holes. My progress was agonizingly slow as I frantically clawed my way up and up, higher and higher. Pulling on a ragged piece of sheet metal as a hand hold, I lacerated my palm deep, to the bone. I ignored the fire in my hand, clambering a path up to the scuffed and dented appliance. I slapped one palm onto the refrigerator door, leaving a macabre, bloody handprint. Grabbing the handle with the other, I heaved myself up until I stood next to the appliance, praying it wasn't a coffin.

Panting, I pulled at the latch. The door swung open easily, and a wave of fetid air washed over me, as though the chamber within had belched. At the bottom of the refrigerator, I found plastic squeeze-bottles of condiments, a six-pack ring with two remaining cans of Schlitz, and some unidentifiable vegetables and meat products that had decayed into a translucent confection of slime, neither solid nor liquid. But no Miguel.

I sagged, my head slumping in relief against the side of the icebox before I turned back to the men anxiously watching me and shook my head.

As I gingerly made my way back down, I took a quick look at my hand. A brisk ooze came from the base of the cut, running down my pinkie finger and dripping to leave a thin trail of blood beside my path. The sheriff jutted his chin at my hand and passed me a red bandana from his back pocket. As I bound my injured hand, the lawman gave Sonny the stink-eye. We all knew storing the appliance with its self-locking door still on the hinges got you a citation. Chagrined, he mumbled to the sheriff, "I'll be back 'n' take care of that after we wrap up."

Scooter worked the dog around the pile, and she acquired Miguel's scent again on the far side. After dawdling there a few moments, she continued on.

The adrenaline burst wore off leaving me shaky, but I stayed glued to Scooter's hip, hyper-vigilant as I grappled with a roller coaster ride of emotions, relief and anxiety battling for supremacy.

Our path roughly paralleled the fence in the direction of the cut hole. The chain link would be intermittently visible, sometimes a little closer, sometimes a little farther, but never disappearing entirely. After a few minutes, the hole in the fence came into view to our right. I stood still, watching the bloodhound, waiting for it to turn in the direction of the gap in the fence. Much to my surprise, though, the dog continued straight, paralleling the fence line, its snuffling path angling back and forth like the arm of a metronome, but tracking persistently in the same general direction. Then the dog was clearly past the hole in the fence, continuing onward further into the interior of the yard. I saw the sheriff wince once he realized the dog was passing the gap. I tried not to think about what that meant as I trudged along behind Scooter and Arabella.

We continued like that for another few minutes, each of us lost deep in his own thoughts. Soon, the corner of the lot came into view where the fence turned from running west to south. I was about to ask Scooter how old a trail could get before Arabella lost it when she locked onto the husk of a blue Cutlass.

Adjacent to a stack of gutted vehicular skeletons, the Cutlass' shell sat off by itself, like a crumpled outcast. Its passenger doors and windows were gone, and the trunk was closed but nonfunctional, the edges buckled and curved so it wouldn't seat true. Two rimmed tires sat atop the trunk, denting it slightly.

The dog jumped onto the bench seats, running her nose along the torn-up vinyl and dashboard, then out again, and wedged her head sideways under the chassis. But instead of continuing down her path, Bella looked excitedly back at Scooter as she looped the car's bare bones, wagging so hard her rear shook, her tail thudding against the rear quarter panel.

I frowned, unsure why she stopped when we could all clearly see the car's empty interior. No signs of Manuel lurked nearby.

Then it dawned on all of us simultaneously.

The trunk.

A wave of nausea washed over me. A roaring came up in my ears and my throat squeezed shut. Scooter reeled Anabelle in, scratching her flanks and cooing at her while he fed her treats from his pocket. We exchanged glances silently. With a sigh of resignation, the sheriff started forward, but I put out a hand to stop him.

I felt like I was walking underwater as I approached the trunk. I heaved the first tire off, tossing it away where it bounced a few times before toppling on its side and undulating to a halt. My vision blurred from tears as I pulled the second tire off the trunk's chipped paint. The drag of the tire's weight coming off popped the trunk open for a moment, maybe three inches, before it bounced closed again, the lock broken.

I took a deep, shaking breath, ragged and hitching. Lips pressed into a tight white line, I steeled myself and lifted the trunk's hatch.

There, face down and knees bent, with his nose pressed into the grimy liner like he was looking at something in the tattered carpet up close, Miguel's body lay before me.

Chapter 23

I sat on an old V-8 engine block some distance away from the trunk, watching while a technician dusted it for fingerprints. Not far off, a driver from the Brewster County Morgue leaned against his rig's quarter panel smoking a cigarette and reading a tattered copy of *The Hobbit*, waiting for everyone to finish so he could transport Miguel's body to the medical examiner.

I couldn't bring myself to leave the spot, as though my presence was the last link to a Miguel who was alive and well. It sounds crazy, I know, but a part of my grieving brain kept whispering that leaving would finalize his death, and by sitting right there on that old engine block I could somehow forestall it.

The sheriff had been walking in slow, small circles, but now wandered over. He squatted in front of me, his face pained and weary. Taking off his cowboy hat, he fingered the brim, then dropped his chin to his chest.

"You up for hearin' what we know Doc? I understand if you'd rather hold off."

I took a long hitching breath. "I'm good enough, I guess."

"Miguel's got two big cuts across the back of his

head, crossing each other, sorta 'V'shaped," he indicated on the back of his own scalp. "Puttin' it together, seems most likely that somebody drove down that trail other side of the fence, saw Miguel back here by himself, cut that hole in the chain link yonder, and killed Miguel with two blows to the head. We found a blood trail and followed it back over about twenty yards south. There's a puddle there, looks like where it must'a happened. Then back out the hole he cut, jumped in his car, and lit a shuck on outta here."

I flinched, trying to digest the information, but the reality of what he was saying hit me all at once. I choked up, then let out a gasping sob, clasping my hand to my mouth and squeezing my eyes shut.

"Listen here, Doc. We still got a good bit of scene work to do. Why don't you head on home and be with your woman? Times like this is family time. By the way, you want me to tell her? I don't mind bein' the one to do it."

I couldn't say anything for a few moments. Tilting my head back to keep from crying, I finally brought my emotions under control. I wiped my eyes with my palm and my nose on my sleeve. "No, I'll tell her. I left a message on our machine when Miguel was only missing. If she's not down here it means she hasn't come home yet, so she doesn't know. It oughtta come from me."

"Fair enough." The sheriff stood, his knees popping, and clapped a hand on my shoulder. "Listen to me. We're gonna find the piece of shit did this to your boy. You hear me?"

I exhaled, long and slow. "Thanks. I appreciate that."

He pursed his lips and replaced his hat. As he walked back in the direction of the car trunk, I heard him mutter under his breath, "And Hector Moreno, for your own sake, I hope you're far away from here."

Henry Judd Carter had hung back a respectful distance while I spoke with the sheriff, and now he approached and gave me a hug. Tall and lanky, with thinning hair and soft eyes, he went to our church, and he'd done the pictures for our Christmas card the year before. Nice man. Quiet and God-fearing. At that moment his sadness was palpable. He said, "Noah, I don't have words..."

I nodded and hugged him back, too choked up to answer.

He broke the embrace and held me by the shoulders at arms' length. "I'll say a prayer for Miguel tonight. Try not to fret. He's in a better place."

Amoret was such a small town back then the sheriff's office didn't have a full-time evidence photographer on the payroll. Instead, they contracted with Henry Judd, the owner of a Kodak store in town who also ran a portrait studio out of the back. He'd earned the job of law enforcement photographer after attending a weekend-long course in El Paso, paid for by the county.

As I left to go home, Henry Judd set about his work. The last thing I saw was the way he'd cock his head to the left or right in between each shot of Miguel's body and the trunk, just like he'd done for our portrait.

Henry Judd would go on to die five years later on Thanksgiving Day. He was at his in-laws in Fort Davis and volunteered to go to the convenience store to pick up God knows what. Poor man was standing at the register with his wallet out when some piece of shit burst in wearing a ski mask, waving a pistol and wantin' all the money. With a gun in his face, the clerk dumped all his bills and his change drawer into a paper bag and passed it over with shaking hands. Henry Judd stood five feet away with his hands up still holding his wallet. The man was about to leave, then supposedly stood there for a second, like he was thinking about it. The clerk said later he walked up to Henry Judd, calm as could be, reached up to take the wallet out of Henry Judd's hand, then shot him once in the throat before running off with only a thirty-seven-dollar score.

It took Henry Judd a couple of minutes to bleed out. I've often wondered what went through his mind in that time, what he had to say to God while he's lying there on the linoleum in between those DIY shelves and staring up at the fluorescent lights, feeling his life ebb away as the clerk shouted in terrified Korean. Was he happy about going to his reward? Or angry that he was going to die over a couple of bags of ice and some Doritos?

Goddammit, I'm sorry ma'am. I know that sounds morbid as hell, but you live to my age and you find those are the thoughts that come to mind more and more when you hear tales about the randomness of life. That's one of the things that always struck me, the— I don't know— *indifference* of the universe, or God, or whatever you want to call it. Even looking back on that day at the scrapyard. While Miguel's killing was – well, actually there was nothing random about that as we're about to discuss. But there's still a million ways how it could've been different. Every day since, I've asked myself, what if Miguel hadn't gone with me to the scrapyard? What if I'd made him help instead of letting him wander around? If I'd brought Maybelline, would she have tagged along with him and maybe prevented it? All questions I'm looking forward to asking the first person I see once I make it through the pearly gates.

The Bones of Amoret

Chapter 24

I came home to an empty house.

Dread at the conversation to come ate at me, winding my guts up like a windlass. I wished I could fast-forward time, to zoom past it.

I wandered into Miguel's room, soaking up the details of our son's life, our son who was no more. The sight of two large wooden chests, brim-filled with Lincoln Logs and green plastic army men, released a tidal wave of memories that made me cringe. Miggy would rise before the sun to build sprawling complexes out of the one and populate them with the other. Angelica and I called the little pieces "land mines" after finding them buried in the shag carpet with our bare feet. I'd sanded and varnished the trunks the winter before when he kept picking up splinters.

The swirls of his Dallas Cowboy bedsheets pooled at the foot of the mattress because we'd abandoned the daily battle over his making the bed. He might have his problems, but that didn't mean he wasn't still a teenage boy and when Angelica once found a Victoria's Secret catalogue under his bed, she'd shrieked. I don't know which made her madder: her son's pubescent urges or my blowing the whole matter off with a chuckle.

I picked up his pillow and held it to my face, sniffing deeply, enjoying his scent while I still could.

Positioned on the wall to be the first thing he saw when he woke up, Roger Staubach reared back to let one go in the ice and snow as Alan Page bore down on him with fingers curled like meat hooks. Staubach, all grit and defiance, knew the airborne Page was a split second away from driving him into the frozen turf with every ounce of his two hundred and fifty pounds. Boys need their heroes, and oh, how he'd loved that poster.

I feared I'd forget those details, the little things that would keep his memory sharp and clear for me. The years to come would bear that out, ma'am, but only partly. My recollections of Miguel might have gotten fuzzy at the edges over time, like a camera that's a touch out of focus. But the good stuff is still there, filed away, where I can and often do go back and access it.

Just then I heard an engine pull into the driveway. Through Miguel's window, Angelica's pickup came to a halt and, slinging her purse over her shoulder, she fetched groceries from the back of the cab. As she bounced up the walk cradling the brown bags, I thought of how she looked so blissful in her ignorance. Two hours ago, life had been about to return to normal for us. Now, I took a deep breath and trudged toward the living room, prepared to destroy her world.

At the front door, she shouted to the house, "*Papi*, Miggy, can you come help me bring in groceries?"

As I came out of Miguel's room, I realized I still held Miguel's pillow— don't ask me why. Taking one look at my red-rimmed eyes, her face morphed into a mask of concern and she asked, "*¿Ay, papi, qué* *es esto?"* Hurriedly, she set the bags down on the end table in the foyer and came to me with arms outstretched, folding me into her embrace.

I broke bad news to people all the time, and over the years I'd developed a ritual, a routine for it. Get to the bad news quickly, don't leave them hanging. But follow it quickly with something hopeful because people needed that faith, that possibility to get them through the dark times to come.

Standing there in the foyer, though, my arms at my side, unable to summon the strength even to hug her back, I could find no words. Try as I might, it was like my tongue had been made inert by the hand of God. I weakly shrugged my shoulders and began to cry.

Angelica broke the embrace and held me at arm's length, mystified and worried. "What is it, *papi*? What is going on? Please, you're scaring me." Then she noticed I was holding the pillow and her expression changed from concern to fear. "Where is Miguel?" She shouted at the empty house over my shoulder, a trace of fright in her voice, "Miguel! *¿Dónde estás?* Miguel?"

Finally, the spell that held me broke. As fresh tears streamed down my cheeks, my voice cracked, but I was able to croak out, "He's gone, baby. Someone killed him."

I felt her grip on my arm weaken as her eyes widened, searching mine, bewildered and shocked. She took two wobbly steps backward, her mouth opening and closing wordlessly. Her back bumped against the wall, and she slid down until she sat on the floor with her elbows on her knees and her hands over her eyes. Then she began to cry, her body wracked by convulsing sobs.

I sat beside her against the wall, my arm around her shoulders and eventually her weeping trailed off to sniffles. Then, in a shaky voice, she asked, "What happened?"

I told her everything. My decision to let Miguel play in the scrapyard, the hole in the fence, the bloodhound's search. I held back only the most grisly of details, summing them up instead by simply saying he'd been killed by a blow to the head.

She clasped her hands in the way a child prays, palms flat and pressed together, and brought the fingers to her lips, her thumbs under her chin while she listened. At the end of my account, she rubbed her forehead, slowly shaking her head until she squeezed her eyes shut and gulped at the air. "Do the police have any idea who might have done this?"

"McHenry said something about Hector Moreno. They'd been looking for him already even before this."

She nodded her head.

"Angelica, I'm so sorry. If I'd only told him to stay with me-- "

"No, *papi. No te preocupes*. If there is anything life in Sinoloa taught me, it is that when someone is planning on killing, the only way to stop them is by killing them first. If what the sheriff says is true, if it was not today, it would have been tomorrow or the day after that. Please do not think I blame you for what some—some animal has done to our son."

It was folly for either of us to think we would sleep that night, and at midnight I got up and went to the living room in my bathrobe. The flue, unused since the previous winter, screeched when I cranked it open and I built a roaring fire. After a few minutes, Angelica came out in her flannel pajamas and joined me on the couch, mute as she lay her head on my chest and her hand on my stomach. I pulled the blanket up to swaddle her and encircled her bony frame in my arms before kissing the crown of her head. We both stared into the fire, listening to the hiss and snap of the cedar logs and watching the sparks corkscrew up into the chimney, content with the other's presence amid our own thoughts.

In the morning, I made scrambled eggs just to have something to do, trying to take refuge in a routine. After staring at the fluffy yellow mound, though, neither Angelica nor I had an appetite and we put the plates down for Maybelline and Rope Tail. The dogs devoured the food while I cleaned up my mess and Angelica went back to the living room. She pulled down an old photo album and flipped through the pages, caressing the photos.

Still in my robe and slippers, I went to the mailbox where a four inch stack of windowed envelopes and fliers waited patiently. Back in the kitchen I poured coffee and flipped through the stack, sorting the mail on the kitchen counter. I was on autopilot, so much so it took a moment to notice the heavy white square in the middle of the stack.

It was the back of a Polaroid picture.

Curious, I turned it over.

It was a picture of Miguel before his killer had stuffed him in the trunk, the scarlet colors muted and Polaroid-fuzzy. Judging by the fact that the pool of blood on the packed dirt behind his head was only the size of a softball, barely visible, it had been taken mere moments after he'd hit the ground. Miguel's face was wrinkled as though disgusted, like in death he smelled something putrid, and one eye stared skyward while the other looked off to his left. By the angle, his killer had stood directly over him and squatted to take the picture. I looked up and watched as Angelica, her back to me on the living room sofa, continued her progress through the album, too preoccupied to notice.

This message had been for me. Not for Angelica, not for the sheriff, not for the newspaper. From what I knew of Hector, he was violent, quick to anger, a grudge-carrier. But did that mean he was capable of killing a child as an act of retribution? That kind of blood lust, that need for vengeance spoke to a moral rot I wanted to think I could have sensed when in his presence.

He now knew the police were looking to question him in Blaine's disappearance. Would he have taken a risk of the kind that killing Miguel in broad daylight would entail? And then send me a Polaroid just to taunt me?

As I pondered these questions, another thought occurred to me. Could Miguel's death be related to the mule and the backpack full of stolen dope? Could Pablo have been wrong, and instead of punishing me directly could a rival cartel member have sought to punish me in this most visceral of ways? Lord knew the cartels never had any hesitation about going after family members when they thought the situation called for it. Had Miguel paid the price for my stupidity?

Giving the Polaroid one last glance, I put it in my robe's pocket and said to her with as much nonchalance as I could muster, "I just made coffee. You want some?"

Chapter 25

Parents aren't meant to put their children in the ground.

All in black, we interred Miguel on a raw morning five days later. With a biting wind in our faces, Angelica held her hat to her head with one hand and her skirt to her thighs with the other as the pastor read some scripture. Side by side at the gravesite, we stood before that pitifully small, varnished casket enduring the pain.

You have kids, ma'am? Twins, no kidding. Sure, I'd love to. Aw, look at 'em. Yeah, seven's a great age. They still believe in Santa and haven't started rolling their eyes at everything you say yet.

Well, I hope you never go through something like it, but on the day of my son's funeral, my grief manifested in the strangest way. The little details stood out in bold, and my mind was— I guess you'd almost say it was cataloguing them, filing them away for later so I wouldn't have to experience them in real time.

I remember the chubby mortician wore a bad toupee yet still managed to have a dusting of dandruff on the shoulders of his black suit. I can still picture the artificial turf carpet over the dirt pile, pockets of hard caliche mixed in with the clay and sand peeking out from underneath. Overhead, the blue canopy's bottom edge undulated like cartoon waves, and I can still recall the snapping sound they made in the stiff breeze. All those little details persist even to this day.

I counted twenty-seven people at the burial, most of 'em Mexican. Some were my patients, some Angelica's friends. Shy Mike and Jimmy Wayne attended, giving me brief nods of support when we made eye contact, and Chebo attended with his family. It came as no surprise so few *gringos* attended. Two funeral homes served the town: *Funerales La Paz*, which catered to Mexicans and which Angelica had chosen, and Sunset Funeral Home, used by the town's white folks. I suspect when the announcement went out of which funeral home was being used, lots of people just— well, just sort of assumed. But brown or white, we all wound up in the same cemetery. One might say there's a lesson in there somewhere.

We'd been home long enough to change and settle in when the doorbell chimed. A moment later, Angelica and the sheriff's voices drifted back to me from the foyer.

"Afternoon, ma'am. I hate like hell to intrude at a time like this, but can I come in?"

"I just buried my son this morning, Sheriff."

"I know, and I promise I wouldn't be here if it wasn't important. If I could just talk to y'all, I promise to get out of your hair quick as I can."

Her voice moved in the direction of the kitchen, sounding like she left him to close the door behind him. "Would you like some coffee?" she offered automatically.

"No thank you, ma'am, I'm hopin' not to be here long enough to drink it." Joining me in the living room, he took off his winter coat and scarf and hung them over the back of his chair before taking a seat across from me.

"How you doin' Doc?" His gaze held a look of genuine concern, not just a man making small talk.

I tried not to let my voice sound as tired as I felt. "I ain't braggin'. What can I do you for?"

"I can see how wore down y'all are so I'll get right to it. I been puttin' a lotta thought to this, why someone would've targeted Miguel."

"You think someone 'targeted' Miguel?" Angelica asked as she returned with her own mug and sat next to me.

"Of that there's not a doubt in my mind, ma'am. But, excuse me for sayin', why would somebody want to kill a little retarded boy? There ain't too many reasons, near as I can figger, but up 'til now I been workin' under the assumption this was somebody with an axe to grind against you, Doc." He saw me wince and hurried past it. "But there's things about that don't make a hell of a lot of sense, though. If that was the case, why not come after you directly?

"The reason I'm here," he continued, "is I'm wondering if there ain't another possibility we been overlooking."

That statement cut through my weariness like a blade and my guard immediately went up. "What're you thinking?"

He shifted his weight and leaned in with a look of satisfaction, as though he'd solved a riddle. "What if Miguel was killed because he saw or heard somethin' he shouldn't have?"

"I do not understand. What is it that he would have seen or heard?" Angelica asked, a tightness in her eyes and an edge in her voice.

"Anythin' that made a man so nervous he'd do

somethin' as risky as killin' a boy in broad daylight at the scrapyard," McHenry said matter-of-factly.

My first reflex was to feel relief, that the spotlight of attention hadn't swung back to me. On that emotion's heels followed intrigue, though. I, too, had been under the impression Miguel's murder was a big middle finger to me. The thought it may have been a way of tying up a loose end had never entered my grief-addled brain. It made sense, though, I had to give McHenry that. "So what kinds of things're we talkin' about?"

"When I was noodlin' this over, somethin' kept poking at my brain, like a little voice in the back of my mind that there was somethin' I was missin'. I slept on it— well, not slept. But finally it come to me. Doc, remember what Billy James had to say when we was out lookin' at Blaine's car, all burned out in the canyon?"

My thoughts went back to that evening, but too much had happened in the interim. "You're gonna have to help me out here."

"Billy James said, 'What if Blaine did this himself?' What if he ran off and just didn't wanna be found? We been workin' under the assumption all this time this was all impulsive, that Blaine was killed and dumped Jimmy Hoffa-style. But the fact remains, Blaine's a smart man, smart enough to plan this out if he was so inclined."

He ticked off on his fingers as he spoke. "Wait for a weekend his wife's gone so he's got a head start. Maybe squirrel some money away ahead of time that he can live off of? Possibly set himself up with some wheels that don't nobody know about so he don't gotta worry about drivin' a known car? He sets it all up, and it looks to be goin' off without a hitch. Then somehow, someway, Miguel sees him afterwards.

Maybe he's stalking you, Doc. Maybe he's delivering that anonymous note to me. Whatever. Suddenly Miguel sees him and recognizes him. I could see it that he doesn't know what Miguel's capable of. What would happen if Miguel starts tellin' people that he saw Blaine? Would they listen? Maybe he thinks he can't take that chance, and he decides to clean up the mess. More I think about it, more possible it seems. If Blaine's still alive that is."

I took that in, re-energized by this possibility. Not wanting to get my hopes up just yet, I tried to poke holes in the idea. "But Jesús saw the man who torched Blaine's car head down the creek toward my property, not back up the road to the highway. Let's say Blaine left himself another set of wheels or arranged a ride in the way you're talkin'. Common sense says he'd head to the main road either way."

"Way ahead of you. Lookit here." He reached behind him into the pocket of the coat hanging on his chair and retrieved a new copy of the topo map we'd examined at my cabin. Unfolding it, he laid it over the magazines decorating our coffee table.

I leaned forward to inspect the map, stroking my cheeks in thought as Angelica looked over my shoulder, also drawn in by this possibility. McHenry'd already outlined in yellow the dry creek bed, and in pink the fence lines around my property. When I saw he'd highlighted a squiggly line in green on the north end of the map, I knew where he was going with this.

He tapped his finger on the green line. "This is how Blaine could'a done it." For the first time, I heard the first nibbles of excitement in his voice.

Angelica looked puzzled, unfamiliar with the landscape depicted on the map. "I do not understand. What is that green line you are pointing to?"

"That, ma'am, is a little chicken shit— hell, I don't even want to call it a road, it's more like a trail, all overgrown and rutted. It's on the next property north from Doc's ranch. Undeveloped land. Some Jew lawyer owns it, lives in— what, Midland is it?" he asked.

"Odessa," I corrected.

"Fine, Odessa. But here's the thing, ma'am. We know whoever torched the Jeep on Mariano's property followed the creek bed east in the direction of Doc's property. We been assumin' that after a few miles when the man came to the fence line that separates Mariano and Doc's property, he just crossed it and continued east onto Doc's property. But what if the feller only followed the creek to get to the fence line? Because once he found that fence, if he come up out of the creek bed and turned left to follow the fence line north—."

"— After about two miles, that fence line'll lead him to within fifty yards of that road," I finished.

The sheriff leaned back in the chair and steepled his fingers, for the moment a poor man's Poirot. "So y'all think about this. Maybe Blaine sees all this on a map of the area. Maybe he even knows that road would be a good place to stash a car 'cause the landowner never comes 'round, lot better than leavin' it on the side of the main highway where folks'd see it or some deputies might stop and poke around. Problem is he knows that after he torches his car, he's got to find his way to the second vehicle on that primitive road in the dark across country he's unfamiliar with. So what's a solution for that problem? Head to the fence line and use it as a guide. If he can read the map good enough to set all this up, he'd 'a known that once the fence line ends, he's only gotta bushwhack his way another fifty yards or so in the same direction, and *boom*, he's right there at the car he squirreled away ahead of time."

As we looked at the map, a thought occurred to me. "Thing is, Sheriff, I've seen that road on the map, but never been down it. And like you said, the owner never maintains it. I don't even know if it's passable."

"I ain't been able to talk to the landowner yet to drive it and see for m'self. I don't wanna go on his property lackin' his permission without what it's absolutely necessary. He's supposed to call me back later today."

"Would you mind if I tagged along?" I asked. "I'd be curious to see."

"Absolutely."

"So what about Hector, then?" I asked.

The sheriff's expression changed from intrigue to vexation. Crossing his legs, he drummed his fingers on his boot. "Much as I hate to say, statistically speakin' he's still the most likely one to be responsible for killin' Miguel. You know, all that 'The simplest explanation is usually the right one,' business."

"Occam's razor," I said.

"Right, that. Him and Miguel was on your property around each other, so there's an opportunity there for Miguel to have seen or heard somethin' that Hector figured he needed to fix. Or he might have just done it as a way to punish you. As far as whether he might'a killed Blaine, the boy's got a motive and a track record of violence, sounds like he had the opportunity, and he doesn't have an alibi. Looks like he tried to misdirect us toward you, and then when we found out he took off and went to ground."

The sheriff stood to refold his map, and I held his coat while he slipped his arms into the sleeves. Trailing him to his truck, we hunched our shoulders against the chilly wind.

He said, "Goddam, it's cold as a cast iron toilet out here. You best be gettin' back inside. I'll call you later after I hear back from that lawyer." He cranked the engine and I stood by politely waiting for him to back out. He paused, though, staring straight ahead without putting the truck in reverse. Then he rolled his window down and waved me over.

"I wasn't gonna say it in front of the boy's momma, Doc, but there's one other big problem I got with the Blaine theory, and it ain't got nothin' to do with all these logistics. I'll tell you if you've a mind to hear it."

"What's that?"

"Now I'm just thinkin' out loud here, all's I'm doin'."

"I understand. Go on."

He looked back toward the house in a way that was unseeing. "I could buy any man who's as unhappy as Blaine was for as long as he was wantin' to just hit the bricks. I could even see my way to believin' all this cloak and dagger stuff that it would'a took to make himself disappear, the way we were talkin' 'bout in your livin' room."

His eyes came back to mine. "But here's the thing, Doc. It takes some kind of a bad man to go killin' like was done. This wasn't some run of the mill heartless bastard, pullin' a trigger on a gun, doin' it from a distance. That I could buy easier, y'know? No sir, this took bein' up close and personal. Close enough that whoever did it would smell Miguel's sweat, would smell the shit-stink when the boy's bowels let go. They would'a heard that dull crack when his skull caved in, like the hollow sound a eggshell makes when you break it open. That's a lot harder to do. And to a child no less.

"The Blaine Beckett I knew wasn't that kind of man. But now I'm left to wonder, was what we were all seein' every day for years some kind of a mask?"

Chapter 26

McHenry's speculation rattled around my mind after he left, opening new doors of possibility. His theory that Miguel may have been killed for something he saw made intuitive sense at first blush, and I'll admit I prayed for this to be the case since it would absolve me of the responsibility I felt for the boy's death. I felt twinges of guilt for my selfishness in thinking that way, but it was nothing compared to the gut-churning blame with which I'd saddled myself since the scrapyard.

The creativity the lawman had demonstrated in constructing a scenario in which Blaine may have engineered his own disappearance impressed me. I'd always respected McHenry and recently had reason to fear him in that regard. And I had to say, looking at the map and hearing him explain his thoughts, it certainly sounded plausible. I hoped the investigation would move in that direction, as a finding that Blaine was behind it from the beginning would also obviate the possibility that innocents might be swept up in the desire to lay blame.

After the sheriff left, I ran by the feed store, then dashed into my clinic to grab a stack of files so I could do my billing— folks were understanding about my clearing the clinic schedule for a while, but the paperwork wouldn't do itself. After a few more errands, I made it back to the house just in time to put one of the casseroles we'd received from a neighbor into the oven when the sheriff called once again.

"Say Doc, I just heard from the feller owns that piece of land north of your ranch. I'm gonna head out there now and check that road out. You still want I should swing by and pick you up?"

"Yup. I'll see you in a few." After I hung up, I checked in with Angelica, asking if she wanted to come too. She shook her head, saying she felt like being alone for a while. When I heard the sheriff's rig pull in the driveway I leaned over to give her a kiss, reminded her about the casserole, and moments later he and I were headed outside town toward the empty desert.

"Lawyer told me it's a split rail gate we're lookin' for, got a black and white 'no trespassing' sign on the fence post. Took him a while to find the combination to the lock he got on it, but he managed." McHenry's eyes flicked between the road and a dark blue scrawl on his calloused palm before he extended the hand to me. "Can't read my own goddam chicken scratch. That third number look like a two or a seven?"

"I thought doctors were supposed to be the ones with the unreadable handwriting." I steadied his wrist and squinted. "Think that's nine, one, seven, eight."

He tapped the wheel with his thumb as we drove in silence. Then he said, "I'm not gonna lie, Doc. There's a part of me really hopes this was all Blaine's doin'. You're a smart man. I don't just mean book smart, neither. You know people."

I stayed silent, watching a cluster of crude oil pump jacks bob away, sucking the desert dry.

He *tsk*'ed his head. "Even if you won't admit it to

me, I 'spect you been feelin' this too. I know when men get to be our age, there's somethin' what happens in our brains, like a switch flips, makes you believe things are changin' for the worse. But just 'cause every generation of men before us says it, that don't mean there ain't a grain of truth to it. This here that I'm talkin' 'bout now, Doc, it's somethin' out on the horizon. I can sense it rollin' in no different than when you smell rain on the way. It's an ugliness if I gotta pick a word. I don't know what brung it to Amoret but it took root, and now it's trying to grow, like a goddam cancer.

"Time was, didn't matter who you were. Wetback, roughneck, state senator, nun; we all knew we was all on the same side, everybody just tryin' to carve out a livin'. This desert, beautiful as she may be, it's a relentless place. Relentless and unforgiving. It didn't make no sense to fight 'mongst ourselves. That was just wasted energy, 'cause when you were through fightin', the desert was still there waitin' for you." He interrupted himself to slow for two buzzards pecking roadkill on the yellow stripe, the splattered remnants of a coyote carcass. The two birds lazily hopped a few feet away and flapped their great wings at the disturbance, the end feathers looking like fingers for a moment as McHenry gave them a wide berth.

This kind of talk always made me feel older than my years. "I know the ugliness you're talkin' about. But it doesn't do any good to lament it. It's up to men like us to push back on it best we can," I said.

"We're doing the Lord's work, you and me, each in our own way."

I wasn't so certain. "There's work to be done without a doubt, but whether it's the work of the Lord or the devil I'm not sure I can say."

I immediately regretted my momentary candor, but he continued on unperturbed. "I'm the first lawman in my family. My people come here fifty years ago, started off in the cinnabar mines down in Terlingua, my Grandpa and my uncles. Tough men, all, I tell you what. They were willin' to charge hell with a bucket of ice water. I can remember listening to 'em tellin' stories 'bout the tunnels, them all the while not knowin' they was slow dyin' of mercury poisoning from bein' down there.

"Anyway, my whole life, I seen brown and white workin' together, livin' together, side by side. The only enemy was the land. It was all we knew, so we never thunk twice about it. But deep down in my bones I can feel that changin'. I don't know if it's big city ways pushin' in on us, the outside world, or what. It sure as shit ain't what I'd call progress."

As the road's gate hove into view, his last words on the subject were, "Let's just say, times what they are, I'm hopin' to hell Hector didn't have nothin' to do with this."

"I'll tend the gate," I said. The truck idled twenty feet away as I crunched over the gravel on the highway's apron. A chill wind rattled the gate as I straddled the pipe rail cattle guard and picked up the heavy chain looping the split rails to the fence post.

Then I saw something out of the ordinary, something that gave me pause. I reached out to touch it, then thought better, pulling my hand back slowly. McHenry saw me stop and stare, a quizzical look on my face, and cranked his window to ask, "Goddam, what's goin' on? Look like you seen a turtle sittin' on a fencepost."

I waved to him, calling out so I could be heard over his engine, "You're gonna wanna see this."

Brow wrinkled in curiosity, he climbed down off

his running board and sauntered over. Grimly, I pointed at the chain.

The combination lock's shackle had been cut, then looped back through two of the chain's links to keep the unlocked gate from drifting open and drawing attention. From the highway, it would appear all was well. It wasn't until you got right up on it that you could see the cut lock.

"Well I'll be damned," McHenry said. "Cut just like the lock on the gate leading onto Mariano's property when we found Blaine's Jeep burned out." With a thumb he pushed his cowboy hat back on his head before putting one hand on his hip. He thrust his jaw sideways, left and right, for a moment while he thought, then said "Don't touch that, Doc." He went to his truck and retrieved a Ziploc evidence bag from his toolbox before picking up the lock with his bandana and dropping it in the bag. Climbing back in his cab, he steered the truck across the cattleguard and through the gate once I'd opened it. I looped the chain into a crude half knot so the gate would stay closed as he called the office on his radio.

Beau Alexander picked up. "What you got goin' on, Sheriff?"

"I need you to head out here after all. Looks like somebody cut the lock on that lawyer's gate. Somebody who ain't an old man like me's gonna have to walk the trail all the way from the gate to where it meets up by the Doc's fence line lookin' for anythin' somebody might'a thrown out their window while they was drivin' along. Walk the left side goin' out and the right side comin' back lookin' for stuff."

"Like—?"

"Like things somebody might'a thrown out a vehicle window before blowin' town. A wallet, keys, trash that might still have fingerprints, anythin'."

"Yessir, will do." McHenry hung the mic back up, and we headed down the overgrown, rutted trail.

Rough but passable, the road rocked us side to side as we bounced along. At one point a wash had scooped a divot in the road, but it was no problem for the sheriff's four wheel drive. Dried and withered trees lay partially across the road, victims of forgotten storms. Their brittle branches clawed at the sides of the truck as it inched past, screeching, like nails on a chalkboard.

Fifty yards to our left, I could see my east-west fence line, four strands of barbed wire strung between beau d'arc posts paralleling our path. It felt funny seeing it from that angle, like walking down a familiar street but in the opposite direction.

Finally, the spot where my fence line turned south hove into view. Tapping the sheriff on the shoulder, I pointed and he killed the engine.

The wind had died down, and the activity warmed me. Twenty feet apart, McHenry and I covered the ground to the fence's angle slowly, scanning the sand and rock for anything that looked man-made. We came upon the skeleton of a rabbit, picked clean by varmints and ants. The sheriff considered it for a second, then flipped the sun-bleached bones over with the toe of his boot. Dragging his heel through the soil, he turned over dirt until he'd satisfied himself the skeleton hadn't been placed there to mark some buried object. His lip downturned, he gave me a shrug and we continued on.

Once at the southern fence line, I ducked between the wire strands like a boxer climbing in the ring. A barb caught my back, ripping a small hole in my canvas jacket and scratching my skin.

"You okay?" McHenry asked, but I waved it off.

With each of us on one side of the fence line, we walked the two miles to the dry creek bed's crossing, not seeing anything that shouldn't have been there. I half-expected to see some signs of Jesús Barrera: an old campfire site, or some discarded plastic shotgun casings, but even those were elusive.

After we'd returned to the truck, McHenry pulled a plastic gallon jug of water from the back of his cab. As we took turns pulling on it, his gaze never wavered from the southern fence line.

Well, ma'am, I'm no mind-reader but I'd be willing to bet he was trying to picture Blaine picking his way across the desert pan in the dark, following that fence line in the moonlight, looking for that road and some truck he'd placed there in advance, holding keys to both the vehicle and a new life. From the expression on his face, he was trying to will it so.

Arthur Herbert

Chapter 27

"So then we come to find the shank of the lock cut on the lawyer's gate just like on Mariano's."

Jimmy Wayne let out a low whistle at this news as he pointed the panel truck south under a moonless sky. A rim of frost dusted the edges of the windshield, resisting the wheezing heater as we made our way to the river crossing. "Sounds like you and McHenry had a big day yesterday, then. So he really thinks Blaine's behind all this?"

I nodded. "That's the way he's talkin'. Says he's still lookin' for Hector though."

Shy Mike said, "Hard to believe it's only been three weeks since that asshole disappeared. Feels like forever."

Leaving Amoret, we found ourselves sandwiched between a pair of big rigs. The one in front had the oval-shaped chrome rear of a tanker truck, so we knew we'd be following it for the whole route, there bein' no place to deliver gas until Presidio. All we could see of the rear truck was a wall of headlights that reflected off Jimmy Wayne' side mirrors and illuminated our faces in the cab like footlights. Strange as it sounds, it made me feel like we had company out there, a feeling that wasn't unwelcome right then. We stayed that way for the hour it took to hit the highway's dead end, where the pair of eighteen wheelers turned right for the half hour drive to Presidio while we turned left to head to the rendezvous.

A small quarter ton GMC truck that'd been behind the rear big rig now fell in behind us, trailing briefly for a few miles until we slowed down at our familiar spot on the highway's crest. As Jimmy Wayne pulled onto the shoulder and flipped on his hazards, the pickup blew past, the only vehicle in sight in either direction. We watched until its taillights winked out in the distance.

Jimmy Wayne said, "We got a half hour yet. I'm gonna keep the heater runnin'." The small luminescent dashboard clock indicated it was almost five o'clock.

From our vantage point, we couldn't see the river yet through the darkness. "Cut the headlights, maybe see if we can get our night vision back," Shy Mike said. Jimmy Wayne obeyed, leaving just the dull yellow glow of the running lights on the asphalt.

Shy Mike yawned then said to Jimmy Wayne, "You're awful quiet."

Staring straight ahead, he replied "Just tired. Didn't sleep good. We had a fight last night. Me and Loretta I mean."

"What 'bout?" Shy Mike asked.

"She's talkin' 'bout her momma movin' in with us now that her daddy passed."

"Ouch," I said.

"You gonna do it?"

"Might have to before it's over with."

"No goin' back once she's in the house," I said.

"What's got into you? I thought you ran that house," Shy Mike teased.

Jimmy Wayne said, "Don't you either one try to tell me your woman came to you askin' that, you'd tell her no. Any man been married long enough'll tell you. Sooner or later, comes a time you just gotta bend over, grab your ankles, and take it. This is one of those times."

"It ain't any such," Shy Mike said. "Least ways not for a man who knows how to win an argument with his wife."

"What d'you think, Doc?"

"There's two theories when it comes to arguin' with a woman." I paused. "Neither one works."

Shy Mike snorted, but Jimmy Wayne still looked serious. "I only wish we'd come to a final decision about it, that's part of it. Like it is now, we got to have this argument 'bout once a week."

"I got news for you," Shy Mike said. "If you told her 'no,' and y'all are still discussing it, that means a final decision's been made, you're just too dumb to know it."

I smiled, enjoying the banter. Frankly, it felt good to be talking about something, other than Miguel and Blaine and Hector and the sheriff. A pair of headlights blinked to life ahead of us, interrupting the two men's nattering.

I said, "If you two'll stop flirting for a minute, it's showtime. C'mon, Jimmy Wayne, you're up. Chop chop." The headlights were still over a mile away.

"Fuck a duck," he muttered, killing the engine and climbing out of the warmth of the cab. Hurrying to the hood, he popped it and bent over waist deep into the engine's guts, pretending to inspect the motor as the other vehicle approached through the darkness. Shy Mike and I had our view blocked by the hood, but we waited patiently for the vehicle to pass. The silence stretched for thirty seconds, then a minute, then ninety seconds. When the other car still hadn't passed us, I slid over to the driver's seat and cranked the window down. I stuck my head out and the cold wind stung my face, like so many wasps.

There was no sign of the other vehicle. Just empty road continuing toward the southeastern horizon in the cold gray predawn.

From under the hood, Jimmy Wayne peeked over his shoulder and saw the same thing. "Hell's bells, where'd he go?"

Shy Mike said, "He must'a turned off. That or maybe turned around. Either way, Jimmy Wayne stand clear, I'm startin' her back up again." He reached across me and cranked the engine, then huddled his hands in front of the heater's vent.

Jimmy Wayne stepped up onto the running board but didn't get back in the truck yet. His weathered face bore a look of unease. I felt it too.

"Hand me those binocs, would you?"

I passed them through the window, and Jimmy Wayne brought them up to his eyes. He stayed that way for what seemed like a long time but was probably less than ten seconds. "Hard to say in this piss-poor light, but I think that's a dust cloud off to the north side of the road 'bout two hunnert yards out."

That was enough to make me climb out of the cab. "Let me see."

With the binoculars up, I leaned on the truck's side-view mirror, bracing my forearms to steady the image. Right away I saw what he meant. Off the north side of the highway's shoulder was a puff of brown dust, just a few feet above the ground but definitely there. The ground looked flatter in that spot than the surrounding desert pan, like there was a dirt road leaving the highway. It disappeared behind an outcropping of rock, a small mesa that continued on toward the northern horizon. The vehicle must have headed off in that direction.

"Any idea what's down there behind that rock?" I asked.

"Nothin' if I recall correctly. Just one big hunk of empty all the way to the horizon," Jimmy Wayne said.

"Maybe the landowner checkin' up on things?" Shy Mike volunteered.

"Or maybe the Border Patrol up in those rocks watchin' all of our dumb asses. Probably arguin' right now 'bout who's gonna cuff who," Jimmy Wayne said.

Unease nipped at me while I searched the rocky outcropping for signs of activity. Was it possible that McHenry's confidences had been a setup? That his openness in sharing information and theories had been a subterfuge to get me to let my guard down and do something stupid? I recognized this line of thought as paranoia, but as the saying goes, paranoia is a healthy attitude if they're out to get you.

I swung the glasses back to my right, towards the Mexican side of the river. Everything looked gray as ashes except the silver ribbon of the river. Across the rippling water, beyond the slate shelf and ocotillo bushes and creosote scrub brush, I could see a stand of juniper trees atop a ridgeline a half mile away. Chebo liked to use that juniper stand as a landmark because the cluster's silhouette was visible for almost a mile on the other side of the ridge making for easy navigation. I knew that was the spot from which Chebo would eventually appear, but at the moment no one was in sight. The wall of trees stood silent, uncaring about our drama.

"Tell you what we're gonna do," I said. "I'm gonna get out and wait here. I want you two to pack up and head down the road a piece. Once you pass that outcrop of rock there where the vehicle turned off, slow down and take a good long look. You see the Border Patrol, Johnny Law, or anything else that doesn't look right, you keep going, all the way home to Amoret. If whatever's on the other side of that rock looks kosher, just turn around and come back to this spot, and we keep waiting for Chebo."

"You want us to leave you here?" Shy Mike looked at me in confusion.

"We gotta have some way to let Chebo know what happened. If I see y'all keep drivin' on, I'm gonna head across the river to catch Chebo before he crosses, and we'll just abort for today. Me and him'll turn the group around and take 'em back to the safe house. I'll call y'all later, and we can sort out what you saw and what we gotta do to get those folks across the river another time. What do y'all think?"

"I like it," Jimmy Wayne said.

"Sounds like a plan," Shy Mike told me.

"Jimmy Wayne, let me borrow your ski cap. Case I get stuck out in this weather for a while."

"Help yourself."

He handed me the winter cap, then hopped up into the cab. I flipped my collar against the wind, and jammed my hands deep in my jacket pockets, standing on the gravel apron while Jimmy Wayne dropped it into gear. The engine rattled as they pulled out, and I watched the red taillights head down the road in the direction of the rock formation.

The panel truck crawled forward, letting gravity pull it down the hill's gentle incline, the engine at an idle. Fifty yards, then one hundred. I hopped up and down to stay warm while I watched and turned to check my six. No headlights were coming from the other direction. For now, this stretch of road belonged to us and the mystery vehicle.

Once Jimmy Wayne made it past the outcropping of rock, his brake lights lit up the gloomy dawn. The truck sat idling for a long moment, belching white exhaust into the cold air like a smokestack as Jimmy Wayne and Shy Mike sat in the cab and studied the scene on the far side of the rock outcropping where it was shielded from my view.

Then the reverse lights came on, and I felt a sense of relief as the truck began to back up, making a shrill beeping noise that cut through the desert silence.

But then Jimmy Wayne pulled the truck up short again, stamping on the brakes so hard the truck swayed a moment.

Suddenly the reverse lights disappeared and with a rev of the engine, I saw the panel truck creep forward, pulling away, then accelerating slowly as it headed off down the highway.

Apparently Jimmy Wayne and Shy Mike wanted no part of whatever they'd seen on the other side of those rocks.

"Well that's it then," I said out loud. They'd aborted the run.

Facing a long hike in that cold, I grumbled to myself as I picked my way down the short, crumbly slope. The overcast delayed the morning's burn off of the gray, and it didn't look like I'd throw a shadow for a while. After clearing the declivity, I weaved my way through the ocotillo toward the river and the stand of junipers atop the ridge on the other side, damn near a half mile away.

A shape emerged from those very trees, still too far off to see features, but I recognized the plodding gait as Chebo's. Two people emerged from the stand of trees behind him, then three more. I could see him reach into his pack and hold something to his face. Once he'd glassed no sign of the truck and that it was me walking towards him across the caldera, he pointed at me and then held his left arm up bent at the wrist with his fingers curled inward in the shape of a question mark, our hand signal for, "What's going on?"

I pointed to him, "You," then crossed my arms over my chest with the palms open, "Wait there." I placed my opened palm across my eyebrows, "Look," pointed at the rock formation where the truck had disappeared, "Over there." He said something to the group, then trained his field glasses toward the outcropping of rock.

Stinging drops of sleet began to fall, thumping heavily against my jacket and sliding down the back of my collar. Jamming my hands deeper in my pockets against the cold, I hunched my shoulders and picked up my pace across the flat river plain.

Glancing up, I saw Chebo hold his hands steepled in front of his face, then drop them open palms down like an umpire calling safe. "Everything looks okay." I nodded, and he retrained his binoculars at the rock outcropping to monitor the situation.

I wiped my nose on the rough canvas of my sleeve, the tip already numb. The silt barked each time my boot broke the surface, a rhythmic fracturing that would have been relaxing if not for the miserable conditions. The land seemed to break away from the river, and with nothing to stop it, the breeze turned into wind, slicing at my face. The dread of walking twelve miles through that weather grabbed me hard, squeezing me. Far ahead, the wind rippled the water's surface, like schools of fish swimming in manic bursts. The ocotillo bushes around me undulated, obeying an invisible hand. As the wind skated along the river break it whistled, low and spectral, like a phantom's moan. My teeth chattered.

I plodded along, concentrating on putting one foot in front of the other as a way of blocking out my aggravation. At the time I came up with this idea in the truck's cab, I hadn't thought it likely things would come to my actually making the walk back to the safe house with Chebo. I'd made the walk several times before, of course, but this was going to be a hassle. Not just the walk, itself, but the return. Sometimes I came back to this same rendezvous spot where one of the boys would pick me up and drive me home. Twice, I'd had to get a ride to Ojinaga sixty miles upriver and just walked back across the river bridge to Presidio like a tourist who'd gone for a day visit. This may be hard for you to believe now, ma'am, but back then, all *gringos* had to do was flash a driver's license if your stated plans were to shop or carouse, and half the time they didn't even bother checking that.

I was already planning logistics when motion in my peripheral vision caught my eye. Glancing up, I saw Chebo waving his arms over his head to get my attention. When he saw he had my eye, he pointed at the rocks, then crossed his arms over his chest, but this time with his fists balled up.

The signal for "danger."

It took a moment for this to register. After Chebo's first all-clear, the brutal conditions had caused a mental fog to set in, blunting my situational awareness. My brain was as numb as my feet, and it took a moment to cough to life, like a cold engine.

It was just then I heard a crack, and the unmistakable sound of a bullet whizzing past my head. It caromed off a rock with the high *whing* you hear in the movies. I knew that sound, and instinctively threw myself to the ground. I laid there prone on the desert floor, elbows bent and hands splayed in front of my face. My fingers dug ten tiny ruts in the sand.

I looked back and to my left at the outcropping of rock. Twenty feet high for most of what I could see, it had a perfect field of fire. Even if I tried to make it back to the highway, the incline was too shallow to hide behind, and the asphalt was wide open. I'd have to try to make it across the river.

From high up in the rocks, a muzzle flash preceded the sharp crack of a rifle. Six inches in front of my face, my left hand exploded in agony and a bloody spray of sand filled my eye with grit.

He'd gone for a head shot. This was no warning, nobody was sending me a message. I knew if I stayed there any longer I was going to die.

I scrambled to my feet and ran one-eyed across the flood plain, ignoring my hand for the moment. I judged it to be two hundred yards to the riverbank, and my shortest path took me at an angle away from the shooter so that I'd be putting distance between me and him.

My limited vision caused me to miss an obstacle in my path, and I stumbled but didn't fall. Another rifle shot, this one whizzing in front of me. I remember thinking he must be using a bolt action judging by the time between shots.

I dove into the carrizo cane along the river's edge to catch my breath and let the stitch in my side abate, but only for a moment. I was three hundred yards at that point from the muzzle flash. Still not enough distance that it would take a real marksman to hit me. Not out here in the land of the pronghorn where a successful kill shot routinely took four hundred yards or more.

I hazarded a quick glance back up the Mexican side of the river toward the juniper stand. Chebo and the immigrants had scattered back into the trees, disappearing like ghosts once they heard the report of a rifle.

Another gunshot echoed across the caldera, and this time the bullet zinged into the reeds directly behind me. He couldn't see me at the moment, but the divot in the cane would be unmistakable, a big black hole where I'd trampled the vegetation down. May as well be a goddam bulls-eye, I thought.

Gathering myself, I took a few deep breaths then bolted from the cane. I could see ripples where a shallow gravel bar occupied half the width of the river and headed in that direction, splashing across the ankle-deep water until I reached the main channel. I took a running leap into it, arms pinwheeling like a long jumper.

I broke the surface and landed thigh-deep, but my momentum pitched me forward and I was underwater. The cold ripped the breath from my lungs, and I caught a quick glimpse of a hazy red cloud billowing from my wounded left hand. Then I was up on my feet and running again, slogging across the river's channel with loud wet splashes as the current dragged at my legs. Another crack and water sprayed my back. Three great, lunging steps, then four, then five, then I was back on a muddy flat on the other side of the river, scrambling toward a log, driftwood deposited on the Mexican shoreline during higher waters. I dove behind it and caught my breath.

Laying there panting, I shimmied in place so my bulk would remain sheltered behind the log and examined my shaking hand. What I saw made me grimace.

The laceration I'd sustained from climbing the sheet metal pile at the scrapyard was no longer recognizable as the bullet had shattered my palm and the knuckles at the bases of my ring finger and pinkie. Both digits were only attached to my hand by thin strips of skin and they dangled loosely, no longer under my command, their herky-jerky movements looking like puppets on a string.

Pulling a bandana from my pocket, I folded the fingers in against my palm and bound them in place, then crawled on my elbows and knees for several yards, the length of the log. At this point, a smaller mass of bare branches had been caught up in the debris, making a jumble of sticks dense enough that I thought I could safely take a peek. Barely raising my eye level over the log's smooth-skinned husk, I still couldn't see the shooter.

I turned my attention to the stair-stepping landscape up to Chebo and the juniper trees. I saw a path I thought might allow me to dart from shelter to shelter until I was out of his range. All it would require was covering one last stretch of open ground, roughly fifty yards, to an earthen mound. Once I was behind that defilade, I would be in the clear.

The problem was, from his vantage point, the shooter could see that too. And I'd given him enough time to reload. He'd had several shots to gauge the distance. Plus, the wind had died down, making his shot easier.

I was up and sprinting, weaving my way through the underbrush, my eyes fixed on the berm. I heard one crack, then a white-hot lance tore through my right leg, kicking it out to the side and spinning me around. I hit the ground hard and landed on my bound hand. I was paralyzed for a split second by the pain. If he'd been firing an automatic, to this day I think I'd have been dead. But the few seconds he needed to work the bolt and reacquire me in his scope were all I needed. I was able to run on the leg, and when he fired again I saw a spray of earth where the bullet dug into the berm in front of me. I dove headfirst, neither knowing nor caring what was on the other side of the earthen mound and crumpled into a ball. I was safe.

Chapter 28

Panting, I stared up at the overcast sky with my one good eye and waited for my heaving breath to subside. Sleet pellets tapped my upturned face like cold fingers, but at that moment I didn't mind, the pain confirmation I was still alive. My soaked clothes clung to me and a film of sand coated me head to toe, as though I'd been dredged in it.

With a groan, I sat up and looked at my leg, just below the knee. Two holes edged with curly-cues of ragged denim stared back at me, one on the outer half of the calf and one the inner. Blood stains crept around the circumference of my leg, getting larger before my eyes.

Through the pain and adrenaline, my instincts kicked in, training so ingrained my mind stored it in a red box that read, "In case of emergency, break glass." I dug out my folding Buck knife and slit my jeans. A slow venous ooze emanated from the wounds, purple-black in the overcast, but nothing with a pulsatile arc or bright red color that would have suggested an arterial injury. Gingerly, I flexed my knee and ankle once, then again. My calf burned as though branded by a drunk ranch hand, but my leg worked, so I figured my tibia wasn't broken.

Untucking my heavy flannel shirt, I managed to pinch it taut awkwardly with my lobster claw of a hand before cutting off the tail and binding my calf. Cinching the knot revved the pain into a new gear and I turned onto my hands and knees, my back arching hard as I vomited my breakfast onto the sand next to the blood stain. A long tendril of snot dripped while I retched, undulating with the movements of my head before dribbling to the ground. My mouth ran thick with saliva. I spat into the earth to clear the taste, and I have a clear memory of thinking I ought to just piss and shit in that spot to complete the spectrum of bodily fluids I'd sprayed onto that poor stretch of sand.

I collapsed onto my back again, but only for a second before I heard the sound of an engine starting up. I peeked over the edge of the berm and scanned the stretch of caldera and highway. Noise carried in the stillness of the desert's silence, and I could hear the motor had a knock. From the sound, I could tell it was bouncing as the engine would whine for a split second when the tires cleared the ground.

The vehicle appeared from around the base of the rock outcropping. It was way too far off for me to see the driver, but I got a decent look at the make and model: an old GMC-style pickup, looked to be a light color with a dark stripe down the side.

"I'll be goddamned," I said. It was the same truck that'd followed us down from Amoret, trailing along behind the rear eighteen-wheeler. I recognized it from when we pulled over at the rendezvous. The son of a bitch doubled back after he saw us set up shop on the road's shoulder.

While I watched, the truck sped across the uneven desert pan toward the asphalt, so fast and so hard he risked bending a tie rod with each impact.

Then he made the concrete, fishtailing as he pointed the vehicle away from me and toward the horizon.

From the juniper trees on the slope above me, I heard Chebo call out, *"¡Oye! ¡Cabrón! ¿Estás bien?"*

"I'm still looking at the right side of the grass," I shouted back. "Don't move. Let me see if I can walk."

I thought it unlikely the sniper would have left someone behind with a rifle to try and take another shot, but Lord knows I didn't want to take any chances. Bad luck had combined with bad choices enough for one day.

A nearby rock facing was shielded from view of the river, so I crawled in that direction before trying to stand. I walked my hands up the rock, then leaned back against it, both hands out and my good leg bearing my weight. I slowly eased pressure onto my injured leg. It hurt like hell, but it held. I looked around but didn't see any wood. "Hey, bring me down a crutch from those junipers, would you?" I yelled up at him.

"Por supuesto, one minute."

As the thudding sound of chopping commenced, my adrenaline surge ebbed. In its place, the cold threw itself at me. An icy numbness crept up my legs and arms, and I began to shiver uncontrollably. "Start working on a fire too," I shouted up in Chebo's direction. "I'm not sure how far I can walk like this."

Chebo hopscotched from cover to cover carrying a sturdy, Y-shaped branch. Frost accumulated on my jacket and in my wet hair, crinkling and flaking when I moved. The cold was unbearable.

With the crotch of the stick in my armpit, Chebo looped one arm around my waist and used my belt as a handle while I leaned on him. He was much smaller than I, the top of his head only coming up to my shoulder.

"Feel like I'm leanin' on goddamn Napoleon. Mind you don't bang my hurt hand," I said through gritted teeth.

"Speaking of me banging things, how's your mother?" he asked.

Together we inched our way back up the slope toward the junipers and the rest of the group. Twice I had to pause, shivering so violently I worried I'd fall and take a tumble. Our progress was excruciatingly slow. The tendrils of white smoke drifting up through the tops of the junipers ahead seemed to draw no closer no matter how much ground we covered. I willed myself forward, concentrating on nothing more than working the crutch while putting one foot in front of the other.

"How big a fire'd you make?"

"Big one."

"Tell them make it bigger."

"It's already a big one."

"I don't give a shit, tell them make it bigger."

He shouted ahead, *"¡Amigos, hagan la lumbre más grande!"* Then he smiled. "Just like a fucking *gabacho.* 'Chebo, make me a crutch! Chebo, make me a fire! Chebo, make the fire bigger!' Next you going to tell me do some yard work for you too when we get up to the trees? *Chingao.*"

In spite of the brutal cold and the throbbing in my leg, despite my one eye still clenched shut and filled with grit and blood and a mangled hand, I snorted a laugh. That was one of the great things about Chebo. He could always make you feel better.

It took twenty minutes to cover the ground, even though it was only a hundred yards uphill. In a clearing among the junipers a waist-high fire blazed, the green wood billowing white smoke to be snatched by the breeze. It swirled across all points of the compass where it burned my lungs and watered my good eye. Steam rose off my clothes as I sat by the flames. I sagged with relief at the warmth.

"*Agua, por favor.*" Someone handed me a plastic bottle, and I irrigated the paste of congealed blood and sand from my caked-shut eye until I could see. I handed it back with a nod of thanks and scooched closer to the fire. Feeling crept back into my arms and legs, accompanied by needle points of pain stabbing my skin. With my vision clear, I took in the spectacle around me.

Twelve Mexicans, mostly teenagers, crowded the space around the fire looking scared and forlorn. Murmurs circulated through the group about the gunshots and the *gringo* who was a bloody mess. Their faces all bore the same expression, some unspoken variant of *what fresh hell can this be*? Heads tilted together in low conversations.

"Chebo, tell 'em they're not in any danger, that the sorry sumbitch who did this was after me and not them. But in all the commotion, the truck had to leave to go back to Amoret. We won't be able to move 'em across the river today."

"Who was behind this, do you think?"

"I don't know, but whoever it was followed us down here from town. That's how they knew where we were."

"Okay, so what is the plan?"

"For the moment, y'all are gonna have to walk back to the safe house and spend at least one night there while we figure the rest out."

"What about you?"

"Ain't no way I can make twelve miles on this leg. Plus, I gotta get to a phone and call Angelica to warn her to leave the house, that she's in danger now, too. Once I stop shiverin' I'm gonna make it back to the highway down there and flag down a ride to the motel. I can call her from there."

"Not to tell a doctor what to do, *mi amigo,* but you look like you need a hospital, not a motel."

"I'm gonna tell her swing by the clinic and pick up some things. 'Tween me and her, we can get this fixed up without me having to go in to the hospital, stir up a lot of questions. Gonna be plenty enough of those as it is anyway, and I can't very well go telling McHenry about what I was doing down here when all this went down. While I'm at the motel I can let Shy Mike and Jimmy Wayne know about this shit show too."

Chebo translated quickly and I could see mixed emotions on the teenagers' faces, relief at not being in immediate danger from the shooter, co-mingled with frustration at the prolongation of their ordeal as well as a repeat of the hike. To compound everyone's annoyance, the sleet picked up in intensity. I was dreading the prospect of leaving the warmth of the fire, but I knew I wouldn't feel at ease until I'd spoken with Angelica, and she was on the road.

Feeling this urgency, I stood and tested the leg. My stiffened limbs screamed at me. Chebo came to my side but I waved him off, stressing the leg as I hobbled around the flames. It was gimpy as hell but it held, and between the crutch and the knowledge I'd be going downhill I nodded that I thought I could make it to the highway solo. Limping over to Chebo, I gave him a bear hug that swallowed him up. "Thank you, *mi hermano.* For everything."

He squeezed me hard, then clapped my back twice. "*Vaya con Dios, primo.*"

It took a supreme act of will to tear myself away from the warmth of the fire. The cold rushed back in, engulfing me like an incoming tide. I focused on making the walk into small goals. I would pick out a rock, and limp to it. Then I'd pick a sharp angle in the trail, and limp to that. I made my way further downstream, taking myself out of range of the sniper's nest just in case. Soon, I found myself at the river's edge in a spot where ripples indicated a gravel bar. I splashed across, only getting wet to mid-shin.

A raw wind raked across the desert floor, blowing into my face as I hobbled on my crutch the two hundred yards between the river and the ribbon of asphalt. I slipped once making my way up the hard scrabble of the declivity, my arms windmilling before I regained my balance. A small avalanche of loose gravel tumbled down the slope where my good leg dug a divot, and when the stones and earth came to a stop, I heard a blessed sound: the far-off rumble of a big rig, heading in my direction. I bent at the waist and clawed my way up the last of the slope with both hands, damaged fingers and all, until I was on flat ground. I hopped one-legged across the gravel shoulder and stood in the opposite lane, waving my arms over my head at the approaching headlights of what looked to be a Freightliner hauling a flatbed of K-rails. I heard the air brakes engage with a *ksh-ksh* sound, and the eighteen-wheeler ground to a halt. Its truck stacks coughed black diesel exhaust as it idled on the road's weather-beaten blacktop for one bloody mess of a man.

What's that? No ma'am, between the cold and the fear and the pain I hadn't really taken a minute prior to climbing up into that big rig's cab to consider the shooter's identity. It wasn't until I was thawing out in front of his warm air vents knowing the exertion of walking was behind me that I began to ponder that question.

While the cartel was still a possibility, a sniper-type assassination wasn't their style. Gangland soldiers would have more likely just pulled up behind us where we idled on the shoulder in the darkness and shot all three of us in the cab, leaving our corpses for the law to find. No, I figured it had to have been Beckett or Hector squatting up in those rocks, and— the sheriff's theories notwithstanding— my money was on the latter.

I carefully made my way down off the running board of the rig, and after a last wave to the driver limped toward the motel's office, my sock squishing with each step from the bloody ooze.

The jangling of the bell over the front door announced my arrival, startling Elijah as he dozed in a La-Z Boy behind the counter. A compact man with thinning hair, he'd grown what little he had long. The net effect made him resemble Ben Franklin, except Ben Franklin never had a neck tattoo of an M-16 with the words "The right arm of freedom" below it.

With the help of an origami of tin foil molded to its rabbit ears, a small black and white television behind the counter showed a re-run of Midland's Friday night wrestling. Pink streamers fluttered from a heating grate above the TV. The room felt toasty, like a cocoon.

I reached across the counter and snatched Elijah's phone. "Need to make a call."

He came to the counter and eyed me up and down. "Goddamn, Doc. You're a sight. Everythin' okay?"

"Depends on what you mean by okay. I'll explain in a minute."

Looking worried, he peered over my shoulder at

the empty parking lot then reached under the counter where I knew he kept a sawed-off with a pistol grip. "Anythin' goin' on I'm gonna need Gladys for?"

"No, you're fine." Despite my reassurance, he kept his hand under the counter while I dialed our house, but I got the machine. At the beep, I said, "Baby, if you're there, it's me. Pick up. It's an emergency."

A moment later, her voice came on, sounding sleepy. "*Mi amor*, what is it? Is everything okay?"

I said, "No, but it will be. Listen close, 'cause I want you leavin' the house within thirty seconds after I hang up."

Chapter 29

I was dreaming about Miguel.

In the dream, he was frantic and speaking to me in a language I couldn't understand, a look of abject terror on his face. Unable to sit still in his panic, he bounced and whirled like a fly trapped in a jar. On one knee, I kept asking him to switch to Spanish or English because I couldn't understand him. He fell silent, staring past me and I felt a tap on my shoulder. I turned to see a man's shape standing over me, his face obscured in shadows. His arms dangled at his sides, his body at a slight angle, like an Old West gunfighter about to draw. He oozed menace and I braced for an attack. Without taking my eyes off the man I flicked open my blade as I yelled over my shoulder at Miguel to run, run as far and as fast as he could. When he didn't answer, I turned to find him lying on the ground, face down, in the same pose in which I'd found him at the scrapyard. We were alone once again, and I felt the familiar sensation of dread wash over me as I called for help while squatting to render aid. Suddenly we were back at the pick up point by the river, on the flood plain between the river's banks and the road. I feverishly performed CPR, alternating between chest compressions and mouth to mouth, and screaming for help. But the emptiness was as silent as the bottom of the cold, deep river.

Suddenly I became aware of a distant sound. Someone nearby was clicking rocks together, rapidly and in sets of three. I spun in place, scanning the area to identify the source of the noise. The sound grew louder. Whomever it was banged the rocks together with real effort now, still in sets of three. I screamed, "Whoever you are, come help me!" but the unseen source ignored me.

I snapped awake. I had a brief, blurry moment of disorientation, my head still hazy. It came back to me, my limping away from the motel office to my room, my stripping nude as I turned the heat up as high as it would go, my crawling under the sheets. As the events flooded back, I heard another furtive train of three knocks on the plywood door.

I threw back the blankets and saw a sweaty outline of my form on the sheets as well as blood stains the size of dinner plates from my calf and hand. The room's window unit labored mightily, rattling to meet my demand for heat. The room was sweltering now, humid and sticky. Checking my watch, I'd been asleep for almost two hours.

I hobbled to the peephole and saw Angelica hugging herself against the cold. I opened the door and she rushed in, dropping a large black trash bag inside the doorway before hugging me fiercely. She kissed my neck, then hugged me again. I heard a gritty rattle approach, caster wheels on pavement, and a portly cleaning woman trundled her cart past the open door. She glanced inside the room as she passed but never broke stride at the sight of a bloody, naked man in the embrace of a beautiful woman, as though it happened all the time.

"The most awful thoughts have been going

through my head as I drove here," Angelica said as she kicked the door closed with her heel. She stepped back and wiped her eyes. "I cannot believe that I almost lost you too."

"I'll be all right, but we have some work to do. You sure nobody followed you?"

She nodded her head.

"How about all the things on the list? You get everything okay from the clinic?"

"*Sí, mi amor.*" She took the trash bag into the bathroom and I heard the squeak of faucets turning. "It will be best for me to work in there," she said in an assertive tone.

Soon, I lowered myself into the bathtub's steaming water, groaning with pleasure. Next to me, she sat on the commode's closed lid and used the toilet tank for an instrument tray.

She drew up two syringes, one with antibiotics, the other with tetanus vaccine. Wiping my deltoid with an alcohol swab, she asked, "Who did this, do you think?"

I winced both times she stuck me. "Maybe Hector. Maybe Beckett. Maybe somebody pissed off at Pablo's people?"

"Let me start with your hand." She unwrapped the bandana binding my hand wound, then scowled. My fourth and fifth fingers were dark purple and useless, dangling flush with my palm and each still attached to my hand only by a thin strip of skin just past the knuckle. They flopped left to right as I rotated my hand back and forth to examine the damage, obeying gravity rather than my brain. Spikes of bone stuck out into the space where my fingers had been, the remnant edges of the wound black and macerated.

"Could have been worse," she said as she wound

her long hair into a knob on the top of her head. Donning sterile gloves, she drew lidocaine up into a syringe.

I showed her where to inject the nerves in my wrist, and in less than a minute my entire hand went from throbbing to silent, as though the mangled tissues belonged to someone else. She painted my hand in antiseptic, and with a sterile pair of scissors and forceps began snipping away the dead muscle and tendons. With her hair up and reading glasses perched on the tip of her nose, she could have passed for a librarian.

"How much danger do you think we are still in?" she asked as she clipped the thin tissue bridges holding my fingers on. She casually tossed the fingers into the bathroom's trash can like used tampons. I looked at my purple fingers at the bottom of the can's crinkled plastic liner, and it dawned on me I'd never need to trim their nails again.

"Well, I don't think the asshole did this is going to walk up to us on the sidewalk and throw down in front of God and everyone, if that's what you're askin'." I leaned my head back against the lip and studied the ceiling while she worked. The drywall had a brown water stain that radiated out like ripples on a muddy puddle. "He did it out here for a reason, from a distance, so no chance Shy Mike or Jimmy Wayne could ID him."

"Is this enough?" she interrupted.

I took a look. "Trim that tendon there back a little more," I instructed. Once she'd done so, I slid under the water for a moment to slick my hair back, then blew my nose to clear the sting of the bathwater. "Christ almighty does this water feel good."

"Quit moving. You will make me slip with the scissors, and then you will be missing three fingers instead of two."

"Yes ma'am." My stomach growled audibly. When was the last time I'd eaten? I'd have to see to that soon. "Now, I'm not stupid, I know what we do out there on the river isn't exactly a secret. Hell, it wouldn't surprise me to find out McHenry knows and chooses to look the other way. The bigger problem we got is whoever did this can get to you easier than he can get to me."

"You know I am no stranger to looking over my shoulder," she said. Her tone was more matter-of-fact than brave. Which, now that I think about it, would amount to the same thing, I guess.

"That's one of the things I love about you, but that doesn't mean we need to go takin' any more chances than we got to. 'Til this gets sorted, I'd be a lot more comfortable with you stayin' out here. It's not the Taj Mahal, but I suspect you've stayed in worse. What do you think?"

"*Claro que sí*," she agreed.

"Good. I'll sleep better."

"What are you going to tell the sheriff?" she asked as she appraised her work.

"I'll come up with some bullshit. Even if he knows what we do out here, I don't wanna go rubbin' his face in it. Might put him in a bad position."

With all the dead muscle and skin removed, she nodded her head in satisfaction. She exchanged the scissors for an instrument that looked like a small pair of garden shears.

The shears snipped neatly across the jagged edges of the fractured finger bones leaving two healthy cut surfaces, nubbins that looked like cut ivory sticking out of the base of the wounds. She poured a splash of Betadine into a liter bottle of saline, and after replacing the cap, poked a number of holes in the screw top with a hypodermic. This transformed the bottle into a small waterspout which she used to spray the open wounds, irrigating them with disinfectant.

Watching her rinse the dirty wound, I said, "When I was a resident doing this, we used to say, 'The solution to pollution is dilution.'"

"Hmph."

"After I get back to town, I think I'm gonna try to find Francis and have a talk with him. Maybe he knows something about where Hector's at."

"Just promise me you will be careful." The irrigation finished, she began suturing the edges of the wound together, pulling the now-healthy skin edges over the cut edges of bone, handling the instruments with precision using the technique I'd taught her when she first came to work with me.

"I'd say I always am, but, well—" I jerked my chin at my three-fingered hand.

When she cut her last stitch, I held the hand up and examined the suture line. "Nice spacing, edges everted-- almost looks like you know what you're doing."

"I had a good teacher. Now let me see that leg."

Take a look here, ma'am. Yep, that's her handiwork some forty years later. The scars aren't the prettiest, but it sure as hell worked. See here, the way she rotated the finger pads up, gave me a nice little cushion there? Lord almighty, that woman was somethin' else.

I dry-swallowed two pain pills and hobbled to the edge of the bed where I pulled the phone into my lap and propped my leg up so it wouldn't throb. I rummaged in Angelica's purse and found a pen and paper, then dialed Amoret's directory assistance.

"Phone number for Francis Beckett please."

I could hear typing on her keyboard, followed by, "I'm afraid that number is unlisted at the customer's request. Is there anything else I can do for you today?"

"Shit. Okay, how 'bout Michael Culverson then?"

More typing, then, "Hold for the number please." I scribbled as Angelica came out of the bathroom and gathered my bloody clothes and the medical waste into a trash bag. She sat on the mattress, caressing my lower leg. Now that she didn't have the first aid to occupy her mind, a worried look clouded her face.

"I am going into Terlingua and pick up supplies, plus clothes for you to wear home."

"Thanks. I wasn't keen on explaining this look if I got pulled over on the way back to Amoret."

A smile crossed her face for a moment, then she turned serious again. "How long do you think for me being here?"

"I'm not sure. A week, maybe? Lots of things happening right now, so it's kind of hard to say. Nobody else knows you're here, and let's aim to keep it that way. I'll figure something out for getting you a vehicle in the next couple of days."

She leaned forward and kissed my thigh, then slung her purse over her shoulder. "Get some rest while I am gone."

"Wish I could. I got lots of phone calls to make. Rest'll have to wait."

"Anything else you need from me before I leave?"

"Come to think of it, a tug would sure hit the spot right about now." I moved the phone off my lap and scooched down in the bed with a lascivious grin.

Closing the door behind her, she rolled her eyes, muttering, "Unbelievable."

I left a message on Shy Mike's answering machine, and when I next called Jimmy Wayne's number he picked up on the third ring.

I got right to business. "Once y'all cleared that rock outcropping, what'd you see made you keep driving?"

"Saw the vehicle sittin' close to the edge of the rock, looked like the driver'd pulled over and parked as soon as the rock blocked our view of him. Me and Shy Mike figgered since he didn't drive up and offer help when he saw the hood up on our rig, it likely meant he wasn't a civilian. We couldn't see hide nor hair of him, figured he's up in the rocks by then more'n likely, watching. Put all that together, it just didn't smell right. We both agreed, right thing to do was keep drivin'. How 'bout your side of things? Anythin' I need to know 'bout after we pulled out?"

"I should say so," and proceeded to catch him up on the events after they aborted the pick up. I told him everything except for Angelica's presence at the motel.

"You ain't pullin' my leg? I'm gonna be pissed off you're pulling my leg," he said.

"I'm serious as cancer."

"Well I'll be goddamned. "

"So listen, this is what I need from you. Get ahold of Shy Mike and Chebo and make a plan for getting that bunch over here by yourselves ASAFP. They're kids from what I saw, scared shitless and miserable after making that walk twice foul weather. Just let 'em know the doc won't be available."

"You think that's smart?"

"I don't think it's dumb. This more'n likely was about me, not y'all. If I'm not there I think y'all will be all right. Also, tell Pablo to get ahold of me. He needs to know about what happened, too. Last thing, can you take Maybelline and Rope Tail to your place for a while? They get along with you."

"Sounds good. You gonna be around town?"

"I will be tomorrow." I needed to find Francis Beckett, to persuade him to tell me anything he could about how I could find Hector before the police. I wondered how hard it'd be to find Francis with all that was going on.

As the universe was about to show, it turned out not to be hard at all.

Chapter 30

I awoke at four in the morning to make the drive back to Amoret. I dressed quietly in the dark, then after kissing Angelica's shoulder I went into the stillness of the desert night. The delicate buzz of the neon sign reached across the parking lot, and the motel's profile was quiet and dark, as though the building itself slept.

My headlights swept across the walls and windows, then fell off the corner's edge into blackness. On the gravel apron, I startled a coyote trotting across the cracked asphalt. It froze in my high beams, its eyes glinting like red marbles as I slowed down to avoid it. For a moment, the coyote acted nonchalant, curious even, staring back at me with its ears perked forward. Then, the spell broke and it loped back in the direction from which it came. Silly as it sounds, ma'am, I felt a camaraderie with the animal, like in being the first to lay claim to the new day we shared a secret from the rest of the sleeping world.

It was still dark when I pulled into my clinic's parking lot an hour later. Even though the space was only designed to hold ten cars, the distance between my truck and the front door seemed vast and exposed. I was jumpy, I won't lie. That nugget of fear, the one that starts in your chest and settles deep down in your balls like silt, it was something I hadn't felt since 'Nam.

I got my key ready while still behind the wheel and barely broke stride in entering the front door. In the charts behind reception, I dug out Francis' manila folder and scribbled down his phone number and address on a scrap of paper. Hurrying now, I left to get a room at the Motel Thunderbird about a mile from the clinic, a place where my parked truck would be shielded from sight of the street. Once inside my room, I set the alarm for eight o'clock and was instantly asleep.

When the alarm jangled, I paused long enough to stretch and run my tongue over my fuzzy teeth before calling Francis' number. I got his answering machine, but I didn't want to leave a message. Not yet anyway.

Next, I tried Darla's. As it rang, I cursed myself for being in too big a hurry and not thinking things through. It'd look funny, my calling to see if she could give me a clue to her son's whereabouts, and had I been thinking I'd have come up with a convincing lie ahead of time. While the phone rang, my mind clutched at possibilities, quickly rejecting them all as preposterous sounding. I was just about to put the handpiece back in its cradle when she picked up.

"Hello?"

"Uh, mornin', Darla. It's me."

"Oh, thank God you got my messages. How soon before you can come over?" Her voice was thick with worry. Intense, maternal.

Caught off guard, I said, "Hang on, back up. What messages? I been out of town for a couple days."

"I called your house and the clinic. It's Francis.

He's not well, and he's refusing to go to the Emergency Room."

"What do you mean, 'not well?'"

"He's feverish, his stomach hurts, he's breathing fast-- so fast he's having trouble talking. Max and I told him we're going to call an ambulance, but he refuses. He keeps saying that if paramedics show up he'll send them away, that they can't make him go." Her voice hitched. "Oh, Noah, I'm so scared."

"Why won't he go?"

"He won't talk to us about it. Can you please come talk some sense into him? He thinks so much of you."

"Sure, I'm on my way."

I bought toiletries on the way and cleaned up in a Texaco bathroom. When I got to Darla's, she was already standing in the doorway watching the street for my arrival, hugging herself tightly and fretting. She took my hand and led me— or to be more accurate, yanked me— to the east wing of the house and up a scissored staircase. "This is Francis' old bedroom. Max went to the apothecary."

There was a time when I'd have teased her for her pretentiousness in using that word, but now I just said, "Sounds good."

In Francis' sick room, the morning sun backlit thin red curtains, making the room glow a bright crimson. It was obvious Darla had been right to worry. Perspiration soaked the pillow around Francis' head like a halo, and his styled hair lay slicked against his forehead and cheeks. Despite the sweat, a thick duvet bundled him to his stubbled jaw. When I entered, his glassy eyes crinkled with a wan smile and he attempted a half-wave, but the effort exhausted him and he let the hand drop with a thump.

"Doctor Grady, thank you so much for coming," he mumbled through shallow breaths. "I was hoping I'd get to—" but a coughing jag interrupted, the rales sounding wet and ragged. He wiped his mouth from a box of tissues. "I was hoping I'd get to see you."

His exertion in forming words made me tired just watching him. I half-expected each rattling breath to be his last.

"Darla, you mind givin' us the room?"

"Of course." But before stepping out she hugged me fiercely. On tiptoes, she whispered in my ear, "Please take care of my son."

I reflexively hugged her back and caught a whiff of her perfume as I did so. For an instant, the smell transported me, evoking memories that flashed across my mind's eye. In spite of myself, I felt a pang of— not regret. Maybe a better word is curiosity? Wondering of things that could have been? It's testimony to the connection we shared that even in that moment, with my boy dead and in the ground, my woman in hiding and my wounds still fresh, her scent could do that to me.

I snapped out of it with a jerk, a realization of proximity to danger, like finding yourself surrounded by high voltage lines. I broke the embrace first and awkwardly held her at arms' length, passing it off by giving her a wink. "I'll come find you when we're done." She nodded, and once hidden from Francis' line of sight by the closing door mouthed, "Thank you."

I pulled over a straight-backed chair and took a seat, then threw an arm over the top as I crossed my legs. Neither of us said anything for a few moments, then I picked up a well-thumbed copy of *The Picture of Dorian Gray* from the nightstand.

Flipping through the novel, I asked

The Bones of Amoret

conversationally, "Reading Oscar Wilde on your death bed? Little bit of a cliche, don't you think?"

He smiled and doubled the pillow to prop his head. "It's nothing of the kind. His words have been a source of great comfort to me of late."

I turned the open book over on my thigh. "What all have you told your mom?"

More coughing, then, "Everything. She said she had her suspicions but hadn't wanted to pry. She's such a good person. Oh my, what happened to your hand?"

Holding it to the lamp, a small spot of blood had seeped through to stain the white bandages directly over the sites where my fingers had been.

"Fella clenched up when I was doing a rectal exam. Snapped 'em clean off."

He laughed at that, the guffaw accompanied by a rattle deep in his chest. "You need to work on your bedside manner."

"No, next time I just won't do the rectal exam like I'm trying to get the last pickle outta the jar."

He laughed again, then winced. "Don't. It really does hurt to laugh."

I was silent for a moment, then said, "You know you don't go to the hospital, you're gonna die, right here, in this bed. Soon."

He smoothed the sheets with one hand, a feeble smile on his face as he looked around at the flowered wallpaper with a fond expression.

"I know so many people who were unhappy with their childhoods. Until very recently I thought I was one of them. For a while I just thought that was the default human condition. When you're a child you spend your life watching June vacuum in pearls and Ward helping the Beaver with his homework in a smoking jacket, and you think that's the way everyone else's house is, you know? You're too young to know better. What I would have given for an episode where they caught the Beaver masturbating in the bathroom to a tattered copy of *Playgirl* he found in the woods. Can you imagine?" He giggled.

Becoming more serious, he said, "You know my mother is still in love with you, don't you?"

I didn't say anything.

"Do you still love her too?"

I thought about it for a moment. "I suppose I do. Feelings like we shared are like the tide. Sometimes high, sometimes low, but always there."

"I would have loved having you for my father," he said, real melancholy in his voice. "I can't tell you how many times I've thought about that over the years."

"Regretting things isn't the way you want to spend your last hours. There's no point to it."

"I suppose you're right but indulge me. Why didn't she ever walk out?"

"Her and your dad don't believe in divorce. Well, I don't know what they actually believe, but the Church says it isn't right, and that was enough for them."

He sighed. "I think both she and I are dying. I'm just doing it more quickly."

I snorted. "If you're getting metaphysical, we're all dying."

"You know what I mean," he shook his head with downcast eyes. "It makes me sad to think of the years of happiness she's missed out on. And not even just her, but me too." He paused. "Is there ever any chance you would go back to her? Now that my dad's dead?"

"You don't know what your dad is or isn't."

"Don't be coy. Would you give any thought to going back to her now?"

"I'm happy now."

"That's not an answer."

"Fine, then, if I've got to spell it out in so many words, no. I'm happy with my woman and have no present or future plans to go taking up with your mom again. Our moment's passed."

He studied my face like a poker player, then said sadly, "I believe you."

"Good. And I wouldn't worry too much about your mom's future happiness. She's a good-hearted, beautiful woman with a lot of money. Every swingin' dick in the county's gonna be linin' up. She'll have her pick of men. If that's what she wants that is."

Francis' eyebrows shot up. "You think she might be gay?"

I laughed, "No, no. I mean between me and your dad she may just have had her fill of the bullshit that goes along with having a man in her life."

"'A woman needs a man like a fish needs a bicycle.'"

"Pithy. Sounds like something you read in here," I said, tapping the book's cover.

"No, I can't remember where I read that, but it wasn't Oscar."

Changing the subject, I said, "You know, I never got a chance to thank you for coming clean about Hector to the police. But for you, there's a good chance right now I'd be sitting in the clink instead of this chair. Took a lot of guts."

He picked lint off the sheets, flicking it away. "It's hard when you're in love with a monster."

"Seems harsh, don't you think?"

"There's been other things. Things I didn't feel the need to share with anyone."

"You know where he is right now, don't you?"

He continued as though he hadn't heard me. "His anger was like gangrene, it just slowly spread, defiling anything healthy it came in contact with. I thought I could change him— speaking of cliches— but that wasn't hope, it was delusion."

"Francis, look at me." His eyes locked on mine. "If I promise not to tell the police, where can I find him? I promise not to hurt your man, but I need to know."

"Why would you feel the need to promise not to hurt him?" he asked with his first look of concern.

"I put my son in the ground last week. I don't think it's crazy talk that someone might worry I was gonna take matters into my own hands. But that's not what this is about."

"What is it about, then?"

I hesitated. "Could I just say I need to talk to him, and we leave it at that?"

He lay back with his eyes closed and was silent long enough I thought he may have dozed off.

Then he said, "I have your word?"

"Yes."

"He's probably at a motel in Ojinaga, *Casa El Vaquero*. It's next door to the bar where he and I first met. We use it for some of our getaways. If he's not there then I have no idea."

"Fair enough. Thanks."

I put the book back on the nightstand and leaned forward, hands clasped, and elbows on my knees to try one last time. "You know your momma isn't gonna forgive me if I can't talk you into going to the hospital, today, like right now."

He reached over and patted my folded hands. "I know. But I just feel like, why bother? I know what's coming. I've read about this, this— disease, what to expect. The final minutes sound horrible. Did you know at the end, you feel like you're drowning? What am I saying, of course you do. I just want to get it over with. Going to the hospital would be dragging it out, like pulling at the Band Aid slowly. I'd rather just rip it off."

"Even if you don't want to be treated, if you go to the hospital, I can try to make the end more comfortable."

"Please don't tempt me. I've made up my mind about this, and I want to die here, surrounded by the familiar." His eyes grew moist. "I know that if someone were to look at my life from the outside, there's not much about it that would suggest the word 'dignity' has been a concern of mine. But that's what I want now, here, at the end."

"I think you're being too hard on yourself."

"Actually, I would argue I'm not being hard enough. 'One should die proudly when it is no longer possible to live proudly.'"

"Nietzsche, right?"

His eyebrows shot up even though his eyes were only half-open. "I'm impressed. Although I don't know why I should be. You know, Doctor Grady, you are without a doubt one of the most interesting people I have had the privilege to know in this Godforsaken wasteland. In the space of ten minutes, you've gone from cracking jokes about rummaging in a man's rectum to recognizing quotes from German philosophers." He snatched at the tissue box and clamped a Kleenex to his mouth just in time to beat a rough coughing fit. Francis tossed it in the bin with the others, but not so quickly that we didn't both notice a few small crimson flecks on the white tissue.

I stood and cricked my back. My leg and hand were throbbing again, but I didn't want to be seen taking pain pills here.

"Will you be back before I'm gone?" he asked.

"I don't know. Truth is, I'm not sure how much more time you've got left. We're probably talking a few days, but I can't swear you'll make it to sundown."

He accepted that. "Thank you for not lying to me. If this is the last time I see you, I want you to know that I think I loved you more than my own father. That kind of hard honesty is one of the reasons why."

I bent forward and hugged him, feeling his damp t-shirt sticking to his back. Burning up with fever, he was skin and bone, like hugging a pillowcase full of tree branches.

"I would have enjoyed having you as my son, Francis. And the last piece of advice I'll pass along is, give yourself a break. What you're facing is hard enough without beating yourself up while you're going through it. You're a good man."

I broke off the hug and went to the door with hope. Hope, that is, that I hadn't lied to him about what would happen if and when I found Hector.

Chapter 31

I found Darla, hands interlaced on top of her head, pacing at the bottom of the staircase, anxiety fueling her need for movement. She took two rapid steps in my direction, but my expression betrayed me. She stopped short, frozen. Her face asked the question.

Slowly, I shook my head, lips pursed.

Her eyes squeezed tight as her face collapsed in on itself, and her shoulders began to shake. I came to her, pulling her in close, encircling her in my arms. Muffled against my chest, she managed to say, "This can't be happening." The grief crept up on her, building without an explosion.

Unable to help myself, I gave her temple a kiss, then pressed my lips into her hair with its silver tiger stripes. Out of the corner of my mouth, I said, "I'm so, so sorry."

We stayed that way, swaying slowly together on the linoleum for what felt like a long time.

Later, when we were in the living room, I asked, "You sure you wouldn't rather be alone right now? Feel like I'm intruding. This is family time."

"No, thank you. I welcome the distraction. Besides, you're like family." She wiped her eyes with a tissue. "Oh my God. What happened to your hand?"

"Long story for some other time."

"Are you okay?"

"I will be." Wanting to change the subject, I asked, "Want me to build a fire?"

"That would be wonderful. I made coffee, would you like some?"

"Read my mind, thanks." I went to the patio and pulled split wood off the stack. Through the last of the morning mist, Max's apartment was dark. I thought that strange. The old man had been gone longer than a run to the pharmacy should have taken.

The flue's hinges settled with a clunk, and I arranged wood on the grate in the firebox. Above my head, a young Blaine and Darla.looked back at me from a picture on the mantel. In black graduation gowns under a melancholy sky, with tight-lipped smiles they held their diplomas to their chests. His eyes looked dour and serious, as though he wanted to get on with life's business, while Darla had a blunt expression, like she was filming a hostage video.

Turning on the gas, I scratched a match and tossed it into the firebox where it ignited with a muted *phoomp*. By this time Darla was back, and I took my seat next to her.

"Max's been gone a long time. He okay you think?"

"I suspect the pharmacy was just an excuse. He just found out a few hours ago that his only grandson is gay and dying. He's probably struggling with that, and knowing Max, more with the former than the latter." She scooched closer and draped my arm across her shoulders. Feeling me tense up, she said, "Relax, handsome. I just need some human contact right now."

Buds of yellow flame licked at the edges of the

wood. The snaps and hisses of the fire made a relaxing counterpart to the chirps of morning song birds.

"I just don't understand why he doesn't want to fight this."

"That's not who he is. Ask me, though, he's got something better than the energy to fight."

"What's that?"

"He's got a sense of peace about it. Way more, frankly, than I think I'd have in his situation."

"He's an old soul," she said.

"He gets that from you," I said. I rubbed her arm, then stood and took the poker from a stand by the hearth. I rearranged the logs and the fire flared.

She asked my backside, "What does it say about me that I don't miss Blaine?"

Still poking at the fire I said, "Pardon me for sayin', but to my eyes that's the last thing you should feel bad about right now."

"I just feel like a hypocrite, going through the motions of what people expect, acting like I'm broken up about it. Truth be told, it feels more like a roommate broke a lease."

I opened my mouth to speak, then thought better of it and closed it once again. She could see my reflection in the glass cabinet of the grandfather clock, though, and asked, "What?"

"Nothing."

She leaned forward to see my face better, then said, "Don't give me that. What were you going to say?"

"Seriously, nothing," as I stood and wiped my good hand on my jeans.

"Noah Travis Grady if you don't spill it right now-- "

"Goddammit, this isn't why I came over here."

"Don't curse in my house. And what isn't why you came over here?"

"Can you please let this drop?"

"No. Now you're starting to make me mad. What's going on?"

I sighed. "There's new information 'bout Blaine's disappearing act. Sheriff thinks he may not be dead after all." I explained all of the new information McHenry and I had discovered.

Once I'd finished, she sat looking off into the middle distance. I asked, "Darla, maybe you can help with something I haven't been able to figure out. If he's alive, why go to all this trouble of disappearing? Why wouldn't he just walk out?"

For the first time, a note of real anger crept into her voice. "I'll tell you why. Because he knows his meal ticket would disappear."

"I thought about that, but it stops now anyway, right? How would he benefit from doing it this way?"

Instead of answering, she set her glass of wine down and stood, pressing the heels of her palms into her eyes. She paced, genuine fury creeping into her voice. She asked, "Oh, how could I have been so *stupid?*"

Baffled, I asked, "What? What is it?"

She ignored my question, continuing to curse herself. "That has to be it. And after Juan *specifically* warned me--"

"Who's Juan?"

"Juan Modesto, the Studdard family's accountant." She stopped pacing and her eyes darted around the room without seeing as she thought this through. "I bet you that's what he did. My God, how could I have not seen this *coming?*"

"Sit down and explain what you're talking about."

"I'm sorry, Noah, but I'm too angry to sit." She

stood behind the couch, unconsciously kneading the top edge of an expensive-looking throw pillow with one hand.

"Blaine always took care of the household finances. I can hear him saying it now, 'That's the man's job.' In my angrier moments, I wanted to ask, "You mean the man's job is overseeing the woman's money?' but of course I never did.

"Several years ago— well, Francis was just starting kindergarten, so longer than that even— I had to go sign some forms for the trust with Juan. He worked for us for most of his career until he dropped dead of a heart attack in his office."

Biting her thumbnail, she said, "After we took care of the signatures, he asked me how Blaine was doing. I gave him my sort of stock answer, the one I gave to anybody who ever asked after him in that superficial way people do. After I gave him the polite answer, he paused, then asked if we were having any discord."

"What made him ask?"

"I'm getting to that. His question took me aback, frankly. My reflex was to lie and say no, everything was fine, but then I remembered something you told me once, that the three people in your life with whom you should be completely honest are your doctor, your lawyer, and your accountant. So I said something nonspecific. Something like, we had our disagreements but what couple didn't? Blah, blah, blah. Then he asked me how involved I was in our household bills and finances. I told him not very.

"I'll never forget what happened next. He asked, 'Truthfully, how much do you trust your husband?'

"I was shocked. I stammered something about how I trusted him as much as I needed to or some such, but what I really wanted to know was why was he asking?

"Juan told me that our situation was rife with potential for trouble. A woman with lots of family money and a meager knowledge of the marital finances. A savvy husband with a low-paying career who manages things. A rocky relationship.

"I had to admit that described us, but then I asked what kind of 'trouble' he meant.

"Then he told me, 'Blaine siphoning off money and storing it somewhere that only he knows about.' Quietly building a little nest egg just in case things with us didn't work out."

I found my thoughts racing in anticipation of where this was going.

She continued, "I have to admit I dismissed Juan's concerns at the time because I never really thought Blaine was capable of doing something like that. Or that even if he did try, that he'd be capable of keeping it hidden. Naive as it sounds now, I had this momentary vision of him moving out and then trying to buy a five thousand square foot house in Amoret on a professor's salary, or something equally stupid.

"But what never occurred to me is that he might try to do something like this. If he were to just disappear, try and start over somewhere else far away, it would make perfect sense. He knows it wouldn't occur to me to look for any missing money, and he knows that I'd continue taking care of Max."

I interrupted there. "Speaking of that, how close are you and the old man?"

She thought for a moment. "The Blaine I know would have been worried about Max. I'd never just cut his father off, that wouldn't be the Christian thing to do. Max and I are close. Or at least, were close. He's been— I don't know, aloof? Ever since the investigation started and he found out from the police about the letters, and your and my past, our subterfuge that went on for so long—." Her voice trailed off, silently following the thought to its conclusion. "I know the way the town views Max, but there's a side to him that y'all don't get to see. He can be charming. Blaine knew there'd always be a place here for Max no matter what."

"So you think it's possible that Blaine set up a backup plan for himself, some kind of financial parachute that he's pulled the rip cord on?"

With grim resolve, she said, "I'll tell you this, I intend to find out."

Chapter 32

I hung the "Do Not Disturb" sign on my doorknob at the Thunderbird before making the short drive to our empty home. I figured there was a good chance the shooter was watching the house, so using my driveway was out of the question. I parked two blocks away along the elementary school's curb, then trotted through an empty lot and crossed an alley to approach my house from the rear. My chain link fence jingled as I clambered over it into our backyard, the early morning stillness making the noise feel louder than it was. I skulked to my patio and pressed myself against an exterior wall as I scanned the back sides of my neighbors' houses. All appeared quiet.

We kept a spare key in a faux rock among the stones lining Angelica's rose garden. Several ants crawled on its surface, so I flipped it with my boot and peeled off the reservoir's cover. Hundreds of ants exploded from the cavity where the key was kept, a writhing mess that crawled onto my boot. Cursing, I brushed them off the leather, then kicked it over to the faucet jutting out the back wall of the garage.

Rinsing the insects out of the rock's cavity, I solved the mystery when I found the key well packed full of decaying jelly beans. The sugary detritus left a soupy, sticky rainbow caking the key at the bottom. I smirked for a moment at this last little surprise from Miguel, but on its heels came a wave of melancholy, another reminder of our loss. It felt like a part of me was gone, a phantom pain, like an amputee. The grief hit me hard, threatening to overwhelm me before I shook it off.

I closed the back door behind me and stood stock still, listening. The ticking of the grandfather clock floated out from the living room, but the house was otherwise quiet. The hushed darkness felt creepy, less so from the stillness than the solitude. I couldn't remember ever having been completely alone in the house before, no Angelica, no Miguel, no Maybelline or Rope Tail. It was as though the hand of God had tilted one corner of the roof up like a dollhouse and snatched everyone away.

I moved silently through the unlit house to the office, keeping away from windows. My gun safe squatted in the back corner of the study, dark green and menacing. As high as my nose and four feet wide, it weighed eight hundred pounds and took four grown men to move. I twirled in the combination, and gave a spin to the door's handle, like the wheeled helm of a schooner.

By West Texas standards I was an amateur, with a handful of long rifles and shotguns that suited our love of hunting birds and antelope. A small assortment of handguns occupied the top shelf, a necessity in a time and place when break-ins by addicts looking for narcotics were common.

By way of example, ma'am, one family doctor I knew, Jerry Reinfeldt, practiced in Abilene, suffered a burglary in the middle of the night while Jerry and his wife and kids were home asleep. The junkie smashed out a garage window, then cut himself crawling through the jagged glass, lacerating his forearm to the bone and slicing his radial artery in the process. He managed to make it into the main house where he ran around shrieking like a banshee and spurting rooster tails of blood from his arm.

Jerry came out from the bedroom, still in his pajamas and fuzzy-headed from sleep, to see this scabby crank-head running laps around the floor plan, covered head-to-toe in blood. He charged Jerry, who proceeded to shoot him once in the leg with his old service revolver, fracturing his femur. The junkie went down like a chubby kid on a seesaw, and Jerry walked over and put a tourniquet on the psychotic would-be burglar's wound before calling the cops. That's not even the crazy part. After he got out of the hospital, from the jailhouse he got some fancy-pants Austin lawyer who sued Jerry for shooting him, saying something about how as a doctor he should have recognized that the man didn't constitute a threat, being already injured. Then Jerry's insurance company started in talking about how it'd take more money to litigate the case than they were asking for. Sons of bitches settled. I know what they say, that all you need to sue somebody is a typewriter and a filing fee, but goddamn...

Sorry, ma'am, there I go wandering off again. You'll have to excuse an old man his indulgences. But I swear to God, if any child of mine told me they wanted to be a lawyer, I'd ask them if they'd looked into being a piano player at a whorehouse first, 'cause that's more honorable work.

Once in the gun safe, I took down a Desert Eagle I planned to leave with Angelica, figuring if it was good enough for the Israelis it was good enough for her. For myself I pulled out a MAC-11 Pablo had given me when we started working together. I'd told him at the time I thought it unnecessary, but fortunately he'd insisted. After placing both in a duffle bag along with a box of ammunition apiece and two extra clips, I returned to my truck and departed Amoret for the long ride south to the Mustang Motor Court.

Ninety miles later, I picked up Angelica at the motel. While I napped in the passenger seat she drove my truck four hours to El Paso, the nearest place where she could rent a car in anonymity. After we'd finished the transaction and I'd given her the pistol, she drove back to the Mustang in a nondescript compact. I watched her taillights disappear, feeling better that she was armed and mobile.

At Francis' suggestion, I drove through Ojinaga on my way back to Amoret and swung by the Motel Vaquero looking for Hector but he hadn't checked in under that name, and no one matching his description was staying there at the time. Finally, before heading out I made a slow loop through the parking lot looking for a GMC pickup that resembled the one I'd seen at the river crossing but had no luck. Disappointed, I headed back to Amoret.

Back in town, I drove by Shy Mike's house to pick up my mail. By the time I tossed the rubber-banded stack onto the passenger seat, I needed my headlights to make it back to the Thunderbird. Ravenous, I'd picked up some tamales on the way and stuck them in the room's microwave. It hummed in the background while I retrieved the duffle with the MAC-11 from the truck and set it on the floor by the door, then after a moment's consideration, took the gun out and left it on my nightstand just to be on the safe side. A warm glow of satisfaction for what I'd accomplished that day lightened my mood, and as I flipped through the usual stack of credit card and utility bills the smell of tamales wafted into the musty air, making my mouth water.

I was thinking about the logistics of the next few days when I came across a plain white envelope buried in the middle of the other correspondence. The microwave dinged as I tore it open. Inside was a piece of paper with a familiar line of lowercase type, a message that made my appetite vanish:

you can't hide her forever

Chapter 33

Events were picking up momentum, like a crested roller coaster feeling the first pull of gravity.

Sleep was slow to come that night. The darkness was near total, broken only by the parking lot's vapor lights peeking around the edges of the blackout curtains. On the dresser, the glowing red numbers from a clock lined up in the scratchy sheets' valley made by my toes. I became aware of background noise. The rumble of traffic on the highway. The hum of the window unit battling the chill. The adjacent room's muffled television through the thin walls.

Bare-chested, with my fingers interlaced behind my head and the sheets at my armpits, I watched the minutes roll by while I ruminated on recent developments. I kept turning them over in my mind, examining them from different angles, trying to spot some fact, some clue I'd missed. Shortly after one o'clock, I turned on the bedside lamp and propped myself on a pillow to re-examine the anonymous typewritten note and the Polaroid of Miguel's death scene for the hundredth time. I stared at them, wishing I could see whose hands they'd passed through previously, like those hands had left behind some kind of an echo that would reveal itself if I stared at the picture and the note long enough.

This'll sound strange to say, ma'am, but I never really considered giving them to McHenry. I knew there was no chance whomever was behind this had been so stupid to leave fingerprints— the note sent directly to McHenry saying I'd killed Blaine was proof enough of that. But I had the sense that I'd fallen off McHenry's radar, and I was nervous that knowledge of the picture and the note would refocus his attention on me. Even more than that, though, I didn't see how passing them along would help my situation. With every passing day, I became more confident the cartel wasn't behind Miguel's death or the sniper attack on me. I've already mentioned the assassination at the river crossing wasn't their style. And as far as Miguel's death went, the more time passed without knowing the killer, the less likely it was the cartel to blame. While killing family as retribution was pretty standard for them even back then, they wouldn't keep the motive quiet. Hell, often as not they'd do it in front of you to make sure the point got across. What they sure didn't want was you wondering who'd performed the execution, because that meant you hadn't gotten the message. That was the whole point after all. For you to know.

That meant it was either Hector or Beckett. I'd come to learn both men harbored violent streaks, and each held a grudge against me. Both men had devastating personal or familial secrets break out in the open in the last few weeks— Hector, his sexuality, and Beckett my decades-long affair with Darla. Might that have driven either of them to feel like they had nothing left to lose? Or was McHenry right and they were driven to desperation by something Miguel had seen, desperation enough to cave in a child's skull?

One final thought nagged at me, ma'am, nibbling

at the back of my brain. I have to say I'm a little embarrassed to mention it to you, although given what you've already learned about me I surely don't know why I should be. I kept coming back to the question of what I would do if I found out the answer to these questions to my satisfaction? Could I trust myself not to become an instrument of vengeance? And was that really why I didn't want to share the picture and the note with McHenry? To give myself the choice, should I find out the truth before the law? I tried to get rid of those thoughts, as though I was sucking venom from a snakebite.

I wanted to get a jump on the day and firing up my truck that morning I thought I'd start by checking on Francis. Darla answered the door in the same clothes I'd seen her wearing two days before.

"He's gone, Noah."

"Oh, Jesus. When?"

"About an hour ago."

She looked dazed and turned to go to the living room leaving me to close the door behind myself. There were no tears, no grief, no crying. A thick blanket of exhaustion seemed to smother all of her emotions.

She smelled of sweat and grime, all of her normal fastidiousness stripped away. She took a seat in the breakfast nook where a mug with a tea bag's string steeped on the table, a look on her face that back in 'Nam we called "the thousand-yard stare."

She said with a tone that was flat and numb, "I guess we need to call someone. It seems strange to call an ambulance, though. Is there some kind of rule that you can only call an ambulance for someone who's living? How does this work?"

"Plenty of time for that. He's not going

anywhere." I grimaced at my poor choice of words, but she didn't seem to notice. "Where's Max?"

"Out back in his apartment. He's still struggling with all of this." Then she leaned back with her hand on her forehead and her eyes squeezed shut. "Oh, God, I completely forgot to tell him."

"Relax. You want me to go let him know?"

"Would you mind? I don't think I have it in me at the moment."

"Absolutely. I'll take care of this. You lie down for a minute and rest."

I walked her over to the couch and laid her down, then pulled the Afghan off the back of the sofa and covered her. She curled up with her head on the plush armrest and closed her eyes. Back in the kitchen, I poured a cup from a cold pot of coffee and stuck it in the microwave. By the time it dinged, I heard soft snores from the couch. Leaving the coffee on the counter for the moment, I went to be the bearer of bad tidings once again.

The massive oak's grackles argued in loud clacks and whistles as I climbed the three short steps to the apartment's porch and rapped gently on the brass knocker. I heard a metallic ratchet inside, the sound of someone getting out of a recliner, and the Venetian blinds in the window next to the door tented into a long, thin diamond for a moment before snapping shut once again and the door jerked open.

At that moment if Max and his days-old stubble and cowlicked hair had entered a looking-like-shit contest with me, it would've been a photo finish. He'd missed a buttonhole on his rumpled cardigan, making it bow in the middle and mismatching the tails at the bottom. The point of one collar stuck up carelessly on his chambray shirt, like a finger testing the wind. Rank air wafted past, and over his shoulder

I could see unwashed dishes stacked high in the sink. While his appearance may have been slovenly, though, his attitude was defiant.

"Son of a bitch. Get off my porch, you miserable home-wreckah."

"Look, Max, I didn't come back here to fight. I got some bad news."

Looking over my shoulder toward the house, he asked, "Where's Dah-la?"

"Inside. Max, listen. There's no easy way to say this so I'll just say it. Francis died 'bout an hour ago."

His gaze shifted back to me, and his eyes locked on mine. His eyebrows wrinkled as though he didn't understand my words, then his mouth silently opened and closed a few times, like a fish on a dock. He reached out slowly and at first I thought he was going to put his hand on my shoulder. Then he grabbed a handful of my t-shirt with surprising strength and pulled me toward him. Still in slow-motion, he balled his other fist.

"Max, take your goddamn hands off me." I grabbed the hand that was pulling my shirt. The tendons stood out like cables. His knuckles blanched white, his age belying the strength of the muscles rippling beneath his liver-spotted skin, and he reared back. He stood in that pose, his eyes bright with tears and still locked on mine, lips peeled back in a snarling fury that exposed his dentures, unmoving except for his inexorable pull on my shirt.

I shouted, "Max! Enough! I don't want to fight you, Max! Goddammit, let go!" I heard a soft rending as the fabric of my shirt tore. I grabbed for his other wrist, trying to keep his cocked fist at arm's length. "Max! Look! Stop! This won't bring Francis back!"

His muscles relaxed, and for a moment I thought my appeal to reason worked. His eyes softened, the glare of hatred morphing into something else. At first I thought it was resignation, then I realized his eyes were no longer seeing me, that he was looking through me, past me. His muscles went beyond relaxation to limp, and his arms drooped until they dangled at his sides. His mouth never stopped opening and closing, but now it was the motion of an infant when you play here-comes-the-choo-choo with a spoonful of apple sauce. He slid forward into my chest and sagged. Reflexively I caught him by the armpits and laid him gently on the ground.

It looked like we were going to need that ambulance after all.

Chapter 34

Some strokes pluck at the brain's functions, altering fine movements in ways so subtle only an especially attentive neurologist can detect them. Not so for Max's stroke, though. It wreaked havoc on his mind, crashing through his motor strip like a car plowing through a storefront's windows. He lost movement of the right side of his body and landed on a ventilator in what passed for an ICU at Big Bend Regional with me as his doctor. For the first forty-eight hours after his event I fought off spikes in Max's blood pressure, spikes that represented assaults of the body on the brain, like barbarians charging the castle walls. When it comes to someone's blood pressure after a stroke, you manage it with the Goldilocks method: not too high, not too low. It's got to be just right.

Darla transitioned from holding vigil in a room at her house to another one at the hospital. Still wary of being stalked, I restricted my movements to the evenings and handled as much business by phone as I could while staying away from windows with clear lines of sight.

When I arrived to make my evening rounds on that second day, I first encountered Max's nurse at the front desk. "Any excitement?" I asked.

"No drama," she said. "Listen, you need to chase

Missus Beckett outta here. Poor lady's exhausted."

"It's on my to-do list. Anything else?"

"Lotta visitors, mostly family and friends from their church. Plus a stranger. Hoo, mama. He got my motor runnin'." She fanned herself with a magazine.

"That right?" I asked as I reviewed Max's rhythm strips.

"He was some kind of handsome, dressed to the nines, expensive watch on his wrist. Smelled good too. I swear, the men of Amoret could take a lesson. Just somethin' as simple as smelling good makes you stand out 'round here."

"Come to pay his respects?"

"I guess. Strange, though. When he come in, him and Missus Beckett hugged, then he pulled her over to the corner and they had a talk real low what I couldn't hear. Went on the longest time, maybe thirty minutes. When it's over, he took her hand in both his, give it two slow pumps and just this little nod of the head. Then he just walked out, but not before giving me a little smile on the way." Hearing this, I wondered if my prediction to Francis of suitors lining up to chase Darla had begun.

In Max's hospital room, I found Darla where I'd left her the night before, sitting in a folding chair watching the rise and fall of the accordion-shaped billows that our primitive ventilators used back then. Her eyes roamed over the hoses attached to a thin plastic tube that disappeared between Max's lips and down his throat, a literal lifeline. Silk tape formed an "X" where it secured that tube to Max's face. We'd had to shave him to get the tape to stick.

Darla worried a tissue in her hands, then used it to wipe her red-rimmed nose. "Good evening, Noah."

"Evening. Sounds like Max had a quiet day?"

She made the sign of the cross. As she watched

me examine him, she asked, "Is he going to be okay?"

"Don't know, sorry to say. Situation's still in the process of declaring itself." I checked his pupils with a pen light, watching them go from big black basketballs to pinpoints. "He wakes up some whenever I lighten up his sedation, so there's that. We got a saying 'round here. 'Time takes time.' Wish I could be more precise."

"I feel like Job." The poor woman looked shell-shocked.

"You been getting any rest? Those folding chairs beat sittin' on a rock, but not by much."

She gave a half-shrug.

"Why don't you go on home, then? Max doesn't know you're here what with all the sedatives I've got in his system. Go sleep in your own bed. We'll give you a shout if anything changes."

She put her hands in the small of her back and stretched, then yawned as she rubbed her eyes. "I think I will at that."

"Good. In fact, I'm takin' my own advice. Doctor Loury is covering the ER next couple days and said he'd look after Max so I can head out, recharge my batteries."

"It's not just this." She gathered her purse and overnight bag.

"Oh?"

"I got a visit this morning from the forensic accountant I hired. Well— that Grandpa Robert hired. Anyway, it looks like the man's already found evidence of missing money, going back several years. He has a lot more work to do, he said, but it looked like it could be a couple million dollars, going back to probably the summer of sixty-nine from the look of things."

The mystery of the well-dressed stranger was solved.

Once I'd finished going over Max head-to-toe, I gave the nurse some orders and swung by the ER to update Loury on the plan for Max. Ten minutes later, I was behind the wheel heading to my ranch in the dark.

The county road was empty, but I still felt exposed as I parked inside the barn, and I held off turning on the interior lights. In the darkness, my hearing grew more acute, marking the pulse of life around me. The soft flit of bat wings overhead, like silk sheets sliding across one another. The chirring of invisible cicadas. A whinny from the stable. The far-off howl of a coyote. I found comfort in these sounds, less alone.

I pulled the barn's sliding door closed and meandered to the stable. In the moonlight I debated which horse to take, and when Clyde nickered at me I took that as a sign. Slipping his bridle on, I briefly stopped at the saddle shed before leading him the hundred yards down to my cabin where I tied him to the hitching post.

The slat steps squealed as I mounted them. On the porch, I turned back and scanned the surrounding escarpment. I loved the way the winter moon painted the rock and sand and scrub, making the landscape both familiar and alien, all cobalt and chrome.

I stood still, head swiveling. There was just the rasp of my old Mackinaw coat's stiff fabric. I could see my breath.

It wasn't until I turned back and got right up to the cabin's front door that I saw it. The darkness of the cabin's interior disguised a thin line traveling across the front door's bottom right windowpane, fine as a spider web, almost like it'd been drawn on the glass.

The window had been busted out. Right next to the door knob.

My blood immediately ran cold.

I froze with my keys in my hand, halfway to the lock. Too late, I realized that to anyone sitting in the cabin's dark interior, I was silhouetted against the moonlit prairie, a target the same size and shape as the ones you buy at the gun range. I may as well have had five concentric rings around my center mass.

I squeezed my eyes shut, realizing if it was going to come, this was the moment. I braced myself for a flash of light and a muzzle's bark, the sight and sound I'd take with me to heaven's gate. In that split-second, I wondered if I'd feel it. Would the bullet hit me like a baseball bat? Or would it cut through me effortlessly, like a ship's bow slicing across the waves? When a few seconds passed in silence, the roaring in my ears subsided and I sagged, feeling shaky. *Better to be lucky than good*, I thought.

I paused to think the situation through. No one knew I was out here, not even Angelica, and no one had followed me in a vehicle, of that I was certain. The likeliest scenario was the window had been broken hours or even days before, but I still unslung the MAC-11 and brought it up to my waist, then held my breath when I keyed the lock and stepped inside.

A quick scan of the tight space showed I was alone. Shards of glass from the window pane lay scattered across the wide plank floor, crunching under foot, the sound of bones breaking. I decided to deal with the mess later. Right then I just wanted to gather my gear and get out as quick as I could.

In the makeshift kitchen, I grabbed those few things I'd need for a couple of nights in the back country. A coffee pot and skillet, a Coleman lantern and a roll of bedding, coffee grounds and lard. I set all these items on the table in the dark, when from the corner of my eye I noticed something awry, like a missing tooth.

The two hooks on the wall sat empty, and my grandpa's scattergun was nowhere to be seen.

I made a mental note of the larceny, but immediately went back to gathering supplies. Truth to tell, I wasn't worried about the threat represented by the missing shotgun since I had the scars to show it was a sniper's rifle I needed to fear. Lord knew I'd have plenty of time to ponder the gun's theft over the next few days.

Ten minutes later, I was packed up and tied down. I ran by the barn to pick up an old iron-sight, lever-action .30-30 from the cab of my truck. The long rifle was overkill for the rabbits and javelinas I intended to subsist on for the next couple of days but would be a better option for game than the MAC-11. I slid the long rifle into my saddle's scabbard and nudged Clyde to set off into the desert darkness.

Past my cabin, I followed a game trail for two clicks until it petered out, then just bushwhacked northeast, taking it slow in the darkness. Clyde ambled along, picking his way across the hard scrabble as I led him toward a cliff face in the distance. Once we reached the looming wall of rock, I turned Clyde to skirt the long talus of shale scree, far enough off the broken rock fragments at the base of the crag that his footing wouldn't be an issue.

After fifteen minutes along that path, we came to our destination: a slate shoreline, long but thin, close to where a creek cut through the flood lands heading in the direction of the river. The shale there was pockmarked with *tinajas*, water holes drilled into the soft rock by the Comanches hundreds of years before but where even now one could generally count on finding water. Several generations of cowboys and outlaws had maintained a bustling camp at that spot before abandoning it around the time of the first world war. The only remains were a crumbling adobe hut and an overgrown wooden corral, it's hand-hewn posts resembling frail gray ribs and looking like a good wind would turn the whole mess into kindling. It'd be a perfect place to lay low for a couple of days.

I unloaded my gear and built a small fire. It'd rained during the day, but with a splash of Cub Scout juice from the Coleman's well to help it along, the wood caught. Despite the hour, I made coffee while trying to clear my mind, alternating my front and back sides to the fire for warmth. I stifled a belch, then laughed at the reflex. With no other human being around for miles, I still automatically displayed the niceties of married life, testimony to how thoroughly Angelica's civilizing influence had taken hold of me.

In the morning, I mounted up and went looking for my breakfast under a gloomy scrim of clouds. Clyde made it up onto a windblown ridge south of the cliff face without much difficulty, and we meandered through a field of thorny chaparral that was usually thick with rabbits. I missed one, then shot two. Scrawny, but together they'd make a meal, so I called it a hunt and turned Clyde to camp. Cutting through the field was an old wagon road that'd get us part of the way back without thorns, so I took pity on Clyde and followed that path as far as it would take us.

As I came up on another wash, a flash of red back among a stand of juniper caught my eye. I stumbled across it, actually, hidden as it was. It caught me off guard, jolting me into the now.

I recognized it as Hector's truck.

I pulled Clyde up short, and in one fluid motion slid the rifle from its scabbard and swiveled off my mount to put Clyde between me and the truck. My heart pounding, I held the pommel in my bad hand, my legs feeling exposed below the colt's belly. Instinctively, I scanned the landscape at my six for a sign of — well, anything. Movement, color, an unnatural profile. But there was nothing. The wind whispered over the rocks like it always had and always would. The country seemed to be watching me, to see what I would do.

I turned my attention back to the vehicle. The rear window's tint obscured the interior. The tires were all-terrain, which explained how Hector'd gotten the vehicle out so far into that austere environment. He'd pointed it into the scrub in a pretty decent attempt at concealment. In fact, I hadn't seen the truck until I was right up on it.

I tied up Clyde and stroked his jowl while I fought off something primitive and ancient, a blood lust. It was looking more and more like through sheer luck I'd gotten the drop on the man who might have killed my boy, and now a desire for vengeance came on strong, washing over me, making my eyes narrow to slits. Under my breath, I said, "You ain't hid no more, cocksucker. You may think you are, but you ain't."

With the rifle leveled on the cab, I cut a fifty-foot semicircle around the truck until I was perpendicular to the driver's door. No signs of a camp marred the ground, no fire ring, no gear. So he was using the truck as shelter.

Through the dark tint I could barely make out a

man's silhouette in the driver's seat, chin on his chest, looking asleep.

I checked my surroundings again. Still nothing out of place. I drew a bead on the profile behind the dark tint and slow-walked up on him. I stepped on a stick that broke with a crack, the sound like a thunderclap in that moment. I froze, cursing myself, but the shape behind the wheel didn't move. I resumed my pace, thirty feet out, then twenty. At ten feet from the truck's door, I caught a vague, new sound. An audible vibration caressed the air, like the soft hum of a transformer.

The hum grew in volume as I crept up on the driver's side, gun at the ready. Gently, I pressed the button on the door's handle and felt it click. Open. I took a last deep breath, then threw the door open with the rifle trained on the driver's head.

Hector's eyes were open wide, the globes bulging, his pupils milky, as though the last thing to go through his mind— besides the load of triple-aught buckshot, that is— was the sight of a ghost. His chin rested on his chest like he was fascinated by the site of gas and brake pedals.

His socked toe remained hooked in the trigger guard of my grandfather's shotgun where he'd braced it between his bowlegged knees. The top of his head was missing, pulverized into a mist of gray matter and skull fragments that stippled the roof of the cab. Holes punched in the thin metal let in beams of indirect sunlight.

Yanking the door open caused a cloud of blowflies to lift off his head momentarily, the hum of their wings ripping the air. Their blue-green bodies glinted in the roof's sunbeams like stained glass in a way that would have been kaleidoscope beautiful if not for the stench. The bloody rundown had dried to black and caked the front of his shirt.

Frantically, I scanned the cab. Hector had to have left some clue, some indication of his guilt before pulling the trigger. I couldn't bear the thought he might have taken his secrets with him, damning himself to silence forever. I felt like I was banging my fists against a vault.

The keys were still in the ignition, and a half-empty bottle of Cuervo stood on end on the bench seat, the cap off, placed there with care. His cowboy boots lay on the opposite floorboard under an open glove box overflowing with papers.

Blinded to all else, I leaned my rifle against the truck's quarter panel and stepped up onto the running board. I held the wheel with my bad hand and reached across Hector's corpse into the glove box. The angry cloud of flies lifted off him once again, the buzz louder as they orbited his corpse and bounced off the tinted glass.

The stench of carrion burned my eyes and settled in my nose, so thick I could taste it. I held my breath as I wedged myself into the tight space between his body and the steering wheel, pulling the papers out one by one, skimming each before discarding it onto the floorboard with his boots. Unpaid parking tickets, miscellaneous receipts, the owner's manual. I worked my way quickly through the pile, seeing nothing that resembled a clue. Cursing aloud as the stack became smaller and smaller, I crumpled them in frustration before casting them in the wheel well. When they were gone, I banged my fist twice against the roof of the cab.

Then I saw it.

A folded piece of paper lay tucked under his right thigh, camouflaged by soaked blood. I snatched at it, but it tore, stuck to the vinyl seat and Hector's denim by gore that had hardened like glue. I released my bad hand from the steering wheel to help and stuck my bad leg out straight behind me to steady my center of gravity. My leg burned with effort as I balanced in that pose, gently peeling the paper away with care until it came free.

It was an old receipt for a fuel pump, folded into quarters with a precision that was incongruous with the sloppiness of the cab. I gently broke apart the adhesions and shook the paper to unfold it.

Scrawled on the back side of the receipt in what looked to be grease pencil were three simple words.

Go to hell.

I wailed a primal scream of frustration and lashed out with the butt of my injured hand, spiderwebbing the windshield.

Chapter 35

The law quickly swarmed my property. Back at the cabin, a deputy took my statement while a technician collected evidence from the break-in. A second tech approached while we spoke and said, "Handwriting on the note's a match with some samples of Hector's writing we picked up from your barn."

"Gotta say, it wasn't much in the way of last words," the deputy said without looking up from scribbling in his notepad. "Who you think he might'a been talkin' to, 'Go to hell?'"

I thought about that. "Whoever found him, seems to me. He was angry at me, the sheriff— hell, the whole goddam universe. Take your pick."

I lent the sheriff's department the use of my horses to get to Hector, but when it came to towing his truck out, the flatbed got stuck trying to make it through a tight draw and had to winch itself out. Finally, the lawmen had enough and someone decided to just fire Hector's truck up, reasoning that since the vehicle had made it in, it could make it out again. One of the techs must have been new because everyone except him agreed he'd be the one to slide in behind the wheel of that rolling slaughterhouse and drive it out. He put on a white, head-to-toe bunny suit and latex gloves, but everywhere he looked was dried brains and blood. I found out later Hector's bowels had let go too, but at least there'd been plenty of time for the cab to air out, so the poor man didn't have to contend with that.

Finding Hector dead by his own hand left me feeling despondent, despairing so deeply it weighed on me like wet blankets. As I sat on the steps of my cabin watching the hum of activity, I feared the only person who could answer the questions to the mysteries about Miguels' death and my would-be assassin had gone the way of all the earth.

It felt like, I don't know ma'am, like that puzzle I'd spoken of earlier starts coming together and you realize some pieces are missing from the box, that you'll never know what the picture was supposed to look like. Hell, you're the wordsmith. I'll let you figure out what to tell people.

Entering Max's hospital room two days later, I found Becky, a matronly nurse wearing a flower-print scrub top whom I knew well, humming to herself as she went about her business. Amid the ventilator's whooshing ebb and flow, she pushed a long, thin straw down Max's breathing tube to suction out his secretions, then injected a medication into the large IV line I'd placed under his right collarbone when he first came in.

"What's buzzin' cousin?"

"Afternoon, Doc," she replied without taking her eyes off the hypodermic needle, its plunger slowly descending.

"Anything new to say?" I opened up Max's ICU flow sheet to let the numbers tell the story of the last twenty-four hours.

"Well, if I squint just right, I'm seeing a man

who's tryin' to get better."

Chewing on the corner of my mouth, I skimmed the flow sheet like a fold-out restaurant menu, picking out data from the hand-inked numbers. My eyes flitted from oxygen levels to urine output to the waxing and waning of his level of consciousness. Together they painted a picture in the same way pixels coalesce into an image.

"Well, I can see where you get that notion. Darla been in to visit today?" I put on my stethoscope, then pulled one earpiece out a few inches to hear the answer.

"She called up, said she'd be here in 'bout an hour."

Replacing it, I nodded and listened to Max's lungs. They were clearer than they had any right to be.

"How long his sedation been off?"

"Since 'bout nine last night."

"Anything else goin' on?"

"One of the three ports on the central line quit workin' yesterday late. Clotted off, from the look of it. Other two're runnin' fine though."

I bit back my frustration. In a central line, three separate IV tubes combined into one large catheter that ran straight into his goddamn heart. It made for easy administration of medications, but they were hell to put in and had to be meticulously maintained to keep them working. It made no sense to get on Becky for it, though, since the lapse hadn't happened on her watch. At least two of the three channels still functioned normally.

"Max, can you hear me?" I shouted in his ear.

He opened his eyes to that, but slowly and without purpose.

"Max, can you wiggle your toes?"

Zombie-like, the sheets at the end of the bed moved once on the left, then again. The right foot sat motionless. But that it was warm, it could have been mistaken for the foot of a dead man.

"Still out on the right?" Becky asked as she emptied the bladder bag.

"Yep. Dead as Dillinger over there."

Behind me, a baritone startled me out of my train of thought. "Does my soul good to see you two up in here." I turned to see McHenry leaning against the doorjamb.

"Figured you'd be out at my ranch with the rest of your posse."

"Them boys's got it under control. How's things with Max here?"

"Hmph. Well, we're following all the latest recommendations for acute stroke care, bullshit though they are. Breathing tube may be out in the next couple days. But somebody like this is like driving an icy road, doesn't take hardly nothin' to throw you in the ditch. Another stroke, a heart attack, blood clot from the legs goes to his lungs. He's at serious risk for all of 'em."

"Well, I know he's in good hands."

I accepted the compliment silently while I wrote in Max's chart.

"Say Doc, you close to wrappin' up? Let me buy you a beer."

"Sure, give me just a second." The offer threw me off-balance a little. Before Blaine went missing, McHenry and I were friendly enough that we'd occasionally invite the other for a cold one at Skinny's, so the invitation wasn't out of the blue. But I still felt the need to treat McHenry with caution. I didn't know what he thought of the facts that Hector'd decided to hide out and subsequently take his own life on my property. I'd gotten the sense over the last week that he'd moved on from considering me a suspect, but now I wondered, did this offer conceal an attempt to catch me saying something with my guard down? I tried to dismiss these thoughts as paranoia but vowed nevertheless to keep my wits about me.

After a few moments of silence, McHenry asked, "Becky, you doin' okay?"

"Better now I've seen you, Lloyd," she said with a sly smile. I'd heard they went to prom together.

"Tell Marcus he best be watchin' his back. I might come up behind him and snatch you off."

"You hush now," she scolded.

"All right, guess I'll quit while I'm ahead."

I nodded to her as I put the chart back in its slot. McHenry put his hat back on, giving her a tip of the brim and a wink as we left.

The sounds of Skinny Dick's welcomed me, salves for my mental bruises. The screech of the screen door's spring when we entered. The click of dominoes. Patsy Cline on the juke. A trio of tipsy-sounding Mexicans arguing in loud Spanish, boisterous in their bids as they played a money game of Moon on the grade school blackboards Dick had cut into tabletops.

The bartender leaned back at an angle, her buttocks against the bar to watch a *telenovela* on the TV overhead. Middle-aged and comfortable with it, she knotted her shirt above her belly button to expose her midriff, like a burned-out Mary Ann from *Gilligan's Island*. I recognized her and scanned my memory for her name. It came to me, Lola. We'd brought her across a year before. She lit up with a smile when she saw me enter.

"Doctor Noah! *¿Te acuerdas de mi?"*

"'Course I remember you. 'L-O-L-A, Lola'," I sang, reaching for her extended hand.

"Richard, he put that song on the jukebox, he say just for me," placing her open palm on her chest.

"Well don't that beat all. The Kinks come to a west Texas icehouse. Now I've seen it all."

"What can I get for you?"

As the sheriff dropped loose change into a cigarette vending machine and pulled the long silver knob, he yelled out "Take a Pearl, if you got it."

"Two," I said.

She slid the top back on the cooler before her and withdrew two long necks, but when I took out my wallet, she waved me off. "*Su dinero no es bueno aqui, señor.*" I smiled my appreciation and joined the sheriff at a rear table.

McHenry took a long pull on the beer, watching the screen where a shirtless man argued with a bride in the middle of what appeared to be a wedding reception. The intensity of the couple's gaze was broken when she suddenly slapped him to ooh's and ah's from the guests.

"Hey, Lola, why'd she slap him?" McHenry shouted.

Turning her head but without taking her eyes from the screen, she shouted back, "He waited 'til she married his uncle to profess his love for her."

"So then why ain't he got his shirt on?"

Still without looking over, she said, "You ask too many questions."

He chuckled, then cocked his head in my direction. "I got the report back on Hector's autopsy right before I come to see you at the hospital there."

"That right?" I picked at the label of my beer.

Taking his notepad out, he flipped to a page in

the middle. "Blood alcohol almost three times the legal limit. No drugs in his system. Trajectory of the wound consistent with what we saw, put the barrel in his mouth. Oh, also, coroner said he had fresh lacerations on his right elbow and back of his hand. She thinks he cut himself busting out the windowpane on your cabin door and reaching in to turn the deadbolt."

I thought about that. The detail made it seem more real. I could picture him standing there at the door, drunk and swaying, rattling the handle and finding it locked before impulsively smashing it out with his bent arm.

"Anything else?"

"Yeah. She put the time of death sometime between Thursday, October thirteenth and Saturday the fifteenth." He returned the pad to his pocket.

While McHenry turned his attention back to the screen, I tried to hide my surprise as I quickly did the math. Miguel was murdered early on Sunday the 16th.

That meant Hector was already dead on the morning Miguel had been killed.

Chapter 36

The sheriff's index finger drew patterns in his bottle's condensation. We sat lost in our own thoughts for a time.

Trying to sound offhanded, I said, "You know, Darla hired a guy to do a forensic audit of her trust fund, said she's worried Blaine may've been building himself a little nest egg. Fella's come back now saying a whole bunch of money's gone missin'. A little here, a little there, thinks it may could be as much as a couple million dollars goin' all the way back to the sixties."

The sheriff opened his mouth to reply but was cut off by the jackhammer roar of jake brakes bringing an 18-wheeler to a halt in the parking lot. Moments later the driver wandered in. Every ounce of four-hundred pounds with a bucket-shaped head topped by a crew cut, the barstool disappeared under him when he took his seat. His name was Casey, but around town he went by "Queso."

The sheriff let Queso settle in before rapping his knuckles loudly on the table's cut blackboard surface. Turning slowly, Queso looked wary when he recognized McHenry.

The sheriff had taken out his pen knife and was using it to trim his thick nails. "Queso, I been gettin' complaints 'bout some long-hauler firin' off his jake brakes in residential neighborhoods in the middle of the night, wakin' everybody up even though there's an ordinance against it. You wouldn't know nothin' 'bout that would you?"

"No, sir," he mumbled guiltily, like a boy whose mother caught him looking at the brassiere models in the Sears catalogue.

"I didn't think you would. But later on when you get back on the horn in that rig of yours, you be sure to let everybody know that McHenry's putting a patrol car out there lookin' for the culprit. You can do that for me?"

"Yessir, Sheriff."

"Good man. Enjoy your beer."

With a look of relief, Queso turned away and we resumed our conversation.

"Yeah, I'd heard about what that accountant was findin'. Darla's been good about workin' with my department. I gotta say, Doc, I've come around to thinkin' this was Blaine Beckett's doin'. Not a doubt in my mind."

"What part you mean?"

"All of it. His disappearing act. Killin' Miguel." He shook his head. "Pains me to say it, but I have my doubts that we'll ever find him, neither."

I felt a flash of anger. "Don't tell me you're givin' up lookin' for who killed my boy just like that, goddammit."

Frowning, he extended his palm, tamping down my outburst. "Settle your ass down, Doc. Nobody said nothin' 'bout givin' up. Case you hadn't noticed, I got my boys workin' enough overtime that we could'a all bought new cruisers for what the city's payin'. I'm just sayin', if the way things are lookin' hold true, there's a good chance this just sorta fizzles out."

He put away his pen knife, and chewed on a cuticle, spitting it to the floor. "If I'm right, and Beckett's out there with a couple million dollars and the only person who knows anythin' 'bout it dead and in the ground—no offense 'bout Miguel, but a fact's a fact—there's nothin' keepin' him here. He could be anywhere from Transylvania to Timbuktu. Less'n he was to slip up bad enough to come to the attention of law enforcement somewheres else, I doubt we'll ever see hide nor hair of Blaine Beckett again."

We watched Queso watch Lola watch TV until we finished our beers, but the mood at the table had turned somber. I no longer felt like socializing, so I put my empty on the bar with a nod of thanks to Lola. As McHenry walked me to my truck, the wind caught the screen door, whipping it open before the spring brought it back with a loud slap.

As I climbed into my cab, a couple on a Harley pulled up next to us, their sissy bar lashed tight with gear. The sheriff waited until they were out of earshot, then propped one elbow on my mirror and leaned into my window.

He gave a heavy, thoughtful sigh. "Doc, I was hesitant to say this before, but I think you deserve to hear it."

I cocked my head, waiting expectantly.

"I know 'bout the work you and Chebo and the others do down there by the river." I opened my mouth to protest, but he raised a palm to silence me. "I'm not trying to entrap you, and truth to tell I'm sympathetic. Hell, if I wasn't wearin' this badge who's to say I might not be right down there with y'all helpin' out. But I am wearin' this badge, so the best I can do is look the other way, and as long as y'all don't go givin' me cause, takin' away my— shit, what'd Tricky Dick and his bunch'a outlaws call it?" He searched his memory, snapping his fingers until it came to him. "Plausible deniability. Long as you don't go takin' away my plausible deniability, what happens down by the river stays by the river far as I'm concerned."

"I'm pretty sure Bingham would want me to say I don't know what you're talkin' 'bout, Sheriff," I said.

"Oh, I guarantee you he would, but that's not why I'm bringin' this up. What I mean to say is that while it's true we're unlikely to ever lay eyes on Blaine again, even if we were to catch him tomorrow, there's no actual evidence to tie him to Miguel's death."

"Miguel's murder," I corrected.

"Miguel's murder. Now, back in the old days, just the appearance of things alone'd be enough for folks around town to have hung him by the neck 'til he was dead. So this is where I'm goin' with all this, Doc. In that line of work you and Chebo got goin' on, I'm sure y'all deal with some rough customers. Men who can go places I can't, and who'll do things I won't. My money is on Blaine runnin' to Mexico. That's what I'da done.

"Now, man-to-man, if you was to use some of those connections you got to try and find Blaine down there and make things right, I can't say I would blame you. In fact, in your position, I think I would'a done the same. I'll deny sayin' this you ever tell anyone, but if you want justice for your boy, that's the only way I ever see it happenin'."

I saw him in a new light. "Don't that beat all. I don't rightly know what to say to that."

With a wistful expression, he looked off down the highway. "Well, let's just say I believe in the justice this badge stands for, far as it goes. But when it comes up short, I think there's a higher call, one that falls between this world and the one comin' to us after we give up the ghost."

I cranked my engine. "You're an interesting man, Sheriff. Take care."

McHenry straightened and slapped the roof of my cab. "I'll say a prayer for you and Angelica this Sunday, as well as one of thanks that we think we know our man and he ain't a Mexican. I worry that might'a lit a fuse 'round these parts."

That night at the motel, my thoughts kept turning back to McHenry's comments. One question had been answered with the timing of Hector's death. I still needed to know whether the stalker was Beckett or the cartel. Suddenly a thought came to me, a possible solution.

The following morning, a light drizzle greeted me as I stood at the base of the rock formation the sniper had used. On the backside where the shooter had parked, a natural path crisscrossed upwards, sort of a natural switch back in the sandstone I could navigate with relative ease.

I slung the MAC-11 over my shoulder and meandered up the path, looking for anything that might hold a clue to the shooter's identity. The path was rocky and open, but at the top I found a natural recess with a shelf. Examining it with a critical eye, I said aloud, "Me, that's the spot I would've picked."

At the front of the alcove, a stone shelf overlooked a vista that included the highway's crest and both sides of the river plain, with unobstructed lines of sight from the shoulder to the logs and rocks I'd used for shelter. With the shelf as a support, the shooter couldn't have had a better field of fire if he'd been allowed to design it himself.

All too easily could I picture the faceless sniper, scope to his eye, strap wrapped round his elbow, drawing a bead on me. The rifle's kick and the muzzle's flash strobing the rock. Working the bolt with a metallic *clack-click-click-clack*. A chill ran through me that wasn't from the cold.

I dropped to my knees and examined every square inch of the alcove's floor. Nothing.

Next, I leaned over the rock shelf. Beyond the craggy outcropping, the slope was rock-rolling steep for thirty feet down to the desert floor. I withdrew back into the niche, then unslung the MAC-11. With the stock unfolded, I braced it against my ribs and leaned out to better view the left side of my field. I fired three shots in rapid succession at the distant gravel bar where I'd once crossed in such a hurry. The explosions of sound in the confined space left my ears ringing, and three small spouts plucked the river surface.

I flipped on the safety and re-slung the gun, then swung my good leg over the stone shelf in a straddle. I tested a toehold in the sandstone with my boot, then gradually let it bear my full weight.

Keeping a tight grip on the rocky bench with my good hand, I swung my center of gravity over the shelf onto the rock face, the strapped gun bouncing off the small of my back. I cradled my bandaged hand against my chest, and let my bad leg catch up with my good one. A few feet down, another spit of stone looked as though it would make a good handhold. I took a moment to prepare myself, then on a mental count of one, two, *three* released my grip and grabbed the stone below. Once my new grip was solid, I shifted my good leg further down. I inched my way along the rock face in this fashion, scanning the hard scrabble around me, working my way toward the ground.

Halfway down, I saw what I'd come looking for.

I bounced up and down for a moment to test my footing and tugged at the sandstone to make sure it wouldn't give when I stressed it. Then I leaned way over, dangling as I reached with my pincer of a bad hand into a crevice where a small ocotillo's roots met the sandstone.

Two brass casings lay caught in the nest of roots. They belonged to the MAC-11. Eighteen inches away from those two lay a larger and longer casing. It would have been hell to find had I not tested where casings ejected from the sniper's nest were most likely to fly.

When I was being shot at on the river plain, the casings would have ejected into the nest every time the shooter worked the bolt on his rifle, pinging off the rocky walls like helium-filled ping pong balls before coming to rest on the ground at his feet. As I made my way from the shooter's right to left, though, sprinting across the river, he'd had to lean out, swiveling the rifle in a way that ejected the brass out into the empty air and down this rocky slope. The fact I'd found no casings in the nest showed he'd retrieved his brass from there, but as I'd hoped, he'd been in too big a hurry to chase any spent casings down the rock face.

I plucked the tarnished piece of brass out from under the system of roots, but the bush's thorns snagged the gauze wrapping my hand. I winced as the tiny spears skewered my wound, entangling themselves in the cotton wrapping like a bug in a spiderweb. I yanked at my hand, but the motion threw me off balance. I unconsciously threw my bad hand out, and it smacked hard off a rock to my left. Stars exploded behind my eyelids, and I clutched my wounded hand to my torso, light-headed from pain.

I clung to the rock face like a bug on a

windshield while I gathered myself. Placing the brass casing between my lips, it tasted like I was sucking on a battery as I continued my slow hand-over-hand downwards. Once back on level ground, I spat the casing into my palm and turned it on end. There, written around the perimeter of the spent shell, surrounding the dimpled base where the firing pin had struck, was written the caliber. ".300"

That meant I'd been wounded by the same caliber rifle as that rarest of models purchased by Blaine from a dealer in Chicago years before. An antique, bolt-action .300 Savage.

Chapter 37

My mind raced as I drove back to Amoret after finding that .300 shell casing. My desire for revenge was real, of course, and I've already told you I'd fantasized about what I'd do to whomever killed Miguel if the hand of God had come down and pointed him out to me. Seems strange now to invoke God for something like that, because I was raised to believe vengeance is the purview of the Lord. I'd always known it was either Beckett or Hector. Now that it appeared Beckett had indeed been the one shooting at me down by the river, my blood ran cold.

At the nurse's station, I found Becky sitting behind the brushed steel countertop charting her nurse's notes, shift change still an hour away. Nowadays, there'd be a monitor in front of her displaying Max's heart rate from his room as a continuous red tracing, his blood pressure as a relaxing blue. That technology wouldn't make its way to Big Bend Regional for another ten years, though.

"Hey Doc. You and Lloyd go howl at the moon?" she asked with a knowing smile.

"Nope, both our howlin' days are over I expect. Thought I'd check in on our boy one last time before callin' it a day."

"You gonna be here a few minutes? If so, I'm gonna grab something to eat in the break room."

"Take your time, I'm good." I reached over the counter and grabbed Max's chart off the rack. I flipped through the pages, skimming, as though it was a magazine at the dentist's office. Through the break room's window, I watched as Becky opened a Tupperware container and turned an overhead television to the evening news.

Going to the supply cabinet, I retrieved fresh bandages to take home for my hand, and a large sixty milliliter syringe. Strolling down to Max's room, I found him just as I'd left him, supine with his eyes closed, the ventilator whooshing and humming as background noise.

I rubbed his breastbone with my knuckles, hard and rough, the pain meant to stimulate him as his body chewed up the last of the sedation in his system. He grimaced for a split-second, then blinked hard a few times, clearing his head.

"Wakey wakey sleepyhead."

Max's eyes locked on mine and flashed in anger as he realized who was standing over him. As long as I live I'll never forget the intensity of the hatred I saw burning there. The breathing tube may have rendered him mute, but his lips could still move, and now they spewed a silent stream of invective at me.

I opened the syringe's wrapper and drew the plunger back until the chamber was full of air. I asked, "You awake all the way, Max?"

While his eyes narrowed with scorn, he gave a subtle nod. I hooked up the empty syringe to the tubing of his central line.

I leaned over the bed rail, my mouth inches from the side of his head. The acrid smell of his sweat filled my nose as his eyes swung full right, searching for me in the corner of his vision.

I whispered in his ear, "I need you awake, 'cause I want you to know it was me that did this." I slowly began pushing the plunger home, injecting nothing but a large syringe full of air directly into the catheter.

In my mind's eye, I could see the huge air bubble traveling down the catheter, through the large chest veins, and accumulating in Max's heart. The black rubber tip on the plunger was halfway through its deadly journey to the bottom when I resumed whispering to him, "See, Max, an air bubble this size is gonna cause a vapor lock in your heart. It's why we make a big deal about bleeding even the tiny bubbles out of the plastic tubing before we hook it up to somebody's IV. Big bubbles like this one are goddam impossible to treat. And even if Darla asks for an autopsy— I know, I can't picture that either, but still— an air embolism's undetectable."

I saw that now the look of fury in his eyes had changed to pure fear. Over and over, he mouthed, "No!" And while I'm no lip-reader, I'm pretty sure I saw, "Please!'"

I hissed, "You should be feelin' it right about … now."

As the air bubble reached a critical mass and glommed up his valves, Max's heart quit pumping blood forward.

His eyes squeezed shut and his back arched. He held the rigid pose for a few seconds as waves of pain ripped through his body. He clawed at the air with his good left hand, straining so hard I thought the canvas wrist restraint might tear. His left knee bent and straightened, spasmodically, over and over. He bit down on the breathing tube, causing the ventilator to alarm. Casually, I pressed the "alarm silence" button, buying thirty seconds of quiet. I knew by the time the snooze button on the alarm expired, this would all be over.

I scooped aside the contents of the trash can and placed the syringe and its wrapper at the bottom where they immediately became just two random pieces of medical waste. The crude bedside monitor we used back then displayed Max's heart rate, one hundred fifty beats per minute, a frenzied rate for a man his age, driven by rage and fear. It held steady, then began to dip, like the stock price of a dying company. Slowly, inevitably, one-hundred twenty ... then one hundred ten. Once it fell below one hundred beats per minute, the rate began to drop more quickly, like an elevator when the cables snap. Seventy ... forty.

By the time Max's heart rate hit thirty beats per minute, he'd gone limp.

Even though I wasn't sure he could hear me any longer, I said, "Bye, Max. I hope that hurt."

Then I limped rapidly down the hallway and threw open the break room door, making Becky jump.

"Goddammit, Max just coded! Help me with the crash cart!"

I went through the motions of trying to resuscitate Max from flatline for twenty minutes, pure theater. Becky, bless her heart, killed herself working on him, slamming one ampule after another of code medications down his central line, unknowingly using what was now a murder weapon. More people magically appeared, taking turns doing CPR, rhythmically squeezing a football-shaped reservoir of pure oxygen into Max's breathing tube, scribing the activities for accurate chart entry later.

The detritus of our efforts made the room look like a disaster area. Ripped open medication boxes littered the floor, and empty syringes accumulated in the bed sheets. The normally organized crash cart sat center room with drawers akimbo and contents scattered. Eventually, I said to the room, "Y'all, we've been asystolic for over twenty minutes. Doesn't look like the good guys are gonna win this one. Anybody got any heart burn if I call it?"

There was no TV melodrama, no people shouting, "Live dammit!" or any such. We were all way too experienced for that nonsense. We all knew, some you get back, and some you don't. In response to my question, they all shook their heads.

I looked up at the clock and said, "Okay. I've got time of death, eighteen-twenty-six. Thanks, everybody." And with that I hobbled out to the desk.

Chapter 38

Two hours later, I stood atop a bluff on the east side of my ranch overlooking rolling acres of empty desert. Swallows darted in and out of the cliff face below me, the soft thrum of their wings caressing the air in bursts. I tossed a handful of pebbles one by one over the edge, watching them *tink-tink-tink* their way down the cliff, buffeted by the wind that bounced and eddied off the rock face before coming to rest on the chert a few hundred feet below. We'd had a cow go missing once a couple years before, and I found her dead at the bottom of that cliff face, busted and broken. She'd managed to make her way up onto the bluff and part of it crumbled under her, leading to a long spill. Just letting her lay seemed the easiest way to go and coyotes and buzzards picked the carcass clean over time. Even now, in the late evening's gloam I could see her scattered, sun-bleached bones far below where a gravel bench met a stand of emory oak.

This was my favorite spot on the whole property, secluded and remote, timeless and forgotten by the rest of the world. I'd never brought anyone else to that spot, not even Angelica. I felt like I had a pact with that piece of land, the way rich people buy stolen masterworks on the black market just to keep them in a vault where only they can view them. Just knowing they possessed the pieces was enough for those folks. That's the closest I can come to explaining my connection to that place.

The spot was hard to get to, the path up there hidden. I'd found it by accident years before after following a set of switchbacks only visible when you were right up on them, and even then it was tricky. The horse I'd been on at the time almost lost her footing at one point, but she'd managed to make it up there where I got a look at a vista so pretty it made me want to close my eyes and stencil it onto my brain, to file it away so I could access it later like a photo in my wallet.

Now, I tore myself away from that view and wandered past my mare into a thicket of juniper where the soil turned softer, more silt and less rock. If you raised a booted foot and snapped the heel backwards into the earth, it would leave an imprint a few inches deep.

The scratchy chirp of katydids surrounded me as I bobbed and weaved through the thicket, pushing aside skinny limbs that clawed at my jacket's canvas with prickly swishes. One supple branch managed to slip past my fingers and whipped back to catch my right eye, making it water. I kept moving and after another twenty yards arrived at my destination.

I pushed through into a clearing in the heart of the thicket, just a few yards wide and about as long. From above, it probably looked like the eye of a hurricane. What was once a patch of sand and grass was now a nondescript pile of rocks, each the size of a football or bigger, a cluster of stones that looked like any of the other thousands scattered across my property and the region. You'd have to have known that it'd been bare up in that clearing once to have taken notice of it at all.

I paced around the pile, inspecting its base. Shallow claw marks in the soil indicated coyotes had gotten after it, digging hard for a bit before giving up when it became clear the rocks wouldn't yield.

Under those rocks, in a grave two feet deep, lay Blaine Beckett in the spot where I'd buried him.

I kicked dirt into the coyote's marks, filling the shallow hole. Then I sat at the base of a tree nearby, my boots crossed at the ankles. My soles almost touched the rocks, and I resumed tossing pebbles, this time at the low-lying stone cairn. As they plinked off the rocks, my mind drifted back to the events of that awful Saturday night.

I'd just finished dinner at the cabin and was fetching well water to wash dishes when a pair of headlights interrupted me, bouncing down the ranch road in my direction and coming fast. Truth to tell, I hadn't recognized Blaine's Jeep, and it wasn't until he braked in a spray of gravel, the chassis rocking from the violent deceleration, that I realized who it was. I stood at my water pump with a bucket in one hand and the other held up to block the worst of the glare from his high beams. When the interior light came on and I saw it was Blaine, my stomach knotted up.

In contrast to the violence of his vehicle's appearance, he got out of the vehicle casually like he was dropping it off at the mechanic. Backlit by the high beams, shadows concealed his face. A stenciled glow outlined his silhouette.

I set my pail down by the water trough. "'Evening, Blaine. What brings you out here?" I tried to sound nonchalant, but it came out wary.

Blaine didn't answer at first. He put his hands in his pockets and looked around at my property, scanning it while he wandered in a half-circle. I thought he might be admiring the landscape. Then again, I thought, he might be looking for witnesses.

I was on high alert, watching his hands. I didn't see a bulge under his jacket, but I braced to rush him if he went for a weapon.

Still trying to sound unconcerned, I asked, "How'd you know to come lookin' for me out here?"

Facing back up the road in the direction of the barn, he said, "My father told me he overheard that redneck friend of yours at the diner saying you'd be out here working all day, that you were probably going to spend the night."

"Yeah? What were you and Max talkin' about then?" I asked.

He turned and faced me straight on, the high beams now lighting him up like spotlights. The last time I'd seen that crazed expression on another man's face, I'd been in the jungle. Wild-eyed and veins bulging, he looked deranged.

"We were discussing what I should do about the fact that you're fucking that whore wife of mine." Seething, he took his hands out of his pockets and began rhythmically opening and closing his fists.

"Settle down, Blaine, come on now. Let's talk this through."

"Listen to me, you son of a bitch— if you think I'm going to— and then with my *wife!* How could you— and for *years!* I ought to—. " The normally articulate professor had transformed into a shaking, incoherent mess. He took a short step toward me, closing the distance from five feet to four.

I spoke in a soft, even voice, as though to a bank robber with his gun to the head of a hostage. "Blaine, listen, I'm sorry for what's happened in the past. But it's over. *Been* over. For a couple of years. I just need you to slow down, take a deep breath, okay? Don't you go doin' nothin' stupid."

Blaine was having none of it. He jabbed a finger at me, stabbing the air. "You and that fucking *bitch* I'm married to are the ones who did something stupid, you *cocksucker.* Nobody humiliates me like that. You hear me, asshole? *Nobody!*" Another angry step toward me.

I continued soothingly, "Blaine, you've got every right to be pissed, and I'm really sorry for what got you here. But we really need to turn the heat down on—."

"*Fuck you!*" he roared. He squeezed his eyes shut and bent at the waist, pulling at his hair with both hands. He'd lost control.

Just as I braced myself for a bull rush, Blaine suddenly froze and became deathly quiet, face pointed at the ground while he held fistfuls of hair. I stood unmoving, not sure what to expect. The only sound was the chug of his engine and Maybelline and Rope Tail barking frantically inside the cabin. Then, in slow motion he released the grip on his hair and lifted his head.

A grin spread across his face. It was psychotic, like a serial killer who'd identified his next victim: wide but no teeth, lips pressed tight. He nodded his head as he spoke, like some truth had just revealed itself to him.

"You don't know anything about sorry, you miserable prick. But you're going to. Yessir, you fucked with the wrong man. You and that little wetback of yours."

I didn't like where this was going.

My face must have betrayed me at the mention of Angelica because I caught a glint of satisfaction in his eyes. "That's right, that wetback *cunt* of yours and her little retard. They're accountable."

My voice went from soothing to steel. "Blaine, I need you to stop right there. You're super red-hot pissed. I get that, and you've got a right to be. But you're entering dangerous territory. I'm telling you, you need to stop talking 'bout my family. Now."

He ignored me. "Yeah, we all know. Everybody in town watches you three play happy family. But people say there's some bad men looking for them back where they came from. Hard men. The kind of men that wouldn't bat an eye about leaving their heads on a pike at the edge of town. And judging by the look on your face right now, I'm guessing there's some truth to that. Am I right?"

"Blaine, I can't be having you talk this way. You're forcing me toward a decision I don't wanna make. I'm not askin', I'm beggin'. Please. Stop."

"We've got money. Probably what made white trash like you come sniffing around my wife to begin with." He spat the words. "Well, let me promise you something, asshole. I'm willing to spend it all to find those men and let them know that if they come to Amoret, Texas, they'll find it worth their while."

It was clear he meant every word. Like two gunfighters in the old west, we stood facing each other, arms at our sides and stances wide. Looking back on it, I think that moment had been the end game for him, that he hadn't thought things through any further than the articulation of that plan and relishing the pain it caused me.

My hand shot out and seized him by the throat. He made a *yurk* sound and grabbed my wrist with both hands, eyes bugging in surprise. Blaine was shorter than me by a few inches and spindly, and I had no difficulty pushing him off balance and spinning him around until the water trough hit him behind the knees.

Fear grabbed him as tight as my grip, and his eyes darted to their corners where they locked on the water level. As I bent him backwards, pushing him closer to the water, he released my wrist and grabbed the edges of the wooden trough in a frenzy. He had no leverage, though, and I slowly overpowered him, pushing his head inexorably toward the trough.

As the back of his scalp made contact with the surface of the water, his reedy breath morphed into a nasal keening sound, high-pitched, like a teakettle chirping. Had my hand not been compressing his voice box, I'm sure he'd have whimpered.

Gradually his hair dipped below the water, then his eyes. I drove him downward, putting my weight behind it. When the water level got to his nostrils, they blew a fine mist of water into the air for a few panicked breaths, like a breaching whale's spout. His hands released the edges of the trough and in desperation flailed weakly at my arm and chest. I could see his mouth open below the roiling surface of the water, his lips peeled back in a skeleton-grin of terror as a stream of bubbles escaped. His frenzied movements began to slow, and the air bubbles thinned out. His hands searched the air but came up empty. He clawed at the breeze, but the white-knuckled hooks of his fingers softened, then went limp.

I kept him like that, head submerged, for another two minutes. When I went to check my watch, tears blurred my vision so badly I had to count it off in my head instead. I knelt there in the moonlight, sobbing like the prodigal son.

I brought Blaine's body to that clearing on horseback and buried him in the inky darkness. Later, I drove his jeep back out to the county road, right past Hector as it turned out. Yes, Hector'd been telling the truth when he told the police he'd seen Blaine's car come and go a couple of hours apart. The distance from the barn to the cabin was too great for him to have seen particulars, but about that one central fact he'd been correct.

My first reflex had been to just ditch Blaine's car somewhere, anywhere, but I quickly realized that wouldn't work. At the time, I didn't know if anyone besides Max knew Blaine had driven to my ranch to confront me. And wherever I left it, I knew I'd be walking back to the cabin. I had to get it off my property to a place where it might be weeks or, God willing, even months before it'd be found. As I frantically searched my mind, I remembered the canyon. When I was considering buying the ranch years ago, Mariano had offered to let me hunt that same elevated deer blind, so I knew it was in the middle of nowhere and hidden from most lines of sight. Fine, I thought. The canyon it would be. Little did I know Jesús Barrera would be watching from a distance, or that Mariano would give some kid permission to hunt that blind just a few days later. Some breaks work for you, some against you.

Once the fact of Blaine's disappearance became known and the car was discovered, I was surprised at first Max didn't go to the police straight away. As I thought about his silence, though, it made sense. Bringing to light his role in sending Blaine out to confront me could have led to Darla's putting his bags on the front porch. He wanted to see me suffer, but not so badly that he was willing to run himself into the poorhouse to do it. Additionally, for a while it had looked like I was going to jail even if he remained silent.

In light of that, it must have driven Max insane with rage when the light of suspicion shifted from me to Hector. By then, he had to have known I'd killed his boy, and I suspect he decided to take matters into his own hands. He wanted me to know the pain of losing a son, and thus his decision to kill Miguel. Max was fit for his age and would have had no trouble overpowering the undersized boy. Then taunting me with the Polaroids and the notes, well— the kind of man that'd kill a child out of a thirst for revenge is a man the world won't miss. That kind of hatred must just run in the bloodline.

For a period of time, I genuinely didn't know whether it was Hector or Max or the cartel that had killed Miguel and tried to kill me at the river crossing. It wasn't until after I was told Hector's suicide predated Miguel's death that I could narrow it down. Then, once I found it was that rarest of calibers, a .300 Savage, that'd shot at me from the rocks, I knew. Max was the one, the cause of it all.

Not that there was any doubt in my mind, but my suspicions were confirmed after Max's death when Darla asked me to help her clear the apartment of his effects. She was in the bathroom going through his medicine cabinet and I was cleaning out his bedroom closet, contending with that old man smell I've come to know in recent years, all cigar smoke and mustiness and moth balls. I went through the pockets of his suits and undid the knots on his ties where he apparently kept them pre-knotted so he had only to drop one around his neck and cinch it up, then laid his wardrobe on the bed for donation to Goodwill. I set aside for Darla a photo album I discovered on the top shelf, and discretely discarded a half dozen old *Penthouse* magazines he'd squirreled away, knowing their presence would tarnish Darla's memory of the old man.

The last item on the top shelf was a weathered shoebox. When I reached overhead to lift it, I felt a weight shift inside, clunking against the cardboard. Puzzled, I lifted the top to find a Polaroid camera sitting on a bed of dozens of photos. Flipping through them quickly, they appeared to go back years. Most were people and places I didn't recognize, but I did come across a few pictures of Blaine in his younger days, some at Christmas, others at the beach, both by himself and standing next to a woman I took to be his mother. I was about to place the box in a stack of effects for Darla when I saw something that made my hands go clammy and my skin prickle with goose bumps.

My trembling hands held a picture of Miguel working on his plywood project in my study as I bent to hug him from behind. The Polaroid had been taken from a few feet outside the window, probably just far enough that Max wouldn't have left footprints in the mulch. My mind raced back to that moment, recalling how our reflections had masked the backyard before I'd seen a mysterious flash outside the window, a flash I took to be lightning but pursued no further.

So Max had been stalking us even back that far, in the first few nights after Blaine's disappearance. I stuck the picture in my pocket and destroyed it later. Feels funny talking about it now. I haven't spoken of it until this very moment, not even to Angelica, God rest her soul.

The theory that Blaine had faked his own disappearance and the finding that he'd been squirreling Darla's family money away for years were absolute gifts from God. On the day McHenry'd come to my house with the map of my property and we'd discussed the road that runs along the edge of the property north of mine, I'd seen an opening and took it when I asked McHenry if I could accompany him out there to inspect it. While he was busy getting the Midland lawyer's permission and the combination to the gate's lock, among the errands I ran that day were swinging by that gate with a bolt cutter and snipping the lock's shank cleanly in two just like I'd done on Mariano's property weeks before when I ditched the Jeep in the box canyon. The second time, though, I did it with the purpose of giving the appearance Blaine had cut the lock while orchestrating his disappearance. Then McHenry and I "discovered" the cut lock shank together a few hours later.

Jesús Barrera and I remained friends for the rest of his life. He died of natural causes out in the back country he so loved sometime during the Clinton years. We never talked again of what he actually saw on the night I torched Blaine's car in that box canyon. We'd both been playing a very delicate game during the one and only conversation we ever had about it back in that dug out scoop of rock on my property. If I had to bet, when the diesel I'd splashed on that clunker roared into flames, lighting me up like the midday sun, he'd recognized me even from that distance. But like I said earlier in this story, I'd earned the loyalty of a lot of the Mexicans in those parts, and if he did recognize me he never said a word about it. I miss that milky-eyed man.

Darla went to her grave thinking Blaine ran off, living off her money someplace where steel drums played in the background. While that thought aggravated her to no end, she did seem happier overall. The single life suited her, at least for a while. She started dating again a few years later, a man about ten years her junior who moved to town to be a Deacon at her church. I'm told the age difference was the subject of some gossip at the beauty shop, but they had a good thirty years together before Covid got her. Blaine's disappearance would have constituted grounds for an annulment had she chosen to go that route, but she was fine with never walking down the aisle again. Once bitten, I guess.

And finally, there's my little Angelica, my angel. In the first rays of morning after that long, awful night, I came home caked in dirt and grime, exhausted and sore to the bone. She was still asleep but stirred when I sat on the edge of the mattress. When she got whiffs of the pungent oil smell of a diesel fire on me and the sour odor of my sweat, her brow furrowed. "Is everything all right?"

I shook my head, and with the flurry of activity done I told her the sad story. Truthfully, I hadn't even thought so far ahead as to game out what her reaction might be. I knew, though, if she said I had to go to the police, that's what I was prepared to do.

When I recounted Blaine's threats and my drowning him, my voice hitched and she folded me into her arms, rocking me and cooing as I sniffled quietly. As my wave of emotion subsided, she held my face in both hands close to hers. She kissed my tears and said, "You're a good man, Noah. Thank you for protecting our family."

I felt something well up, a lightness to my being. No matter what, we were in it together.

Chapter 39

So you'll see now that back at the beginning of this when I told you I've lived a life more interesting than most, I wasn't lying.

I wasn't bragging, or at least I didn't mean to. I'm just saying when you look at my eighty-four years, maybe if you were to stack them up side-by-side against those of most people in Mount Calvary— that cemetery you passed on your way out here, the one off highway 90, next to that little VA clinic— they'd compare favorably.

By the way, when they built that VA clinic back in the mid-nineties, I have never seen such a piss-poor excuse for a medical facility in all my years, and you're talking to a man who delivered more than one baby in a hut. When they first came to me, saying they were short doctors and asking would I help them with coverage, I told them I'd give eight hours a week. I made it five before I shut the clinic down early on my first day. Mislabeling blood specimens, giving patients the wrong medicine, filing charts in the wrong spots— I mean, fuck's sake, if you'll pardon my ... but if you can't handle the alphabet then I don't know how to help you. Well, ma'am, halfway through that first day's shit show, I gathered the nurses around and told them they were headed toward doing to that waiting room of veterans what Saddam and Ho Chi Minh couldn't, and we were done for the day. I went out front and announced to everybody waiting to check in we were shutting it down early and I'd personally give anybody who needed one a ride to the ER. Of course, that was back in the day when you could pull shit like that as a doctor and get away with it. Nowadays, well, it's a different time and I'll leave it at that.

Oh yeah, my life compared to the other folks at Mount Calvary.

I doubt you were thinking it was going to go in this direction, though, huh? I debated what and how much to say to you, kept my options open there at the end by just talkin' about "Beckett", and figurin' if you assumed I was talkin' about Blaine instead of Maxwell, then at least I wouldn't be lyin' to you outright. But I finally decided what the hell. Almost all the folks it affects are dead now and judging by what my doctors are telling me about this prostate problem of mine — well, I'll just say that when I go to the grocery store these days I don't go buyin' the big jar of peanut butter anymore.

I guess I figured it was time.

Try not to judge me too harshly when you write this down. At the end of it all, I felt like Blaine forced my hand. And as far as Max, well, I'm only human. Other men I know are full of bravado, talkin' about how they spent their lives shootin' craps with the Devil himself. That was never me. I wouldn't say I'm humble— Lord knows, lightning would come through this roof right now and strike me down as I sit here talking to you if I tried. But I think I just preferred to keep my head down, just plugging along, and always trying to do something to help the person who was sitting right in front of me be they brown, white, or purple.

And I'll tell you this. When I get up to those pearly gates and Saint Peter opens up that big book of his to the page that has my name written at the top, if that's what he reads back to me, I like my chances.

Acknowledgements

A special thanks to Jane Wigginton, MD for the repeated use of Cross Creek Ranch's solitude to write much of this novel. I agree with you, Jane: the place is special. I'd also like to thank Lisa Vasquez, the CEO of Stitched Smile, for being what I thought a publisher should be when I started this journey. Thank you to Celia Blue Johnson, a truly wonderful developmental editor. The book is much stronger for your efforts. Thank you to William Kent Krueger and Jess Lourey for some of the best advice I've yet received about following the story wherever it wants to go, consequences be damned. And finally, to my wonderful wife Amy. You're so beautiful, sometimes I just want to stand still and look at you.

About the author

Arthur Herbert was born and raised in small town Texas where he worked on offshore oil rigs, as a bartender, a landscaper at a trailer park, and as a social worker before going to medical school. For the last eighteen years, he's worked as a trauma and burn surgeon, operating on all ages of injured patients. He continues to run a thriving practice.

Arthur currently lives in New Orleans, with his wife Amy and their dogs. He loves hearing from his readers, so don't hesitate to email him at arthur@arthurherbertwriter.com.